The Detective's Dragon

by

Karilyn Bentley

Draconia Tales

The Detective's Dragon

Cover Art by *Diana Carlile*

The Wild Rose Press, Inc.
PO Box 708
Adams Basin, NY 14410-0708
Visit us at www.thewildrosepress.com

Publishing History
First Fantasy Rose Edition, 2015
Print ISBN 978-1-5092-0136-5
Digital ISBN 978-1-5092-0137-2

Draconia Tales
Published in the United States of America

The squeak of hinges snapped Parker's attention to the door. Hottie stood in the doorway, one hand on the frame, the other on the handle, a look of determination plastered on his face. A look she was familiar with. A look she saw reflected in her mirror on a daily basis. A look mirrored on her coworkers' faces when working a case.

A look she never thought to see directed her way.

Which was a bit unnerving, but not nearly as unnerving as the realization he'd followed her. He stood in the doorway like he owned the place. Or owned her.

Her limbs shuddered like a car without shocks. He. Followed. Her. Was he stalking her? Was he with the ones who tried to kidnap her? What was he doing here? More to the point, how did she get rid of him? Her muscles might be coming out of a deep freeze, but that didn't mean she could hop off the bed and toss him out the door.

Where was the damn call button?

Parker patted the mattress. Hottie took a step closer. Then another. No button. Her heart shook an uneven rhythm, the beat a warning drum in her veins. Her hand moved faster against the mattress, searching, seeking, not finding.

Damn it.

"Be of ease. I mean no harm."

She stilled, her hand paused mid-pat as if his words flipped her off switch. Deep and soothing, his voice stroked across frazzled nerves, slowing her racing heart. If he could bottle that sound, women would fall at his feet.

Praise for Karilyn Bentley

MAGICAL LOVER

"Ms. Bentley's characters are strong and will defend to the death those they love."

~Aloe, Long and Short Reviews

~*~

WARRIOR LOVER

"I enjoyed the way the author wrote this book and the characters were very realistic. I will be living in this fairytale for awhile."

~Crystal, Romancing the Book

~*~

AFTER THE MOON RISES

"The writing of Ms. Bentley is unique and shows no fear in stepping outside the norm of shifter romance."

~Delane, Reviewer for Coffee Time Romance & More

~*~

WEREWOLVES IN LONDON

"The author has excellent world building skills and leaves the reader with a very good picture of this werewolf society and its rules. This story is a great combination of romance, action, suspense and the paranormal."

~Maura, CoffeeTime Romance

~*~

WOLF MATES

"…had a good mix of humor and action, a good, developed plot for a novella and was a fun read."

~M. Dobson, Sizzling Hot Book Reviews

~*~

"…was a fun book to read."

~Jane, Reviewer for Coffee Time Romance & More

Dedication

To the Plotting Princesses
for helping plot ideas for this story.
You ladies rock!

~

And a special thanks to Phyllis Middleton
for answering questions about all things police.
As usual all mistakes are mine.

~

And to my loving hubby
who puts up with me sticking scenes under his nose
to critique while he's in the middle of a video game.
I love you much!

Chapter One

Death surrounded her in a foggy aura, gray and dense and choking. Her gaze fixed on some point behind him, her expression one of peace, as if she didn't realize death hovered nearby. Or maybe she welcomed its embrace.

Unacceptable.

She belonged to him.

Jamie reached toward the almond-skinned female, hoping she'd take his hand, needing her to touch him more than he needed his next heartbeat. But she ignored him before fading away into the mists of his dreams, leaving behind the sting of rejection.

Sweat beaded his body as he sat straight up in bed. Shadows clung to the corners of the room, chased by the dawning sun. Jamie rubbed a hand over his face. Every night this week he'd dreamt the same dream. The same female. The same aura of death. The same rejection. The only difference between them being the strength of the foggy death aura. With each dream it grew stronger. Closer. More threatening.

He needed to find her. To save her. To mark her as his.

Goddess's toes. Since when did a Draconi male mark a human female as his mate? Especially a Halfling such as himself.

He couldn't do most of the things a full-blood

Draconi could, including turning into a dragon. And now he thought he could mark a female as his mate?

Crazy dreams.

Jamie rolled out of bed and stretched. He waved a hand over the glow lamp on the bedside table, turning it on. Yet another action he needed help with. He had the embarrassing distinction of being the only Halfling he knew who needed their glow lamp spelled in order to work properly.

And to think, when he was a youngster, everyone thought he had the potential to be the most powerful Draconi ever. They based their belief on his coloring, his brown hair and gray eyes, coloring different from the red hair and green eyes of all other Halflings. The only other Halfling with his coloring had been powerful. And dangerous. She'd gained the position of High Priestess and ruled with a magical ferocity not seen since.

He waited his whole life to be powerful. Still waited.

But he could do one thing better than any other Draconi.

Find lost things.

People. Pets. Jewels.

The greater the danger the pets and people were in, the quicker he found them. All except the female from his dreams.

How did he go about finding a human? As a reconnaissance expert, he found abandoned Halflings in less time than any of his colleagues. An image was all he needed to find a lost pet. Jewels called to him like a hatchling to its mother. Humans?

He'd never tried finding a human. Why would he?

But he'd put off finding the dream female long enough. Death almost embraced her in its cold grasp and once that happened, she'd be lost to him forever.

Unacceptable.

Bam, bam, bam! The front door rattled under strong blows, shaking Jamie out of his thoughts. No doubt about who stood outside attempting a break-in. The only question was why his Halfling-finding partner arrived with the dawning sun. Since when was Erik early for a mission?

Jamie scrubbed a hand over his face and stumbled across the bedroom to the door. The gold dragon doorknob slipped in his grasp, but that's what happened when one woke in a cold sweat. After a couple of tries he opened the bedroom door, strode across the main room, and yanked open the front door.

Red-rimmed, puffy eyes stared back a second too long, sleepy thoughts drifting in their depths, as if his reconnaissance partner had rolled out of bed and transported the moment his feet hit the ground.

Nothing new there.

"You're early."

"You gonna invite me in, or do I have to stand out here all day?" Erik yawned, not bothering to cover his mouth.

Jamie stepped back, gesturing with his arm for his friend to enter. "Did you get any sleep?"

"Of course. In a manner of speaking."

A stab of jealousy, hot and painful, slammed into his chest. He knew where Erik had been, what he'd been doing and, if he thought on it long enough, who he'd been doing it with. Lying in a female's arms. Setting his cares free in the pleasures of a bedromp.

If only his life was that easy. Females tended to think of him as a pity romp. The poor little Halfling with no powers. Not a one cared about him for any other reason.

And could he blame them? What female wanted a male with little magic? Who needed the lights and stove in his house spelled by someone else in order to work correctly? Just because he understood their reasoning didn't mean he wanted to act the fool. Giving females up had been easier than he thought. Times like these proved why the Goddess created hands.

If only he possessed magic.

And then what? He'd get females for the opposite reason. Instead of a pity bedromp, they'd romp with him for his power. Still without caring.

Jamie sighed. Maybe if he hadn't grown up around caring couples like Thoren and Keara, his adoptive parents, then he wouldn't mind the lack of love.

"You with me here?" Erik snapped his fingers in front of Jamie's eyes. "I've been talking, and you're standing in the doorway staring into space."

Idiot. Jamie slammed the door shut. "Sorry."

"As I was saying. You got any of those beans we bought in the Southlands?"

"The wake-up ones?"

"One and the same. Where are they? Don't you have the press too?"

"In the cupboard. Top shelf."

Erik poured the small, hard, dark beans into a cylindrical chopper. He screwed the top on the press and used the handle to chop the beans while Jamie started a fire in the cook-stove and sat a pot of water on to boil. Several Halfling hunting expeditions ago, they discovered jaba-jaba beans in the Southlands. Crushed, the beans delivered a powerful stimulant, a wake-up jolt, perfect for early morning duties after a night of little sleep.

No wonder Erik loved the potion.

"Are you going like that? Your lack of clothing is blinding me."

Jamie looked down at his sleeping shorts and back to his friend. "Your fault. You're the one who showed up before I had time to dress."

"You have time now." Erik waved his fingers. "I'll fix us something while you get dressed. You know how the Council hates it when we're late."

He knew how the Council hated it when Erik popped in late. Jamie strove for punctuality. No sense in giving those tasked with the protection of Draconia a reason to think he wasn't qualified to be a reconnaissance expert.

He had enough problems convincing them that despite his middling magic, he could find Halflings. Only the fact he never returned empty handed, and usually returned with additional hard-to-find items, saved him from needing to look for work elsewhere.

Dressing as quick as possible in trousers and shirt, he slipped his knife into his boot. Draconi did not normally carry weapons, relying instead upon their magic, but Jamie's lack of magic meant he needed a weapon. A hidden weapon.

No sense in giving the Council a reason to think he couldn't do his job by flaunting a knife on his belt.

A few minutes later, he returned to the main room where Erik was busy cooking breakfast. The male might not have a punctual bone in his body, but he could cook a mean scrambled egg and sliced ham. Although…

"Where did you get ham and eggs?" Last he checked he only had bread in the cupboard.

Erik raised a brow then shook his head as he turned the ham with a fork. "Forgot you can't just transport food in when you need it."

Right. He should remember how normal Draconi got food. But it said something that Erik forgot about his lack of magic. Meant he did a good job of covering up the flaw.

Or Erik had as hard a time remembering things as Jamie did in the morning.

After a quick breakfast and clean up, the two transported to the Council Chambers, materializing outside the door of the round stone building.

"Ready for our hunting orders?" Erik paused, one hand on the doorknob.

"Ready as I'll ever be." Jamie grabbed the other knob, and they shoved open the two double doors.

A cool draft smacked him in the face as soon as he stepped inside. Marble floors ran into tall stone walls, which in turn led to a high, shadowed ceiling. The impression of cold severity. Unyielding.

Unlike Erik, who straightened and stood at attention each time he entered this room, the ambiance set Jamie at ease. He grew up in this cold room, hiding in the shadows behind a chest no one seemed to notice was there, listening to planning sessions, taking comfort in the presence of Thoren, Thoren's father Balthor, and Keara's grandfather Alviss. His adoptive family would never harm him. Something he couldn't say about his living blood relatives.

Not all Draconi thought Halflings equal to their full-blooded brethren.

"Erik?" Balthor, the Council leader, stepped away from the huddle of Council members, brows forming a vee as he stared at the two. "Do my eyes deceive me, or are you actually here on time?"

"It never hurts to try something different. Sir."

"Keep trying. A morning shock keeps us on our toes."

"Yes, sir."

Jamie ducked his head, hoping no one caught his grin. He remembered years ago, back when Alviss led the Council, how nervous powerful, grown males became in the old Draconi's presence. Balthor failed to impress the same way. But then, Balthor was younger and used a different style of leading. And since the Watcher rebellion, only two and a half Watchers remained on the Council, down from six during Alviss's reign.

He glanced to Enar, the half a Watcher, and Thoren's best friend. The male appeared like any other full-blooded Watcher, tall and blond with piercing blue eyes and a warrior build. His mother, though, was part Draconi, giving Enar a few Draconi abilities.

Less than Jamie's middling ones, of course. A fact that should not put him in his happy place, but never failed to do so. What kind of male did that make him? Keara would be appalled.

Balthor motioned them closer until they stood in the huddle of males. No sitting in carved wooden chairs for this Council. "We have reports of another Halfling in the Southlands."

All right! He needed more jaba-jaba beans.

Especially after Erik's potion this morning.

Balthor told them which village, and they turned to go. "Wait a minute." Jamie turned when his grandfather spoke. "Have either of you heard of any males who are abandoning their offspring in the Southlands? There have been an unusual number of Halflings from there lately."

"I have not." Jamie looked at Erik, who shook his head.

"Keep your ears open, and let us know. Our education programs on this issue don't seem to be working. We need to go after the perpetrators."

What Balthor failed to mention, and what Jamie knew bothered him, was the spell Alviss used to discover the bloodlines of the Halflings died with the ancient Draconi, leaving Balthor with no idea of how to find the Halflings' heritage. Or the identities of their fathers.

Yet another reason to remain celibate. Although unlike the Halflings he hunted for, his blood father had remained in Jamie's life until his death when Jamie was ten.

"Good luck with that, Grandfather."

"I detect a note of sarcasm." Balthor's mouth flattened, but the corners of his eyes crinkled.

"From me? Never."

"Be off with you, now. May the Goddess bless your trip."

With a final nod to Thoren, Jamie walked out the door, Erik behind him.

"You almost gave him heart palpitations showing up on time," Jamie said once the Council Chamber doors clicked shut behind them.

"Was he mad? I can never tell."

How could his friend not realize Balthor jested? "He was teasing you."

"Better that than one of those looks Alviss gave." Erik shivered. "He was one scary-arsed Draconi."

"Yes, he was." Right up until the last month of his life.

"While I must admit appearing for a mission is less scary, I'm not so sure it's a good thing he's no longer with us."

"You miss him?" Jamie raised a brow.

"Wouldn't go that far. He did well handling the Watcher Rebellion and fortifying the borders."

"He didn't do so well stopping males from abandoning their offspring all over the place."

"That's good for us. If not for wandering males, they'd have us strengthening wards. Boring. Waste of my talents."

"You can't use bed talents anywhere but in bed."

"Bloody shame, that."

"But—" Jamie gasped, a sharp pain cutting off what he planned to say. The female from his dreams appeared in his mind, arms raised as if to block a blow, eyes reflecting fear and pain. If he didn't find her now, she'd die.

A growl erupted from his lips.

A male never let his female come to harm.

Wait, wait, wait. She wasn't his female. He didn't even know who she was.

But he knew how to find her.

Just as with everyone else he needed to find, the knowledge of how to find her appeared in his mind as if thrust there by her soul's dying breath.

"Jamie? You all right?" Erik touched his arm. "You get a reading on that missing Halfling?"

"No, not him, my female." Who was not his female. Not yet anyway.

"What?" Erik's eyes flared. "You've been hiding a female from me?"

Jamie rubbed the bridge of his nose. "No. I've been dreaming about her for the past week, and she's in trouble. I have to rescue her."

"Who is she?"

Did he dare tell his friend the female was human? Should he lie? Since when did he lie? "I don't know, but she's human. She comes to me in my dreams. She's dying."

Erik blinked. "A human?"

"Why not? I'm half human. You staying here or helping me find her?"

"Oh, I'm helping. This I've got to see. Where do we go?"

"The caves to the west of the border."

"What's a human doing that close to Draconia?"

"She's not there. That's just how I find her."

"All right, then." Erik grabbed Jamie's arm. "Ready?"

Power seeped from Erik's arm into Jamie, boosting his ability to transport. Yet another thing he lacked, the ability to transport others. He barely managed to transport himself. But over the years as Erik's partner, the two discovered a way to keep Jamie from depleting his magical stores. Rather than Jamie transporting to the find, then returning to tell Erik where to go, Erik's touch simplified things.

Jamie pictured the caves in his mind. Several caves

dotted the landscape, one of which had a waterfall running in front of it, obscuring the entrance from view. His internal beacon homed in on that cave. Jamie threw them into a transport, using Erik's magic to pass through the Draconian ward lines and appear inside the cave.

Water pounded a rhythm into the river below the cave, a relaxing, rolling thunder. The damp from the cave mixed with the piney scent of wood from the trees dotting the hillside.

"All right, scout, you sure the way to this female is here?"

"Yes." Clear as if she stood beside him, he heard the female scream, her cry coming from deep inside the inky blackness.

"Where is she?"

Jamie closed his eyes, and the female popped into his mind, this time with the aura of death enclosing her in its grasp. His muscles tightened as he straightened his shoulders. "This way."

The light dimmed the further they walked into the damp darkness of the cave. Erik formed a blue flame in his palm, and they continued forward, their elongated shadows dancing across the stone walls.

Until the blue flame disappeared.

"Goddess's toes, what just happened? I can't form a flame."

Jamie took a deep breath, hoping to calm his racing heart. A male should not react to sudden darkness with an involuntary squeak. Not male-like at all.

"Try again." Good for him. No squeaking voice.

"I. Can't. Form. A. Bloody. Flame. Nothing. It's like my magic stopped working. I can't do anything.

Can you?"

Definitely a panic moment for Erik. Otherwise his friend wouldn't have asked the obvious.

But it wouldn't hurt him to try.

Jamie focused on his palm, willing a blue flame to appear, the same exercise he'd tried, to no avail, since a youngster in magic training classes. Only this time a flame danced in his palm. He sucked down a sharp breath.

"I did it! I formed a flame!"

"Goddess's toes, scout, how'd you do that when I can't?"

"No idea. Back up and try again."

Shoes scraped against pebbled stone as Erik took a step backward. Blue light exploded from his hand, illuminated his wide-eyed expression. He took a step forward, and the flame died. Back and it appeared. Forward and it died. His eyes narrowed.

"You led us to a titanium vein? Are you bloody crazy?"

Jamie swallowed. Titanium was the bane of Draconi, rendering their magic useless, allowing their enemies to overcome them.

So why, for the first time in his life, could he perform magic?

"It couldn't be titanium. I can form a flame."

"I can't. And there is only one thing that stops my magic, and it starts with a T. So what are you? Some sort of titanium neutralizer?"

The dancing flame tickled his palm, creating a corresponding echo in his heart. "I don't know. We can figure it out later. I need to find the female."

"In a cave? Where I have no magic? Did I mention

the lack of magic?"

"Only several times. It won't kill you. That's how I live."

"You have more than I do at the moment. Maybe I should wait here for you."

"And if I get into trouble?"

Erik sighed. "Fine. But you owe me."

"I'll buy you a pound of jaba-jaba beans."

"Lead the way, scout."

Using his palm-tickling blue flame, Jamie marched through the cave, leading them into a small room off a winding tunnel.

"She's in here."

"I don't see her."

"The way to her is in here. Somewhere."

But where? He closed his eyes, picturing the female, seeing her face laced with fear and pain. Forward. He needed to walk forward. He took several steps to the wall.

"She's in the wall?" Erik placed a hand on his shoulder, and Jamie started.

"Maybe it's a door?"

"Touch it and see."

Jamie reached his hand toward the wall, holding his other palm with the flame close to the stone. Cool stone rasped against his fingers.

"It's just a—" *wall* died in his mouth as the stone gave way, collapsing around him like crumbling mortar, casting him and a screaming Erik into a swirling darkness.

Chapter Two

Detective Ruby Parker sat at the bar, eyes fixated on the ice cubes melting in her whiskey. Alcohol got her into this mess, and with any luck, it would help get her out.

"You look a little down, hon."

Parker raised her gaze and stared at the gray-haired, handlebar-mustached bartender. How did she miss him earlier? Sure, she'd had one watered down whiskey drink, but one shouldn't interfere with noticing the human equivalent of Big Foot. "Damn," slipped out before she could stop it. "Your momma give you steroids instead of milk?"

The skin around his pale blue eyes tightened, and she gave herself a mental smack. *Rude, rude, rude*. But that's what happens after being put on administrative leave and forced to surrender her badge and gun to her captain, instead of being commended for doing the right thing. She released a breath as he chuckled.

"Yeah, hon, that's exactly what happened to me. So what happened to you?" Two large palms rested against the bar on either side of her drink as he leaned forward.

Parker leaned back, one hand slipping to her waist for her gun before she remembered it wasn't there. Besides, he was just the bartender, who'd come on shift sometime after her drink was poured. So what if he was the size of a freaking grizzly.

Nothing to fear. Nothing at all to fear.

She swallowed, trying to coat her suddenly dry throat. "Bad day at work."

Grizzly Bartender leaned back, out of her personal space. "Looks like you need another one."

Not really. But as she had no place to go tomorrow, why not? "Another whiskey."

"Good girl. Finish that one while I pour you the other."

He walked off, and Parker pressed the glass against her lips, swallowing away the sting of hard liquor, relaxing as the whiskey pooled warm in her stomach, firing heat through her veins. Much like a lover. No wonder her partner—make that ex-partner—refused to divorce his bottle.

Country music pounded a beat beneath her feet as if the floor danced a rhythm. Or maybe the pounding was all the dancers. She glanced toward where the happy couples twisted and hopped to the music. Her chest clenched like too-tight handcuffs, ached like a bullet through her heart. She'd had that once. That happy carefree, life-is-grand look. *Once.* Before her fiancé decided she spent too much time on the job and not enough time on him.

She could still see the smooth tanned legs of his lover wrapped around his waist, hear the headboard slapping rhythmically against the wall. In their bed. The bed she shared with him. The lying, cheating jackwagon.

So hell, yeah, happy freaking couples brought out the green-eyed monster she kept stuffed deep inside.

"Here's your drink."

Parker turned around, grabbed the fresh whiskey and raised it to the bartender. "Thanks, man. Where did the other bartender go? He was here just a minute ago."

Wrinkles twitched at the corners of his eyes. "He needed a break."

A prickling slid along her scalp, a warning buzzer firing her intuition. As a detective, she learned to rely on that sixth sense of intuition. But she was no longer a detective, now was she? At least not until she got her badge back.

Which might very well be never.

As she sipped her drink, she stared into the large man's ice blue eyes. He didn't blink, countering her stare with a soulless gaze. How could she have missed those killer's eyes earlier?

Drink much, Parker?

Clearly the alcohol affected her intuition buzzer. She doubted Dave, the owner of the bar, would hire a known killer. Since cops made up a good deal of his clientele, setting Big Foot the Killer behind the bar would be a rather stupid move, and Dave didn't strike her as stupid.

But she knew a killer's gaze when she saw one.

Stop being ridiculous, Parker. Get a grip.

Maybe she should grab her drink and move to a table. One of the many open tables. She stared at the three couples swaying to the beat on the floor. Where did everyone go? When she first arrived, the bar was filled, all the tables full. Parker glanced at her watch. Nine o'clock. People should still be hanging out drinking at nine on a Friday night.

A quick glance showed she sat alone at the bar. Her heart rate quickened as she took another sip. Just as well no other cops hung out here tonight. After the way they accused her of previously concealing the truth when she did what needed to be done—when she reported her partner for coming to work drunk—she didn't want to see any of them anytime soon.

She never thought her captain would take the side of her accusers, would be persuaded to believe she'd allowed her partner to work drunk before and only now reported his behavior to cover her ass.

What kind of a cop allowed another to work drunk? How dare they accuse her of concealing the truth? How dare her captain take those assholes' side?

She'd clear her name and get her job back if it was the last thing she did.

She up-ended her glass, pouring the whiskey straight down her throat. Liquid courage worked better inside her than filling a glass. Her glass slipped on the wooden bar when she set it down, toppling onto its side, an overturned turtle spinning on its back. Parker giggled.

Definitely drunk. Mission completed.

"What do I owe?" At least that's what she tried to say, her words slurred into the land of incomprehensible. She swallowed. Tried again. Grizzly Bartender waved a hand.

"That one's on me. You needed it."

"Thanksh." She stood and grabbed onto the bar for support as the room swayed a dance. How much had she drunk? She only remembered two whiskeys, but two shouldn't make her a stumbling fool.

Getting home just got harder.

"What's the matter, hon? You need me to call a cab?" Grizzly's face loomed close, then retreated, close again, now away. What the hell?

Cold seeped into her fingers where she white-knuckled the wooden bar. A cab sounded great. "Pleash."

He turned, paused, faced her. "Let me walk you outside for it."

"Didn't call."

"Yeah, I did. You watched me. I'll walk you outside."

His arm grasped her elbow, tugging her staggering body toward the door. How did he move so fast? Wasn't he behind the counter, not beside her? She glanced back to her barstool. Bad idea. The entire room swam like a fish in a hurricane.

A wave of nausea punched her stomach and she doubled over. Only to be yanked upright by Grizzly, who shoved the door open and pulled her onto the sidewalk.

Where she promptly stumbled to her knees.

"Fuck," Grizzly muttered.

Her stomach rolled, its contents threatening to escape. Okay. Definitely one too many. Although the last time she drank whiskey, it had been much more than two mostly watered down glasses. And no embarrassing stumbling sessions on the sidewalk. She hadn't felt drunk until that last glass. It was almost like Grizzly gave her something extra in her drink.

But why would he do that?

She tried to yank her arm out of his grasp, but his fingers tightened in a bone-crunching grip. Agony exploded in her arm from where she'd been shot years ago. An embarrassing squeak slipped past her lips.

"You ain't going nowhere, honey. We have

something special planned for you."

Parker tried to move. To run. To get away from this crazy bastard with his killer gaze and steel grip. But her body didn't want to obey her mind's commands and refused to move.

Her knees buckled as if her skeletal system exited her skin, leaving her a limp human rag. To hell with this. She was not going down this way. A surge of electromagnetic energy she normally worked hard to tamp down, but lost control of when scared, exploded from her body, wreaking havoc on anything electrical in its way. The streetlight above them shattered into white-hot shards of glass.

Parker tried to open her mouth, tried to use her vocal cords, but neither worked. Definitely a drug. A drug that left her alert but paralyzed. Unable to move. Unable to call for help. Panic flooded her uncooperative limbs as she stared into Grizzly's killer-cold eyes. No one heard her mental scream.

****

Jamie stumbled, pitching to his knees as the dancing lights slowed their frantic twirl. What just happened? And then he fell forward, palms smacking on smooth stone in a successful attempt to stop his nose from cracking against the ground. A heavy weight landed on his back, slamming the air out of his lungs. Erik. *Ouch.* Who knew his friend weighed the approximate amount of a dragon?

Erik rolled to the side and Jamie drew in a deep breath to prove his lungs remembered their function.

"You all right?"

"Would be better if you were shaped more like a pillow." Erik pushed to his feet, offered Jamie a hand

and pulled him upright. "What about you?"

"Would be better if you weighed a bit less."

Erik returned Jamie's grin. "Where are we?"

"I don't know." Jamie's voice echoed as if he stood in a large cave. But what cave had a stone floor as smooth as marble and just as hard?

A small hiss and a blue flame appeared in Erik's palm. Jamie blinked in the sudden light. Erik held his hand up, turning in place. Shadows bounced off strange equipment sitting on shiny metal tables. Erik raised a brow and Jamie shrugged. High windows looked down upon the cavernous room. He poked the gray floor with the tip of his boot. Not marble. Jamie raised a brow. Erik shrugged.

"You landed us in a strange place, scout. You sure the female is here?"

Prickles exploded along his nerve endings, a warning buzzer of the female's proximity and the cloak of death surrounding her. "She's close."

"Great. Get us out of here."

Jamie spotted a door hidden in the shadows on the opposite side of the room. A tugging sensation drew him that direction as if invisible strings connected him to the female. "Come on. She's this way."

He jogged toward the door, Erik running beside him. Then the blue flame disappeared, plunging them into darkness.

"Goddess's toes! What happened?" Erik stopped, staring at his palm as a thunderous rhythmic noise slammed through the building.

Jamie looked up at the ceiling. What was that noise? Did it affect Erik's magic? If so, how?

"Form a flame."

"What?" Jamie dropped his gaze to Erik.

"Go on. Try."

Jamie held his hand out, palm up and remembered the way the blue flame tickled his palm. Light burst from his hand, illuminating a wide-eyed Erik. "I don't understand."

"Titanium. Just don't know where. Maybe we should stay here."

"You jest. We came all this way to rescue a female—a female who is nearby—and you are too scared to leave the building?" Jamie shot Erik his best are-you-jesting glare. While Erik's lack of magic was a bit worrisome, this place was new and, therefore, an adventure. Jamie loved a new adventure. Especially when it came with a female.

"Me? Scared?" Erik's eyes narrowed, and Jamie grinned. "Just giving you an opportunity to change your mind. Which you aren't taking. So lead on, scout. Find this mysterious female. I'll suffer my loss of magic. The lack of magic hasn't hurt you all these years."

"Being able to use my Goddess-given magic is rather enjoyable." Unusual, but enjoyable.

"Don't let it go to your head."

"Don't worry."

"Well, don't just stand there. Lead us to this female." Erik gestured to the door several feet away and Jamie closed the distance and yanked on the handle.

Nothing.

The flame flickered, casting inky shadows across the metal door. Maybe he could use his suddenly apparent magic to open the thing.

But how?

"Goddess's toes, scout. Open the door already."

"It's locked."

"You are a Draconi. A defective one, I must admit." Erik's teeth gleamed white in the shadows. "But a Draconi nonetheless. And you seem to be less defective the longer we're here."

Jamie gritted his teeth at his friend's teasing. "I am not defective." *Liar, liar, tail on fire.*

"Uh-huh. Just think about it opening. Put your hand on the handle and think about the locks falling away. Unless you know a spell?"

Jamie closed his eyes, palm on the metal door, and pictured the internal workings of a lock. He imagined his magic leaving his body as a white cloud, misting through the small hole in the knob to surround the tumblers in the lock. With a small click, the tumblers fell into place, allowing the knob to turn. He gave the door a shove.

Bright flickering lights flooded the entrance, bringing with it a good dose of noise and a strange stench. For a second he feared the same swirling-light-filled passageway that brought them here had returned to take them home. But only the light moved. Jamie doused his palm flame and blinked in the sudden brightness.

Glowlamps sat high atop metal poles, spaced evenly on either side of a broad street. Strange metal conveyances sped by, each one adding to the pulsing, rhythmic noise. A strange stench hung like a heavy blanket in the warm air.

"What is this place?" Erik's wide-eyed, mouth-open expression mirrored his own.

"I don't know. Have you heard of a place like this?"

"Never. Do you feel that strange vibration?"

"You mean the noise?"

"No, although that's bad too. It's the same feeling as when we were in the cave with the titanium. But unlike then, it feels like my magic is cycling."

"Cycling?" Jamie raised a brow. How could magic cycle?

"It's odd. I can't describe it any other way."

"You all right?"

"Of course." Erik waved a hand, dismissing the issue. "Where's this mysterious female? She better be worth the trip."

A growl ripped the air, and it took Jamie a moment to realize it came from his throat.

Erik took a step back, brows doing a meet and greet with his hairline.

"She's worth the trip." Was that distorted voice his? Jamie swallowed.

"All right, then," Erik cleared his throat, "now that we have that straightened out. How are we going to find her?"

"Same way we always do. She's…" he closed his eyes and tried to filter out the noise. No luck with the noise. But he did pick up the female's signal some distance from them. He pointed in her direction. "That way."

"And how are we going to find this building?"

"Same way we always do." The building smelled like home.

"How are we going to get home?"

"Let's get my…the female, and then we can worry about it."

"How do you propose we do that?"

"Transport to her."

"In case you haven't noticed, I can't form a flame." Erik held out his palm. A small, thin flame flickered like a dying fire. "Huh. Make that a normal flame."

"But you have some power."

"Some. Not normal. It feels…strange. I don't like this place."

"Lucky for you, you don't have to stay here long. We'll find her and return home."

"And I suppose you are going to transport us to her?"

A corner of Jamie's mouth kicked up. *Why not?* Nothing to do but to try. He grabbed Erik's shoulder. "Watch." Jamie slipped into the transport as if gliding through water. No hesitation. No wondering if small particles of his flesh would drop out of space, leaving him scattered to the corners of Draconia. No pain like he often experienced. Nothing but throwing his essence through the air, to soar and dip, to seek and find.

They materialized on a street, this one with less noisy conveyances. Most of the metal conveyances sat quiet in rows as if waiting for the opportune moment to attack. Ugly, noisy beasts. He'd rather face an irate dragon.

"Thank you for not killing me." Erik appeared nonchalant, but the stiffness of his posture indicated a string of tension holding him upright like a support beam.

"Anytime." Jamie slapped Erik's shoulder. Tingles sparked across his skin, a prickling awareness of the female's proximity. "She's close." Soon he would meet her. Soon he would save her. Soon he would…

What exactly?

One step at a time, Jamie, one step at a time. Turning in place, he homed in on her signal, triangulating her location. Only to come to a stop when a scream pierced his mind. His female. And she was in trouble. He spun toward the sound, eyes seeking the source of her scream. There. At the end of the street. Right in the middle of an energy fluctuation, a huge male towering over her prone body.

Steam formed in the back of Jamie's throat, billowed out his ears, and circled his head.

Erik hissed as he saw the scene. "Let's get the bastard."

****

Parker slumped to the sidewalk as Grizzly dropped her arm to cover his head against exploding light fixtures. As usual, none of the shards hit her, but that brought little comfort since her body refused to move and ached like a semi had run her over. In seconds, glass would stop falling, and Grizzly would grab her again.

Then she heard what sounded like a champagne cork popping and two too-sexy-to-look-upon men appeared behind Grizzly. *Appeared.* As in one second not there and the next, poof. Not that she wasted much thought on how they arrived. Her eyes fastened on the taller, brown-haired man, her body responding with a fluttering shot of desire. Which was crazy. In more ways than one. When his gaze locked on hers, her mind froze as if joining her body in its rebellion.

While the black-haired man took a swing at Grizzly, Hottie hurried to her side. Which sent a wave of panic through her that released another burst of energy. Car alarms beeped a ruckus from the parking lot down the street.

Hottie paused, head tilted to the side as he stared at her. Then he knelt, placed his hand on her arm, and everything stilled.

Well, almost everything. Heat rushed from his touch straight to her core, spreading tingles in its wake as hibernating hormones roared to life. But the energy rush emanating from her body calmed.

His low voice asked her a question, but damned if she knew what he said. Between the drug and his accent it was a wonder she even heard him. He seemed to realize her lack of understanding and closed his eyes. Something pressed against her brain, like butterflies trapped in her skull, a gentle beating of wings brushing through her memories. What the hell?

Grizzly grunted as the black-haired man punched him in the stomach, then swung a punch that had the taller man ducking to avoid it.

Hottie opened his eyes, and the fight vanished into background noise. His gaze stole hers as surely as if he committed a smash and grab. Nothing mattered but him. Which was ridiculous on so many levels. "Are you all right?" His heavily accented words stroked across her flesh, a soft brush of feathers on skin.

Parker tried to open her mouth and form words, but nothing worked right. So intent on the man kneeling in front of her, she missed the black SUV that stopped feet from where the black-haired man and Grizzly were fighting. A tall, dark-haired man stepped out of the car and took a step toward her until he noticed Grizzly's fighting partner.

Teeth gleamed white in the shadows as the man from the SUV gaped at the fight. His surprise didn't last long as he reached into his pocket, ran behind the black-haired man, and pressed a Taser against his shoulder. The fight came to an abrupt end as the man dropped to the sidewalk in a heap of convulsing limbs.

Hottie turned in the direction of the SUV, sucking in an audible breath as he looked at SUV man. As if he knew him. Did he?

What if Hottie and SUV man worked together? And the fight was a distraction to gain her trust? But why bother drugging her? And what kind of drug had she been given to still be able to think with a paralyzed body?

She. Couldn't. Move.

Parker tried to scream. To open her mouth and scream her fears. To scream for help. Nothing. Another wave of panic energy swarmed inside her, looking for an explosive release.

Hottie placed a hand on her arm, and her energy wave flowed into his palm and up his arm as a dull ripple of light. Shadows like snakeskin played across the side of his neck, disappearing into his wavy hair. Clearly a trick of the light. Or lack of light in this case.

Grizzly took a step toward them.

Hottie released a growl that reverberated through her skin. He dropped her arm and, in one smooth move, rose to his feet.

Sirens sounded nearby, their welcome wails headed right toward her. About time someone came to her rescue.

SUV man glanced toward the sirens and let loose with a curse.

Hottie leapt at him, clearing the distance between them as fast as a caped superhero. He landed in front of the Taser-wielding creep, one arm cocked back, ready to punch, only to drop to the ground, limbs twitching.

SUV man pocketed his Taser as he shook his head at the downed man. Maybe Hottie wasn't working with him. Or maybe he was, and this was all part of some sick plan. Or maybe she had entirely too much whiskey and was hallucinating.

Yeah, right.

"Leave her, we don't have time," the creep said as emergency siren lights flashed across the darkened street. "This one," he gestured toward the no-longer-twitching black-haired man, "has more potential. We'll return for her when he's secured."

Grizzly snarled at her before helping put the downed man into the backseat of the SUV. Two door clicks later, the SUV sped off, leaving her and Hottie alone on the sidewalk.

Fuck. When she said she wanted to get shit-faced, this was not what she had in mind. What had Grizzly given her? Her muscles ached like she'd run a marathon and then tried cliff diving without a wingsuit. Even sucking down a breath became difficult. But still doable. For the time being.

Panic set in, racing along her veins, sending chills down her spine. Paralyzed. On the sidewalk. After a kidnapping attempt. Talk about the cherry on her messed up day.

Then Hottie groaned.

Chapter Three

The rise and fall of a metallic wail snapped Jamie to attention. He rolled over, his muscles finally obeying his brain's order to move. Pain flickered along over-excited nerve endings as he drew in a breath. How did these people harness a jolt like a lightning bolt into a weapon? Luckily the full-body muscle spasms stopped, but he had no idea how long he'd lain upon the hard stone-like ground unable to move.

To make matters worse, the weapon-holder—who he swore was a Draconi—had captured Erik. Jamie focused on his friend's essence, trying to see how far away he was.

There. To his right. Moving away from him at less than half the speed of a dragon.

Panic quick-stepped his heart, pounding an erratic beat behind his ribs. How was he supposed to get to Erik? How—

Oh, right. In this world, transporting was his friend. All he needed to do was lock onto Erik's signal and transport.

No problem.

Jamie swallowed. Not a problem at all. He loved a good adventure. Although finding Erik in this strange world failed to be the adventure he wanted.

Jamie rolled to a sit, his gaze focusing on the slumped, unmoving shape of the female. How could he not have thought of her?

Right. Burst of corralled lightning from unknown weapon.

What did he do now? His friend was in danger. His female lay injured on the ground. And he'd just been hit by a jolt of harnessed lightning. What should he do? Protect his female or find his best friend? How could he leave either behind?

So much for thinking adventures grand.

A cold sweat beaded across his forehead. The choice hurt, but ignoring the female, his female, hurt worse than leaving his friend to the ravages of fate. Erik was capable of turning into a fire-breathing dragon. The female lying on the ground looked like a fragile doll. What kind of male would he be if he left her on her own? He'd see her to safety and then hunt for Eric.

Jamie tried to stand, thought better of it, and crawled to her side. Her cool skin on such a warm evening surprised him, and her shallow breathing didn't help matters.

"Where is your healer?" Surely these people had a local healer he could take her to.

But she didn't answer. Didn't even move her head.

What felt like eels squirmed in Jamie's stomach as his breath caught. Was he too late to save her? No, she still breathed, and if she still breathed then she could be saved. Provided he could find a healer.

The metallic wail grew closer, intensifying into an ear-piercing screech. Jamie clasped both hands over his ears, as if that would protect his sensitive Draconi hearing. The people living in this place must be half-deaf. How else could they stand the almost constant clamor?

Within seconds, two conveyances pulled up, one a large box on wheels, the other shorter and more elongated, both with flashing round light globes on the top. Two uniformed males jumped out of the box on wheels, while a male with a different uniform got out of the shorter conveyance. All three approached him, firing questions in a language he barely understood.

More clamor. But at least the wailing on the conveyance stopped.

Earlier Jamie dipped into the female's mind, reading her language pattern, translating her words into his and back again. Slow going, but effective at learning a new language if given enough time. But with the new arrivals talking at once, gesturing between him, the female, and the building, learning their language patterns was almost impossible.

Almost.

Jamie gestured between the female and him. "Hurt."

His lone word brought on a new flurry of activity.

The two men from the box on wheels brought out a mattress on wheels. Wheels, wheels, wheels. Everything in this land ran on wheels. And squeaky ones at that. They screeched along his nerves with every turn. And the questions from the remaining male didn't help matters.

Jamie knew he needed to say something, to explain himself, but leftover remnants of the electrical blast coupled with the noises of the town and frantic movements of the males tangled his thoughts and revved his heart rate. A cold sweat beaded on his forehead and he wiped it away with his hand. *Take a deep breath, Jamie. Think.*

He needed to learn the language and fast. And the best way to do that was to dip into one of their thoughts, like he did earlier with the female, but for a longer period of time. The longer he stayed in a mind, the greater the potential for harm, not to mention the impoliteness of invasion.

But he had little qualms about jumping into the thoughts of the male in front of him. Necessity overruled politeness.

The male rubbed his forehead as Jamie slipped into his mind. Lucky for him, this male thought in pictures, which made learning the language easier. By the time the two males placed Jamie's female on top of the mattress and attached some tube to her arm, he understood enough of the language to speak it. Not fluently. That would come later.

But he didn't have to be fluent to tell what happened to the male in charge of security. Or, as the male called himself, a cop. Which was a strange word for those who guarded their people.

"We were attacked." And Erik was stolen. Now that Jamie's muscles stopped tingling, he was more concerned about his female than his friend. Erik was a powerful Draconi. Whose powers seemed to be dampened by this place. Maybe he should be more concerned about his friend.

The sound of metal doors clanging turned his head toward the box on wheels, or as the cop thought, an ambulance. His female had disappeared inside the box. A ball of ice slammed through his stomach, into his veins, frozen shards stabbing his heart.

"Where," he cleared his voice, trying to eliminate the un-male-like high-pitch. "Where are they taking her?"

"To the hospital. She your girlfriend? Wife?"

"Hospital?"

The cop raised a brow. "Where you from?"

"Draconia. Where is this hospital?"

"Where's that? Eastern Europe?"

The ambulance rolled away, taking Jamie's breath with it. He needed to go with her, to ensure her safety, to question the healers at the hospital. At least he assumed hospitals had healers. The cop had thought doctors, but the idea behind the mental picture seemed similar.

"I'm sorry, I need to go with her."

"Answer my questions, buddy, and we'll see about taking you to see her."

Jamie stared after the box on wheels taking the female away. His female. Although thinking of her that way was insane. He didn't even know her name.

But not protecting her, leaving her alone in the box—no ambulance—with two males, went against his base instinct. He could no more abandon her than he could cast a spell in Draconia.

"Thank you for your help, but I must go to her."

"Now, wait a minute…hey!"

The cop reached for him, but Jamie jumped into a transport, disappearing into an invisible cloud, his essence flying toward the female. He landed in a crouch on top of the ambulance. Wind slammed against his body, threatening to topple him, unsuccessful only because he flattened against the roof and cast a spell to hold himself in place.

And it worked. The spell. Worked. A jolt of joy shot through his heart. He, the deficient Draconi, cast a working spell. After years of waiting, of wanting, his magic ran thick in his veins like blood, integral and life-enhancing. And the knowledge invigorated him. A male could get used to this power.

If he wasn't careful, his newfound magic would go to his head. Provided the wail of the flashing globe lights on top of the ambulance didn't kill him first.

How did these people live with the noise? He wanted to clap his hands over his ears, but they were busy helping him hold on to the ambulance, which flew through the streets with the speed of a dragon. Minus the wings. What kind of magic powered this conveyance?

After a ride resembling a flight on a dragon's back but with less wind and more bumps, they arrived at a tall building. Pulled right up under a stone-like awning, the wail ceasing at the same moment as the growling vibration. Perhaps the growl was the magic powering the ambulance.

But he had no time to ponder the oddities of this place as the uniformed males jumped out, running through sliding glass doors with the mattress-on-wheels carrying his female. Jamie released his spell and hopped to the ground. A quick glance showed no one noticed him.

Good to know. Stealth always helped on reconnaissance missions.

Sliding glass doors parted, cold air blowing outward as he walked into the building. The mattress-on-wheels disappeared behind another set of closing double doors, this set metal instead of glass. Jamie quickened his pace, slipping between the doors before they shut.

"Hey!" A blue uniformed female ran toward him. "You can't just walk in here."

Goddess's toes. He needed an invisibility spell. A spell he never bothered to learn once his inability to use magic became evident. But he had tried—with varying levels of success—reaching into a human's mind and blocking himself from their sight. Would it work in this place?

Nothing for it but to try.

Slipping into the female's mind was easy. No resistance at all to a Draconi's telepathy. He found the image of himself in her mind and blocked it.

The female halted, lines etched between her brows, as she stared at him. "Huh. I could have sworn I saw…well, long evening." Shaking her head, she turned and walked in the opposite direction.

Yes! Jamie held the victory shout in his mind. Amazing how well his magic, and apparently his telepathy, worked in this strange city.

All thoughts for another day. Right now, he needed to protect his female and then rescue Erik. A jolt of worry for his friend shook his gut. What if Erik was dead? What if he couldn't find his friend? Nonsense. Finding people was his specialty. Draconi magic ran strong in Erik's veins. No need to worry about his friend.

So why did a chill snake down Jamie's spine?

Probably due to the chill in this building. Powerful magic to turn the warm outside air into a chillbump-inducing cold.

No time to think on the cold air. His standing around already lost him sight of the mattress-on-wheels. Adrenaline fired along his nerves as his heart punched an uneven rhythm.

Jamie closed his eyes and sucked in a deep breath. Focusing on the female, he searched for her spark of energy, her unique flicker of life. There. Not far from him. Holding steady.

He quick-stepped down a hallway with a floor made from a shiny material he'd never seen. So many new things in this city. None of which he had time to ponder. Or explore.

Doors with metallic handles and rectangular windows dotted the sides of the hallway. White-coated, uniformed males and females darted in and out of the rooms carrying strange looking bags and devices. Despite the oddity of both the place and the equipment, he knew this was the healing ward. And what a ward. Keara would love to visit this place and practice her healing arts.

Not that she'd ever get the chance. Females rarely left Draconia.

The room at the end of the hallway beckoned to him, a soul-deep calling. He peered through the window at the white-coated male and female—who he assumed to be healers—as they assessed the injured female. At least he assumed it to be an assessment. Why else would they flash a small light in her eyes and check the fluid bag attached with tubing to her arm?

But were they healing her? Or simply observing her?

He did not see any evidence of healing energy spilling from their palms into her body. Maybe they weren't healers?

Jamie jumped back and tried to act inconspicuous as the two white-coated healers walked out of the room.

His attempt worked as the two only glanced his way before scurrying down the hall, talking about the patient needing a scan.

A scan? But the thought fled as his sight flickered, black spots dancing along the periphery, accompanied by a whirl of dizziness. Jamie slumped against the wall, his fingers curling into his palms, the dull pain enough to keep him conscious.

The vision blotted out the hallway, showing him a scene of the tall giant who captured Erik walking into the female's room. Jamie watched, impotent, unable to move, unable to help, as the giant carried the female out the door and down the hall, the gray mist of death clinging to them like a shroud.

And then the vision disappeared, Jamie's sight returning to normal, his heart pounding like a blacksmith's hammer, his breath the short gasps of the grieving.

Jamie wiped his sweaty palms on his trousers as he stared at the door to the female's room. She was not going to die. He was not going to allow that vision to come true. He had not traveled all this way to wherever this place was to lose the reason for his visit. He could not leave her to her fate.

Jamie pushed off the wall, stepped across the hall and shoved open the door to her room.

Chapter Four

The squeak of hinges snapped Parker's attention to the door. Hottie stood in the doorway, one hand on the frame, the other on the handle, a look of determination plastered on his face. A look she was familiar with. A look she saw reflected in her mirror on a daily basis. A look mirrored on her coworkers' faces when working a case.

A look she never thought to see directed her way.

Which was a bit unnerving, but not nearly as unnerving as the realization he'd followed her. He stood in the doorway like he owned the place. Or owned her.

Her limbs shuddered like a car without shocks. He. Followed. Her. Was he stalking her? Was he with the ones who tried to kidnap her? What was he doing here? More to the point, how did she get rid of him? Her muscles might be coming out of a deep freeze, but that didn't mean she could hop off the bed and toss him out the door.

Where was the damn call button?

Parker patted the mattress. Hottie took a step closer. Then another. No button. Her heart shook an uneven rhythm, a warning drum in her veins. Her hand moved faster against the mattress, searching, seeking, not finding.

Damn it.

"Be of ease. I mean no harm."

She stilled, her hand paused mid-pat as if his words flipped her off switch. Deep and soothing, his voice stroked across her frazzled nerves, slowing her racing heart.

If he could bottle that sound, women would fall at his feet. What was she thinking? Sexy voices and good looks did not mean pure hearts. She should know.

Parker cleared her throat. "Who?" Her voice squeaked like a loose wheel. Another round of throat clearing, and she tried again. "Who are you?"

He smiled.

Her heart started a pounding rhythm, only this time it had nothing to do with fear and everything to do with sexual magnetism. Damn it.

"My name is Jamie. What is your name?"

She wasn't really going to tell him, was she? Her mouth opened, making the decision for her. "Parker." She cleared her throat before her voice got any other smart ideas and started giving him her life story and inviting him back to her house. Which would enter the realm of too dumb to live. She should not trust this stranger, no matter how her body reacted to his presence. "Why did you follow me?"

"I've come to help you."

Help her with what? Taking her to Grizzly and crew? Getting her job back? Maybe he knew what drug she was given, which would help the doctors reverse the effects. Although it did seem to be wearing off, her voice almost normal, her strength returning in increments. But not quick enough to jump off the bed and run out the door. Damn it.

"Help me?"

"You are marked for death."

A chill attempted a slide down her spine but she shook it away, swapping it for a shot of disbelief. "What are you? The Grim Reaper?"

"What is this Grim Reaper?" His brows slammed down.

Parker failed to stop the eye roll. Where was he from to have never heard of the Grim Reaper? Mars? Well, he did have an accent, so maybe she should cut him some slack. "Death personified."

His eyes flared. "I am not this personification of death. I've come to stop your death. Not aid it."

"That's…" nice of you? What did she say to that? "Why?" Because in the grand scheme of things, that pretty much summed it up.

"It is a calling. And they come. You must hurry."

"And how do you expect me to do that?" Being drugged meant hurrying was no longer in her vocabulary. Besides, how did she know he spoke the truth?

He took a step toward her. "I will help—"

Parker shrank as far away as she could. Which turned out to be a whole inch, as if that would help. But she found the call button and put her thumb to good use pressing the thing. What were the chances of a nurse arriving before he reached her?

And the answer would be none.

Jamie placed his hand against her arm, and a fission of electric energy sparked between them. His gaze captured hers, breaking and entering into the deepest recesses of her soul, igniting emotions she thought long dead.

What would it be like to be loved by a man who

could call up these feelings each time she looked at him? To know he would do anything for you? To be put into the local mental institution for losing one's mind over a potential kidnapper? *Wake up, Parker, and stop living in fantasy-land.*

The squeak of hinges snapped her attention from the man who had the potential to be anything from her kidnapper to her lover and focused on the nurse. Thank god for interrupting nurses.

"Did you need something?" The nurse's gaze jumped from Parker to Jamie as she took a step into the room. "Who are you?"

"Her friend. She needs to be moved."

Parker opened her mouth at his gall, but the nurse spoke to Jamie, ignoring her as if she was nothing more than a discarded candy wrapper.

"We're planning on admitting her." The nurse put a hand on her stuck-out hip, her gaze traveling from Jamie's head to below his belt with a slow trip back to his eyes.

Hello, this is a hospital, not a bar, lady. And I'm the damn patient over here. But for once the words stuck to her tongue. Probably because she'd never seen such unprofessional behavior in the ER staff. Shock tended to silence a person.

"Admit her to what?" Jamie's brows furrowed.

Clearly hot as hell didn't mean smart as Einstein. Damn it. Not to mention the real problem here, him answering for her. As if he had some sort of right.

About time she spoke up for herself before flirty nurse and Jamie made all her decisions like she was some sort of child. "Just overnight, right?" For observation, since her muscles seemed to be returning to normal. By morning she should be good to go. Go where was the problem. And one she'd think about tomorrow.

She had more pressing needs now. Like getting rid of Jamie, the potential kidnapper. But did she really want to get rid of him? Of course she did. Right?

What if he spoke true? What if he was here to save her, not harm her? He spoke with conviction, his body language in line with his words, like he believed what he said. So did the local delusional patient. Didn't make him right.

"Yes, overnight. Your friend can come to your room."

"He's not—"

"That would be good." Jamie smiled at the nurse who thrust out her chest like she was some kind of preening bird.

Parker clenched her jaw tight enough to make her teeth ache. How dare he insist on following her. She would...what exactly? Lay here and glare? Hit the call button and hope for a male security guard? Scream like a sissy? As if that would happen.

"He's not—"

"I'll get an orderly and be right back. Don't go anywhere." More eye batting from the nurse at Jamie. And then she slipped out the door, leaving Parker alone with a hovering hottie and a bad attitude.

Her hand ached for the grip of her Glock. "You can't keep following me."

"It's not following. It's protecting."

"Protecting? From what?" The kidnappers? Or was he in cahoots with them and thought he was saving her from something else? His one-brow-cocked gaze raked the length of her body, sending heat straight to her cheeks.

"Yeah, I drank something I shouldn't, but so do plenty of other women with much worse results than this. What makes me so special?"

He pursed his lips together, stared at the ground for a heartbeat.

What was he hiding? Right when her thoughts started spiraling along various scenarios, he spoke. "You came to me in my dreams crying for help. Each night for a week. How could I not seek you out?"

And didn't those words sink straight into her stomach like the tang of fizzy pop. Since when was she a hot man's dream woman?

Yeah, she needed her Glock in her palm so she could use it to whack some sense into her head. What difference did it make if a hot man dreamed about her?

Not one bit. Not at all. *Liar, liar.*

Clearly she ingested a paralyzing agent mixed with an aphrodisiac. Why else would she be thinking such thoughts while lying drugged in the ER with a possible stalker beside her bed?

Parker cleared her throat. "And now that you've found me?"

"You are not safe here. You need to leave."

"I'm in a hospital. With security guards, security cameras and other various eyes." Which didn't necessarily make the place secure—Jamie's presence busted that theory—so maybe he proved his point.

Not that she would allow him to haul her away. If she left with a stranger it would be on her terms.

"Detective Parker?" A familiar voice snapped her attention to the door, and she smiled as Dr. Dover walked in the room. She should correct him of her current lack of badge status, but didn't want to broadcast her shame and anger over today's not-so-pleasant events. Besides, she wasn't giving up her status without a fight. "They told me you were in here. How are you?"

"Dr. Dover. I was wondering where you were."

As a detective, she knew the ER staff almost as well as her own department staff. And Dr. Dover had always been enjoyable to work with, not to mention pleasant eye candy. But he had nothing on Jamie.

Dr. Dover stepped closer to the bed but did a double take, his eyes flaring, with one glance at Jamie.

A low growling filled the room, the sound an animal makes when protecting its own. Jamie stood with his back to her, seeming to have grown in size. Must be a trick of the lighting or a side effect of the drug. Men did not grow larger in the span of a minute.

And then Jamie stepped to the side, out of Dr. Dover's way, his hands scrubbing down his face. With one last glance Jamie's way, Dr. D stepped beside her, resting his large palm against her forearm. Unlike Jamie's touch, his elicited no response, which ruled out the aphrodisiac mixed in with the drug. God only knew Dr. D had captured her attention in the past before the Great Fiancé Debacle.

"They said you'd been drugged?" His gaze cut from her to Jamie and back, his brows furrowed.

She shrugged. "Yeah. Paralyzing agent. It's wearing off."

"Good, good. You'll be admitted…" The rest of his words faded as her attention snapped to Jamie. Who took slow steps to the door, head cocked to the side as if he heard a noise.

A noise in the ER. Definitely something to get excited about.

And yet, her pulse quickened, her muscles tensing under her hospital gown as if they expected to sprint a race. Dr. D continued to speak, his mouth moving, forming syllables her ears failed to convert into meaning.

"…all right? Detective?" Dr. D shook her arm, concern stamped on his face.

The crash of doors slamming into a wall caused her to jump, a shot of adrenaline spiking her system. Loud voices echoed down the hall as footsteps pounded a rhythm against the linoleum floor.

"I've got to go. Multiple vehicle accident. I'll check back…" his eyes narrowed on one of the machines near the bed, his hand reaching out and giving it a thump. "Why is the pulse-ox not working?" He shook his head as he gave it another thump. "How weird. I'll have someone exchange it. Gotta run. They're bringing in the survivors now." A final pat on her arm and he dashed out the door, the click of the jamb lost in the scramble of a busy ER.

Once again leaving her alone with a man she knew little about. A man who was currently pacing a track in the linoleum.

"Have a seat, why don't you?" Parker pointed to the chair stuck in the corner like a disobedient student.

Jamie ran a hand through his hair then did as she asked, picking up the bag containing her clothing and purse before parking it on the plastic chair.

"Do you mind handing me that bag?" So that's where they put her personal items. She needed to check her messages, return the voice mails…

Oh wait. Since she was suspended from the force, who did she have to call? Talk about a sad commentary of her life.

"As you wish." This time she didn't shrink when he walked to her side, placing the bag between her arm and torso.

Jamie returned to the chair, the plastic squeaking as he sat. "You need to leave."

"I need to remain overnight for observation. Leaving is not an option." Especially with you went unsaid.

"They'll return for you."

Her spine morphed into a column of ice, the hairs on her neck rising to escape. How did she know they hadn't already returned for her in the shape of the hottie sitting in the corner?

"How do I know they haven't already?"

****

Jamie straightened as her words sank deep. She thought he aided the kidnappers? Hadn't he explained why he was here? How could she think he meant her harm? He'd traveled who knew how far to rescue her and she still thought ill of him? How could she think his following her meant anything other than protection?

"I said I'm here to protect you from those who mean you harm."

"How do I know you tell the truth?"

"You insult me."

"Well? Think about it. You show up right when I'm being kidnapped—"

"And was hurt."

"How do I know that wasn't planned?"

46

"I would not volunteer for that kind of pain."

"Yeah, being Tasered isn't pleasant, but if done correctly it won't kill you. Everyone knows that. And it makes it easy to plant someone to play on my emotions Make me trust them so then they can lead me to the real threat."

Jamie blinked. How could a female be so distrustful of a male? Maybe the males here did not protect females as they should. He had traveled enough to know Draconi males were unique in their treatment of females.

Just because he understood her view did not mean he wasn't hurt by her words. He wanted her to think of him as her savior, as a male she could trust with her life, not as someone who meant her harm.

Which considering how little he knew about her was disturbing. Almost all males would protect females, even those they didn't know, but the way he wanted her to trust him went beyond normal concern and into the realm of a male who met his mate.

And although he tended to think of her as his female—after all, it wasn't every day he dreamed of a real female needing his help—it didn't mean he wanted her as his mate.

He didn't even know if a Halfling like himself could have a mate. Unlike Keara, who had more Draconi traits than human ones, his middling magic did not bode well for finding that one female created just for him.

It wouldn't surprise him at all to discover a defect in yet another area of his life.

Still, Parker's words shouldn't cause his chest to ache like a malfunctioning heart. Not at all.

"I am not here to harm you. I traveled a long way to save you and whether you want me to or not is irrelevant. I will not allow you to come to harm." He crossed his arms over the ache formerly known as his chest and gave her his best glare.

She stared at him for one heartbeat, two, then her gaze dropped to the sheet, her breath releasing on a sigh. "Fine. My bullshitometer—"

"Your what?" Was this some strange device she had hidden on her person?

"Bullshitometer. My internal gauge for determining whether or not you're lying."

He still had no idea what a meter was, but he got the gist of her words. "I am not lying."

She shrugged. "As I was saying, you're not registering on my bullshitometer, but that's probably due to the drug."

"Or the truth."

Her glare slapped him with caution, and he stopped the urge to scoot back in the chair. The arousal pushing against his trousers caught him off guard. Since when did a female's anger turn him on?

"Just stay there, and don't come any closer."

"As you wish."

Easier than he thought. Especially since he didn't want her to see what was happening below his waist.

Goddess's toes.

Time slipped by with the speed of an arthritic dragon lumbering up a hill.

Parker's eyes drifted closed, her bag tucked in the crook of her left arm like a pillow, her right hand grasped around an elongated piece of metal attached to a thick metal string.

Metal, metal and more metal. Along with a bunch of construction items he didn't recognize. Like the chair he sat in. The metal frame comprising the object caused his magic to surge like titanium did, but it didn't look the same as Draconian titanium. And the hard material he sat on was unknown in Draconia. As were the flooring and the street paving. What an unusual place. He'd love to explore, but protecting Parker until she could travel meant his tingling arse needed to sit on the hard, unknown material for a while longer. Then he could rescue Erik.

Jamie closed his eyes and concentrated on his friend. Panic and pain shot through his body as he homed in on Erik's position. Jamie shot out of the chair like a dragon's fireball, numb and tingling legs threatening to collapse. Grabbing the back of the chair he tottered on shaky legs.

"Bad dream?" Parker's voice stroked across his nerves, concern lacing the words.

"Erik's hurt." Why had he believed his friend could handle himself? Erik's magic didn't work right in this city, as evidenced by his capture and current incarceration. If only he had followed Erik instead of Parker, his friend wouldn't be in pain.

But then, she might be the one injured and captured instead of Erik.

What to do, what to do. Jamie's breath heaved in and out of his lungs as the numbness wore off and he paced around the room.

"I said, who's Erik?"

Jamie stopped by the door, hand mid-run through his hair. "What?"

"Is Erik your friend? The one they took instead of

me?"

"Yes. I need—"

A loud crash exploded from the hall, causing raised voices to exclaim in alarm. He hurried to the door, cracking it open enough to peer out. Adrenaline shot through his veins, shaking his limbs, his throat turning to desert sand.

His vision came true. The kidnappers had returned for Parker.

Jamie leapt to her side. Both her palms came up as if to push him away, but the door slammed open, bouncing off the wall like a thrown dagger. The bearded giant who'd harmed Parker stood in the doorway, a dark shadow of revenge.

Jamie slipped his arms under Parker, said a quick prayer to the Goddess and threw them into a transport.

Chapter Five

Pain slammed along her nerves a second after Jamie grabbed her like he meant to lift her out of the bed. Darkness surrounded her. Grizzly's wide-eyed open-mouthed expression disappeared in a whirl of colors. Thoughts fizzled as agony took up residence in her bones. Gray shapes blurred past, colors streaking like headlights on a time-lapse exposure. Then, with a pop, everything stilled.

Parker concentrated on not screaming. Screaming in fright and pain was for sissies. Even when shot in the arm several years ago she'd held in a scream, locking down the pain by force of will and a tightened jaw.

But this bone-shattering pain went far beyond the burn of a bullet.

Didn't mean she would admit to the low moan breeching her lips. Nope. She would not act like a wimp.

"Are you all right?" Jamie lowered her until her butt and legs rested against what felt like concrete. "Most people have problems their first time transporting."

Good to know her locked jaw wasn't for nothing. But what did he mean by transporting?

Although a glance around the darkened room tripped her heart rate up a notch. They were not in the hospital. How… What… *Oh my god.*

Spots danced on the edge of her vision. They did not just leave the hospital by disappearing like a star of a sci-fi flick. Impossible. Totally impossible. *Then why are you no longer in the freaking hospital?*

Her breathing quickened, pulse pounding in her ears. The dancing spots intensified, swarming into a vision-darkening cloud. *So much for not acting like a sissy.* And then she passed out.

When Parker regained consciousness, the chill of concrete seeped into her back and a blue light flickered, casting shadows across stacks of pallets. A warehouse. How...oh, right. Jamie hadn't really transported her. The drug must be causing hallucinations. Yeah, that was it. Hallucinations. *You know you've fallen down the rabbit hole, Parker, when having hallucinations is the better choice.*

"You wake." Jamie's face swam into her line of vision, blue shadows dancing across his skin as if lit from his hand.

Parker glanced to his hand where a blue flame danced. Nuh-uh. No way. Not happening. Flames did not appear in hands. Let alone flicker blue. Nope. Definitely a drug induced hallucination.

She drew in a deep breath. Since she was hallucinating, this whole room was some sort of mental fabrication. Although why her brain picked a warehouse to imagine was beyond her.

"You are not imagining. The ones who took Erik returned for you. I took you here to protect you."

So much for calm breathing. She almost pulled another sissy out of her back pocket and passed out cold.

Parker swallowed the dry lump in her throat.

"Come again?"

"I transported you here to protect you. I wasn't sure where else to go."

"Why here?"

"We came through this place."

"Through it?"

"Transported into it. Somehow. I've never seen anything like this building."

"It's a warehouse." Clearly she was dealing with someone mentally unstable. While wearing her baby blue hospital gown. Damn it.

"Ah. An over-large storage building. I see that now." He scratched the back of his head. "Are you better?"

Wasn't that the question of the evening? While she no longer felt like fainting, she didn't think she could jump up and outrun him. Lying flat on her back like an invalid was rather demoralizing but might allow her to discover a bit more about her current deluded kidnapper.

Or maybe he wasn't so deluded. If he told the truth and this warehouse wasn't a delusion, Grizzly had found her in the hospital and physics needed a rewrite. Which was enough to give a former detective a case of the shakes.

"Maybe."

He jerked his non-flamed hand through his hair. "I cannot leave you alone, but I need to find Erik. He is hurt."

Her inner detective, the one no loss of title could destroy, spoke. "How do you plan on finding him?"

"I find people. That is my...um..." his brows furrowed. "How do you say?"

"Job? Work?"

"Yes. My job. I find people. Among other things."

A detective. Like her. A grin flirted on the corners of her lips. No, no, no. She would not smile at Hottie. Or think of him as Hottie. He'd kidnapped her. Never mind that he thought he helped her. If only she still held her badge.

Not to worry. She'd have her badge back come hell or high water.

Right after she discovered which Jamie was. Hell? Or high water?

****

Jamie ran a hand over his head. Blue shadows flickered across Parker's face, sparking blue highlights in her straight black hair. Suspicion laced with curiosity ran through the depths of her dove gray eyes. Not the look he wanted, but it beat fear.

Shoving with her elbows, she pushed upright. He reached out a hand to help but pulled it back at her flinch. How did he prove he meant her no harm? Hadn't he already rescued her? What more proof did she need?

Females in this strange place carried suspicion like a healer did her bag of herbs.

But her trust issues weren't his biggest problem. Erik was. How was he to rescue his friend and keep Parker safe?

And get her some clothes. The blue clothing given to her in the healing ward barely covered her thighs and it gaped in back, exposing her nicely shaped bottom.

"I'm not hallucinating, am I?" Parker's eyes narrowed. "You somehow took me out of the hospital."

"Transported you. It's the way we move around."

"We?"

Jamie shook his head. "I need to find Erik. I need to get you clothes. Unless you can go out wearing that?" He gestured to the blue clothing.

"Don't be ridiculous. Just take me back to the hospital."

"I can't. They found you there."

"So Grizzly wasn't a dream."

"Grizzly?"

"The giant who tried to kidnap me at the bar. The one who took your friend."

"No dream. He came for you as I predicted."

"You're psychic then."

"Psychic?"

She sighed. "You can see into the future."

"Oh. Yes. Sometimes." Not often, but enough to trust what he saw would come to pass. "I need to find Erik, but I cannot leave you alone."

"Maybe I can help you."

Jamie blinked, his eyes flaring. A male should never force a female to accompany him. *She volunteered*, his inner voice offered. But still. It was a male's duty to protect females from danger.

Although taking her with him would solve his problem. He could find Erik while ensuring she remained safe from Grizzly, as she called the giant.

Or he could be leading her into danger.

"I find people for a living too, you know."

He caught his mouth before it fell open. "You are allowed to go into danger?"

Her bark of a laugh caught him by surprise. "I'm a police detective. Danger is always there. Maybe that's why I want to help you find your friend."

"For the danger?" Females as protectors? What a

strange land.

"Because it's my job. Or was. Well, it will be again. Anyway, it's probably not the smartest thing to return to my home in case they know where I live. Luckily my clothes and purse traveled with us when you beamed us up, so I have a change of clothes."

Jamie blinked a couple of times in rapid succession, hoping the movement might translate her words. Beam them up? "Do you mean transport?"

"Whatever you call it."

"Ah. Are you able to change clothes?" The thought of taking care of her started a strange tingling throughout his body.

"Provided you turn around and don't watch."

Jamie scooted around, giving her his back, keeping his hand out to the side so she would have some light. He wanted to turn around, to watch the blue gown drop from Parker's shoulders, exposing her breasts. Wanted to see the color of her nipples against the nut brown of her skin. Watch as they hardened at his stare. The bag rustled, the strange material crackling as it moved, snapping him out of the fantasy.

What was it about this female that caused him to slip into fantasy-land when he should be focused on other things? Parker was attractive and it had been awhile since he bedded a female. But seeing a comely female was a common occurrence while on a mission. Until now, it had never detracted from his purpose. What was different about Parker?

"Okay, you can turn around. I'm dressed."

Jamie turned around. Parker sat on the floor, a pale tint hiding underneath the dark hues of her skin. Black trousers framed her long legs, her white shirt had some kind of fastenings down the front and was covered by a blue jacket. Her—what did she call it? Oh, yes, purse—hung strapped across her body underneath the jacket. A sensible style of dressing. Did she wear anything underneath her clothing?

Goddess's toes, he needed to keep his mind on the mission. "Are you ready?"

"Where are we going?"

"To where Erik is being held."

"How do you know where he is?"

"It's what I do."

"Ah, yes. You mentioned finding people was part of your job. But how do you find them?"

"I don't know. I just think about it and the location comes to me."

"Huh. That must be nice."

"It is good work. Helping people." And the jewels were an extra bonus. Not that jewels would be found tonight. Unless he counted the female before him. No, no, no. He needed to stop that line of thought and focus on Erik. Not the feel of Parker pressed against him. Definitely not speculations on her underclothes.

Jamie gritted his teeth.

"Where is he?"

"I'll show you." So she could help find Erik, not so he could feel her body against his.

Goddess's toes.

Extinguishing the flame, Jamie pulled her into an embrace and transported them to where Erik's essence flickered.

Chapter Six

This time the pain of transporting faded as soon as Parker's feet touched the ground. What a great way to move around. And yet, doubts about reality crept into her thoughts. Being with Jamie felt real. The scents, the sounds, the sights, all as she would expect. The transporting thing? Not so much.

A sharp realization stole her breath. If she believed Jamie, if she believed what her eyes showed her, what her body felt while transporting, then she wasn't hallucinating. But how could that be? Who on earth had the ability to shift places? To beam from one spot to the next with a thought?

Parker shuddered. Evidence existed. She might not like the direction it pointed in, but evidence proving a new reality existed. Yet it did not fit into how her world worked. Not at all. And yet. And yet. Her brain tripped over the obvious. Tripped down a path into a realm of impossibilities. She never thought to see the day where she preferred vivid hallucinations over evidence.

"You are not hallucinating." Jamie's voice cut through her thoughts, snapping her back to the present.

She must have spoken aloud. Or he read minds. Yeah, right. But she wanted to believe him, even if it meant a rewrite of physics and every natural law she knew. She wanted to believe he spoke true and his too-hot-for-words self had nothing to do with her desire.

Okay, not much to do with it. Parker believed that look in his eyes. The one that spoke volumes about the truth behind his words. The one she learned as a detective to look for when interviewing a suspect. The one that had never failed her in the past.

Reality as she knew it just needed a reboot. "What do you expect? Until I met you I never realized transporting existed outside of movies."

He grunted, releasing his arms from her waist, leaving her body longing for his touch. Oh great. More evidence for the aphrodisiac in the drug scenario. She swayed, her legs unsteady after the paralyzing agent, unwilling to perform their duty.

Jamie caught her, one arm wrapping around her waist, satisfying her longing. "Do you need to sit?"

"Probably." *Sissy.*

He lowered her to the ground, then stood, turning in a small circle as if trying to discern where they landed.

Wind laced with the scent of rain blew against her face. The hulking dark shapes of the mountains rose in the west, lights from a highway snaked nearby, the hum of cars interspersed with chirping insects. The loud roar of a plane had Jamie ducking, arms over his head.

"It's just a plane. Nothing to worry about."

Parker turned, scooted around on her butt, her attention caught by runway lights several hundred yards from their location. No way. Jamie transported them to DIA?

Denver International Airport sat to the northeast of the city, surrounded by a lot of nothing, the city creeping closer each year. Why would the kidnappers bring Erik here? If they wanted to fly him someplace else, a smaller airport would better serve the purpose. Easier to hide a victim than trying to drag him through security.

Unless they hid him in the tunnels?

Parker snorted. The tunnels conspiracy theorists believed held aliens and other secret government work, the new Area 51 right smack in the middle of Colorado. Some people would believe anything.

"A plane?" Jamie's question snapped her attention from her thoughts. He glanced from the sky to her, his arms no longer over his head.

"It's how we transport. Not as fast as your method."

He squatted before her, brows furrowed. "What is a plane?"

"Like a car." At his blank look, she tried again. "A boat?" He nodded. "A boat with wings."

"Like a dragon."

"Yeah, I guess, but planes are metal and dragons don't exist."

"Dragons don't—" Jamie swallowed. "This place has no dragons."

Why the incredulous tone?

"Only in myths. Did you expect to find one here?" Her breath hitched. Was Hottie deranged? Or was she for continuing to call him Hottie?

Jamie ran his hand over his head as he stared at the ground, taking too long to answer. As if he chose his words with care, deciding how much truth to mix with a lie. "Another metal conveyance. What is it with you people and metal?"

Way to change the topic. Perhaps in his language, whatever that was, a dragon meant something different.

But what? Why hide? Well, that was obvious. If he answered that he expected to find dragons hiding in the fields it would mark him as crazy. Which probably meant he wasn't and just had language difficulties. Hopefully.

"You can't tell me metal's not used where you're from."

"Of course we use metal. Just not to the extent you do."

"And why is that?"

Another hand through the hair. Another pause. Truth or lie?

He shrugged. "Erik is around here someplace. Do you see a building?"

Master of changing the topic. What was he hiding? Was it dangerous? Given enough time she would discover his secrets. "I thought you could find things."

"I can. But I can only get close to the object. The rest is up to me."

"Why? Why not land next to the object?"

He shrugged. "I don't know. But it doesn't work that way. I get close, and then I can find the person. Or thing. But *I* have to find it. It never appears before me when I transport to it."

"No offense, but that's a rather strange power."

"It works for me. Now, do you see a building? Someplace where he could be held? Not too far off."

What she saw was a too-hot-to-be-real man avoid fully answering her questions. The airstrip, security fence, and airplanes almost close enough to touch, faded into the background as she watched Jamie. What was he hiding? No, make that what exactly was he? How did he transport? She'd given up on the idea this was a hallucination. Not even in her wildest dreams had she ever come close to this experience, not to mention it felt real. Definitely not a dream. Nor a hallucination.

So how did he transport? Maybe he was from the future and had some sort of device? *Come on, Parker, do you really think he stepped out of a scene from a sci-fi movie?*

"What about there?"

Parker blinked and followed the line of Jamie's point, straight to the terminal off in the distance.

"Doubtful." He'd have a better chance of being held prisoner in the tunnels.

Parker snorted.

"What do you find humorous?"

"Sorry. That's the plane terminal. It's doubtful he's in there."

Jamie turned back to the terminal, head cocked to the side. He sighed. "Yes, you are probably right. It's a little out of my range. He seems close, but I don't see a place where he could be held."

"Maybe we can't see it in the dark."

"I see well, even in the dark. There are no buildings closer than that one." Again with the pointing toward the terminal.

Nothing unusual about seeing in the dark. Really. Some people just had better vision than others. No reason for a chill to slide down her spine, a warning of the supernatural.

Evidence, Parker. Evidence.

A part entombed within her recognized Jamie as something more than human. He had abilities outside of the norm like she did. He used his while she tried hard to keep hers buried. Extra abilities did not mean she wasn't human. She suspected plenty of others had odd abilities they kept quiet about for obvious reasons. Unlike Jamie.

Otherworldly? Yes. But no reason for chills. The longer she stood in his presence, the less she believed her original thought of him meaning her harm.

Just because she started to trust him didn't mean she wouldn't question him. "Where are you from?"

Jamie turned to face her. "What does that have to do with Erik?"

"Why can you not answer my question?" Maybe she should still be wary of his intensions.

His jaw tensed, lips flattening. "Draconia. Is it possible he's in a cave underground?"

"Where is Draconia?"

"You said you'd help me look for Erik."

"I will. I am. I want to know where Draconia is."

"And if I answer your questions, you will help me find him now?"

"Yes."

"You have not heard of Draconia?"

Parker shook her head. Did he really think if she'd heard of it she'd still be asking where it was?

Jamie gestured to the sky. "How far do these planes go?"

He wasn't changing the subject that easily. "All over the world. Where is Draconia?"

"All over?" His eyes flared. "You have mapped the entire world?"

"Of course." Most of it anyway.

"And you have never heard of Draconia?"

"No. Where is it?"

He ran a hand through his hair, then slammed his

fists against his waist and stared at the heavens. "I do not know. I no longer know. We came through a cave and landed in the storage facility. What did you call it?"

"A warehouse."

"Yes. We landed there. Then I found your essence, you were in trouble, and we went to you. I do not know where we are."

"Colorado. Denver, Colorado."

"This is a country?"

"It's a state in America. The United States of America. Surely you've heard of us?"

He shook his head.

Impossible. Who in the world hadn't heard of America? That sense of otherworldliness slammed into her, spreading through her veins like a Taser zap. He. Was. Not. From. Here. Impossible. Of course he was. There had to be an explanation. *Yeah, Parker, there is one. You just don't like it. Look at the facts.*

First, humans in real life did not transport or form flames in their palms. Second, he didn't seem to know about common things, like planes. Third, and most damning, he had never heard of America.

More evidence. More disbelief. She did not like the direction this interview was taking. Aliens did not exist. Besides, Jamie was definitely a man, no green skin or large eyes like all those depictions.

Perhaps he hit his head, giving him delusions. Even so, that theory failed to take into account the transporting.

"How did you come through the cave?"

"I don't know. I felt you on the other side, touched the wall, and here we were."

"Has that ever happened to you before?"

"Never. Erik's powers did not work once we arrived, while mine did."

"Powers?"

He shrugged.

Okay, then. Transporting and the flame in the palm trick were definitely powers. Much less destructive than her electrical charge when upset. And his words explained his accent and lack of knowledge of planes. He wasn't from here. As in, not from Earth. She licked her lips and sighed. So much for not thinking she hallucinated.

"You aren't hallucinating. Now—"

"How do you know what I'm thinking?"

"You're…" he cleared his throat. "It's on your face."

Liar. He read minds. Another point for the alien explanation. Damn it.

"Now are you going to help me or ask questions all night?"

Parker swallowed. Help an alien. Which of them was more deranged? At least he made for smokin' hot eye candy. She cleared her dry throat. Twice. "He could be below ground. But I'm not sure what's under there. Can you poof in and see?"

"If you mean transport underground, I cannot. Well, I can, but it is foolhardy to try without knowing how far to go or what is there. I could end up stuck in rock."

"Oh. Then I don't know how to get underground, or if there is even an underground."

"Let's say there is. What would be the best way to get there?"

"From the terminal, I'd guess. Unless there is an

outbuilding around here. Or a door stuck in the ground."

"I do not see an outbuilding."

"I have no idea where in the terminal to go. It would be concealed and in the employees only area."

"Erik is closer than the terminal. Perhaps the door in the ground?"

"You look around for a hidden entrance while I sit here. I'm still feeling a little weak."

"I'm sorry. I should not have asked—"

She waved a hand in the air, cutting off his words. "Don't worry about it. Look around. When you find it I'll go through it with you."

He nodded and started walking in small circles, expanding outward, canvassing the area. Every few feet Jamie stopped as if he was trying to feel where Erik was held. What a strange ability. Useful though. Except, apparently, in these situations where being the vicinity did no good.

"Parker? Come here, please." One arm stretched toward her as he looked at the ground.

Parker lumbered to her feet, standing in place until the world stopped spinning. Damn drug. But at least she could walk. Much better than lying in a hospital bed. When she stood next to Jamie, she peered at the ground, trying to see what he found.

"Is that a door in the ground?" He knelt, running his hand across what looked like dirt.

Parker knelt beside him, sucking down a breath as she looked at the ground. No, not dirt. A ventilation pipe, colored to appear as if part of the landscape.

Her heart kicked, pumping a beat as if she'd sprinted after a suspect. "It's a ventilation pipe. Too small to fit through."

"It leads underground?"

"That's my thought."

He popped off the screen covering the opening. "Then hold on."

Jamie grabbed her hand and her body shattered into thousands of molecules, before plunging down the shaft.

Chapter Seven

The room smelled musty despite the pipe bringing in fresh air. Jamie formed a flame in his palm and cast light around the small room. Metal lumps in various shapes stood around the room like statues. No surprise there. He doubted he could go anyplace in this city without encountering metal in some shape or form.

Parker grasped his flame-free hand as if she feared he would desert her. No chance of that happening. The longer he was in her presence, the more he wanted to stay with her. What started as saving a female from harm had morphed into never letting the female go. Incredible. It appeared something in his defective self worked correctly.

He was almost certain he'd found his mate.

Which was next to impossible. His lack of magic led all to believe he wasn't capable of having a mate, of finding the one female destined as his. And she was human. Not to mention, he needed to find Erik and return them to Draconia, not fantasize about mating Parker. *Mind on the task, Jamie, mind on the task.*

He needed to find how to leave this room with its grotesque, lurking metal shapes. Where was the door in all this space?

"Maybe we should follow that pipe." Parker pointed to three metal pipes running parallel about a foot off the ceiling as her voice whispered across his skin. Gooseflesh broke out along his arms, sending sparks straight to his shaft. Not what he needed right now.

"All right." Maybe if he started moving, his Parker induced fantasies would disappear.

One could hope.

The pipes took them deeper into a large open space, the blue flame unable to reach into the shadowed corners. Erik's presence grew closer, lines of pain woven through his essence. Jamie snarled, the Council rule of no involvement lost in a sea of rage. He would rescue Erik. He would wreak revenge on those who dared to hurt his friend. No matter the Council rule.

Some rules were meant to be broken.

"Do you sense him?"

Parker's voice snapped his head around.

As soon as she saw his expression, her eyes popped wide, and she took a step back.

Jamie scrubbed a hand down his face, erasing his snarl. Last thing he wanted was to upset Parker. "Sorry. Was thinking of Erik. He's been hurt."

"You can tell that?"

"Yes. He is this direction." He pointed to the right, listening for her tread as she fell into step behind him.

The closer they drew to Erik, the more upset he became. With the kidnappers. With himself. If he'd only followed Erik instead of Parker.

But by following Erik, Parker would have been on her own, an easy victim for the kidnappers. Why did the kidnappers want Parker? Why did they take Erik instead?

Questions for later. For now he needed to concentrate on the rescue. Revenge could be extracted once he freed Erik.

The vast room shrank to a hallway lined with lights glowing from the ceiling. Not glowlamps, nor were they candles. Yet another oddity about this place. Humming sounded from the lights as if the noise caused the brightness. Their footsteps echoed despite trying to use a light step. Light sank into the dark gray floor as if absorbed. Metal doors—surprise, surprise—lined the hallway, sentries with handles. Jamie stopped in front of one of those doors.

Erik's essence was strongest here.

Taking a deep breath, he grabbed the handle and turned.

Nothing.

Locked. Goddess's toes. Now what?

His heart pounded. How—oh right. Panic tended to make one forget. His magic worked in this place.

Picturing the lock's tumblers in his mind, he imagined them turning and tried the handle again. This time it opened.

The coppery scent of blood assailed his nostrils, mixed with sweat and pain. A wedge of light cut into the darkness of the room, shining on limp black hair and a motionless body. *Erik.*

Jamie's heart seized, his breath a frozen ball of ice behind his ribs. How bad was he hurt? Parker pushed past his frozen, guilt-ridden self, shattering the ice holding him in place. He beat her to Erik, kneeling beside his friend a moment before she mirrored his motions. Her shoulder brushed his arm as she grabbed Erik's wrist, the touch a comforting warmth.

"His pulse is steady." She patted Erik's hand. "Erik, can you hear me?"

Hear, yes. Understand her, doubtful. As far as he knew, Erik didn't speak her language.

"Erik?" Jamie shook his arm, speaking in Draconi. "Can you hear me?"

Erik groaned, eyes rolling behind swollen closed lids.

"I think his ankle's broken," Parker whispered. "Either that or a bad sprain. His boot needs to be removed before it cuts off the circulation."

Jamie glanced to his friend's foot, noting the enlarged ankle, swollen flesh pressing against his leather boot. *Always treat the most pressing injury first.* Keara's voice echoed in his head. In this case, the most pressing injury was determining if Erik's unconsciousness was temporary or permanent. *Please, Goddess, let it be temporary.*

"Erik?" Another shake. Another moan.

"Would you like me to remove his boot?"

"Not now. We're going to move him when he wakes." *If he wakes.*

Parker patted his arm, sparks of heat dashed through his veins, an unintentional consequence of the brush of her skin. At least he assumed it unintended.

Stop fantasizing and concentrate.

"Erik!" Jamie laced his friend's name with a command and sent it aloud and through mind-speak as he shook Erik's shoulder.

Erik grunted and opened bruised eyes. "Jamie?" His voice rasped like a thing unused. "Jamie!" He tried to sit, but Jamie pressed a hand against his shoulder, forcing him to lie still, knowing a bout of unconsciousness made being vertical a dizzying experience.

Erik shoved at Jamie's hand with the strength of a newly hatched young. When that failed, he pointed a finger. "You have to leave, scout. I'm handling this."

"By getting your arse handed to you?"

"You don't understand. You need to go."

"Not without you, I'm not."

Erik sighed, his gaze bouncing to Parker. Panic filled his eyes. "Why is she here?"

Why the panic? Jamie glanced to the open door. Empty except for them.

A crease sat between Parker's brows as if she tried to decipher their words.

"We did not come all this way to leave her to harm."

Erik shook his head, his eyes closing, opening. "She needs to leave. You need to get her out of here. Now."

"We will all get out of here. Now." Jamie drew one of Erik's arms around his shoulders, reached under his friend's legs and lifted.

"Put me down, fool, I can walk."

The swat that smacked Jamie's arm felt strong, no longer feeble. Erik probably could walk if his ankle wasn't swollen the size of a small boulder.

Jamie turned sideways to not hit Erik's head on the doorframe. "Not convinced."

He almost made it to the overlarge room with lurking metal objects before Erik spoke.

"You need to take care of your female."

"I am."

"Then why is she being held with some sort of a weapon against her temple?"

Jamie froze. Which was odd seeing how his knees

wobbled like a hatchling learning to walk. He turned with the speed of an aged dragon, breath caught in his lungs, his mouth dry as a summer wind in the desert.

The bearded giant held Parker, one arm banding hers against her side, his opposite hand pressing a black L-shaped object to her temple. Teeth gleamed, adding unneeded menace to his face. He tightened his grip on Parker and her eyes flared.

"Put him down, and I'll let her live."

Rage filled his veins, a blistering growth taking root in his heart.

What did he say?

Jamie translated with mind-speak for Erik, his attention focused on Parker, on her rapid breathing, the tenseness of her frame.

"Do it Jamie," Erik hissed. "I'll be fine."

All Jamie saw was Parker. All he felt was her fear. All he wanted was to vanquish the one who caused her harm. The pounding in his veins grew louder as the rage overtaking him ran like a beast through his soul. Without taking his gaze from the giant, Jamie lowered Erik's feet, keeping an arm around his friend, until Erik leaned against the wall.

Everything is titanium, Erik's voice whispered in his mind. *I'm useless. But I'll wager a dozen gold pieces you're not.* Glee laced his words, vengeance riding the undertones.

Jamie didn't answer. He couldn't. Parker's fear slammed into his gut like a punch, anger spreading instead of pain. His throat ached, red and raw, as moisture coated the outside of his ears. Steam wisped across his vision. Erik's dark chuckle sounded from a distance, which made no sense as his friend stood only a couple of feet away.

Nothing he would think on either. Parker was his only focus. Parker was in danger. And he was the tool to wield her vengeance.

Ripples crashed against Jamie's skin, waving outward from his spine, down his limbs. His jaw ached, pain spreading into his nose, his face. His lips curled off his teeth. The noise roaring from his mouth sounded inhuman, more beast than male. His fingers cranked into fists.

Ouch! Jamie glanced to his hands, his *claw tipped* hands. Claws like a dragon. Like a dragon defending his mate.

Opening his mouth, he roared, air leaving his lungs in a gush of heat.

Parker's mouth joined her eyes in round disbelief.

The giant shoved her into the wall, double-handed the weapon and aimed it at Jamie.

Parker rebounded off the wall, spun around, and jumped at the giant's outstretched arm.

Bang!

The weapon's discharge echoed in the closed space, reverberating in his ears, deafening him. Pain bloomed along the top of his shoulder, and he roared again.

Parker elbowed the giant in the ribs, fighting for control of the weapon. The giant fired again, but Parker knocked his arm up, causing the next weapon discharge to hit the ceiling.

Glass shattered and a section of the hall went dark as the light exploded. The giant backhanded Parker, who hit the wall, sinking to the ground, a loose-limbed puppet with its strings cut.

A red rage slammed over Jamie's vision, obliterating the pain in his shoulder, focusing his attention on the giant. He hurt Parker. He must die.

Before he formed the thought, his legs moved forward, streaking down the hall, closing the distance from one beat of his heart to the next. Leaping into the air, Jamie extended his claws, ignoring the flashes of light and dull thuds as whatever the weapon discharged hit the walls. He smacked the giant in the chest, shoving him backward, landing on his chest. One clawed hand swiped the weapon, the metal clattering against the floor as it spun out of reach. His next claw slit open the giant's throat, spattering blood in an arc.

The giant gurgled, his hands reaching for his throat in a vain attempt to hold in his life's blood. Another gurgle and he went limp, his frightened gaze sightless.

Breath sawed in and out of Jamie's lungs, steam circling his head, clouding his vision. He destroyed the one who harmed Parker, who threatened his mate. A male always protects his mate. *Always.*

Power coursed through his muscles, pride glowing with victory. He drew in a deep breath, shoved his arms out to the sides, threw his head back, and roared. Glass shattered, raining shards from the ceiling as the hall plunged into near darkness.

Clapping sounded behind him, followed by a shuffle of clothing moving at turtle speed.

"Good going, scout. Now get us out of here before the real danger returns."

Chapter Eight

Jamie blinked at Erik's voice. The only light in the hall came from yards away, from one lone ceiling lamp still shining after his glass-shattering roar.

Roar? Only dragons roared, another ability he'd never accomplished, as defective as his lack of magic. Yet, he remembered the sound escaping his lips like a sword of wrath, the howl of a male protecting his mate. He glanced at the body below him, the throat slit into a gaping maw.

Jamie swallowed. Held his hands before his face. Claws dripped with blood. Claws. Not fingers. Claws. He sucked in a breath, heart thumping an uneven beat. How did he change? Forget the how. Why didn't he change all the way? A partial change was next to impossible. Only Draconi with the strongest magic managed to pull off that feat.

"Come on, scout. Snap out of it. We don't have all day." Erik leaned against the wall arms crossed, resting his injured foot on the toes, one eye reduced to a slit. Despite his nonchalant words and posture, tension rolled off him like a gathering storm. He stood where Jamie left him, a stone's throw away. As if he feared getting too close to Jamie.

Why? Oh, right. Claws. Steam. Roar.

Jamie closed his eyes, drew in a deep breath, letting the air invigorate his senses, cleansing away his rage. Claws retracted, transformed into skin and fingernails. A quick glance to his hands and he sighed in relief.

"I'm all right."

But was Parker? Goddess, how could he have forgotten she lay unconscious?

Jamie scrambled to her side as she moaned. "Parker?"

"Mmmm." Her lids fluttered open. "What? Where?"

"We're underground. You were knocked out. Are you all right?"

She flexed her hands and feet, wiggled her jaw. "Oh, right. I remember. Yeah. I'll be okay. At least I can move." She pushed to a sit, Jamie supporting her back. Her gaze pushed past him, landing on the giant. She swallowed. "Is he dead?"

"He won't hurt you again."

Her gaze lifted to his, eyes flaring. "You killed him?"

Shouldn't she be glad he ended her threat? Wasn't that what males did for their females? Jamie gave himself a mental smack. He needed to stop thinking of her as his. Which was hard to do with his hand supporting her back. He wanted to touch her. Needed to touch her. Like he needed air to live. *Fool*. What was wrong with him?

Maybe he should start by answering her question and keeping his thoughts to himself. Which shouldn't be hard to do since she was human.

A fact he needed to remember.

He gave a brief nod.

"Damn." She ran her hands through her hair. Not

the reaction he craved. A long pause. "Thank you. I think."

"You think?"

"I'm a detective. Despite what you might have heard, we on the police force do not try to kill suspects. We prefer to arrest them."

"Arrest them?"

"Hurry up, Jamie."

His name passing Erik's lips snapped his head toward his friend. Anger at the disruption boiled through him, an unwanted surprise.

What was wrong with him? Perhaps the thrill of using magic, of knowing he possessed powers. He ignored the suspicion his anger issues had more to do with defending Parker and less to do with experiencing the rush of knowing his magic worked.

"We're—"

"I don't care. We need to leave. Now. He's coming back."

Had Erik hit his head? Despite the low light he should see the giant's lack of movement and smell the blood. "He's dead." Jamie gestured to the body.

"Haven't you heard anything I've said? That giant is not the threat. My father is."

"Your father?" All right, it seemed as if partially turning into a dragon eliminated his listening skills and caused his mouth to gap. With effort he snapped his lips closed. "I thought he died years ago."

"You thought wrong. Now, hurry up."

"What is your friend saying?" Parker tugged his sleeve.

"We need to leave. Do you need me to carry you?"

She shook her head, the ends of her black hair

brushing the edge of her jaw. "No, I'm fine. Just help me up." She held out her hand, and Jamie pulled her upright.

He put an arm around her waist, but she pulled out of his grip to kneel beside the giant. She grabbed the black weapon, pushed a button that caused the handle to elongate, looked at what lengthened, and slammed it back into the weapon. Then she frisked the giant, hands moving through his pockets with the speed of a thief.

"What's she doing?" Erik asked.

"I don't know."

When she reached his back pocket, she pulled out a metal rectangle about the size of the weapon's handle.

"Ah-ha. The extra clip." Parker stuck the rectangle in her purse and stuffed the weapon in the back waistband of her pants.

She stood, patting the weapon. "This will come in handy."

"What kind of a weapon is that?"

"A gun."

"Gun?" His tongue teased out the strange word.

"Let me guess." She cocked a brow. "You've never seen one."

"How does it kill?"

"It shoots bullets." She pulled out the metal rectangle. "The bullets go in the clip." She shook the rectangle, or clip. "Load the clip into the gun, aim and fire."

"Like an arrow but smaller."

"Yeah."

"Stop talking and start moving." Erik pounded a fist against the wall, his gaze darting toward the light and back to them, his jaw clenched tight.

"What's his problem?" Parker asked.

"We need to leave."

"Never said otherwise." Her brow furrowed as one hand touched his shoulder below the cut caused by the gun. "You've been hit!"

Blood tickled as it oozed down his chest from the slice on his shoulder. Her eyes caught his gaze and time stilled, the corridor and sense of urgency fading into insignificance. His heart pounded a fast tempo, seeking a kindred soul, each beat pulling him closer to Parker. Her pupils expanded, capturing him in her gaze, promising to never let him go.

Erik's fist pounded against the wall, and Jamie jumped, the communion with Parker evaporating.

"No time for that, Jamie. Grab her and go. He's coming."

Jamie blinked. *Daydreaming fool.*

"Hurry." Jamie grabbed Parker's hand, tugging her toward Erik.

When they got to him, Jamie dropped Parker's hand and wrapped an arm around his friend's waist, pulling Erik's arm across his shoulder. Parker mirrored his movements on Erik's opposite side, her arm brushing against Jamie's as she grasped Erik's waist. Together they hurried into the overlarge area of hulking metal objects, walking as fast as Erik's hobbles would allow.

"You came through here?" A good dose of incredulity rode Erik's words.

"Through a ventilation pipe."

Erik barked a laugh. "You are one brave male, scout. Not sure I could have done that."

Jamie shrugged, flinching as the movement stung

his cut shoulder. "It was a clear shot to the bottom."

"Yes, I'm sure it was. But I'm not sure I could have done the same."

Jamie gritted his teeth. Erik gave him a compliment, not a patronization. "Of course you could. Maybe not here, but you could back home."

"I'm not so sure of that. Do you know where we're going?"

"Of course not. I'm leading you into the unknown."

Erik grunted and hobbled faster. The meager light from the hall faded until inky fingers enveloped them in darkness. Their footsteps echoed in the space, a reverberation of urgency and unease. Jamie formed a flame in his palm, the light casting elongated shadows across their path.

Erik sucked in a breath. "What are those shapes?"

"I don't know." He shook his head. "Everything in this world is made of metal. Parker," he switched to her language. "Do you know what those shapes are?"

"Part of the ventilation system, but other than that I don't know."

Jamie translated to Erik.

His brows popped. "Amazing. These people have ways of pumping air underground without magic."

"Magic does not seem to appear in this world."

"And yet, I feel a small current in your female. A vague buzz where her arm touches my back."

A growl attempted an escape. Jamie swallowed the noise. No need to get upset with Erik. He might have dragoned out minutes ago, but his more rational self knew he could not take Parker for a mate. She was human. Besides, why would she want a Draconi with malfunctioning magic?

His inner beast howled, splintering his heart. Since when did he have an inner beast?

"I think it's right up ahead," Parker pointed to a gap between the metal objects.

Air pushed against his skin, evidence of the pipe's surface opening. So where was the pipe?

Parker pointed to a grate in the wall. "I think we came in through there, but it was a little hard to tell since we just materialized in this room."

"Can you transport all three of us at once?" Erik hopped to the wall and pressed his back against the odd stone-like material.

Could he? "I don't know."

"What did he say?"

Jamie turned to Parker. "He wants to know if I can transport all three of us."

"Can you?"

"I have never tried before." He probably should refrain from mentioning that until today he'd never transported anyone else. No sense in making her more uncomfortable than she already was.

A shout sounded from the hall, voices raised in anger.

Erik cursed. "I told you he was coming, and did you listen to me?"

Jamie peered into the darkness, trying to discern the corridor among the multitude of objects. Would the kidnappers know where to find them? Could he carry all three of them in a transport?

All Draconi—well, all except him, until today— could transport another with them, along with varying objects. But each Draconi had limits on how much they were able to carry, limits usually identified when they were younger—and without the pressure of advancing villains.

Could he carry two others? Nothing but to try.

Jamie grabbed Parker around the waist and reached a hand to Erik. His friend grasped his outstretched palm, hobbling until he hugged Jamie with one arm.

"You'd better know what you're doing, scout."

Jamie ignored the jab, took a deep breath and concentrated on transporting them to the surface. Any moment now they'd shatter into pieces.

Or not.

Footsteps echoed, tinny thuds reverberating off metal, voices joining the cacophony.

His heart pounded as a cool sweat coated his forehead. He couldn't transport. Goddess's toes. He needed to get them away. Now. Before they hurt Parker.

Jamie closed his eyes, drew in a deep breath, and ignored the bead of sweat dripping off his cheek. He would transport them out of here. No other option existed. He opened his eyes, stared at the grate. Remembered the feel of his body as it exploded into tiny pieces.

A beam of light slammed into the ventilation grate, causing Parker to gasp, disrupting his concentration.

"They're over here!" Footfalls darted closer. Swaths of light joined together, exploding across his shoulders like a fire.

A snarl twisted his lip. He needed to save Parker. Steam bubbled in his throat, wisped out his ears, his fingers tingling as claws poked through the skin. He tightened his grip on Parker, pictured the surface, the hum of night, air tickling their skin. This time they flew, their bodies reduced to their smallest components, rushing up the ventilation pipe, soaring above the ground. Like a dragon with no body.

The terminal loomed below, bright lights zooming by as they zipped past. Where to land? Not near the vicinity of the pipe. Someplace farther away, harder for the kidnappers to find. Someplace dark, where they wouldn't be seen.

Which was harder to do than it sounded. Lights and metal objects abounded in this place. He spotted a darkened shadow and materialized in the lee of what appeared to be an abandoned building. Less chance of being noticed.

Erik stumbled against the side of the building. "For a minute there, I didn't think we'd make it."

"Are you okay?" Parker spoke simultaneously, her fingers touching his upper arm, blotting out Erik's words.

"Okay?"

"You're bleeding. It looks like you were just grazed, but that is still bound to hurt like hell."

Jamie inhaled, hoping the inbound air would help interpret her words. What a strange language. Nothing to do but ask. Even if it made him seem a little odd.

"Grazed? Hell?"

"The bullet cut the top of your shoulder but did not go into your body. That's the best scenario. But it still needs treated. As does your friend's ankle."

"Treated by a healer?"

"A doctor. Yes. We need to go to the hospital."

"That's where you were. Right?"

"Yeah. But we need to try a different one. I'm still

supposed to be in St. Anne's. We'll go to Denver General. They're good with gunshot wounds."

Erik cleared his throat. "You need to let me in her mind so I can learn the language."

Jamie growled, a low-pitched warning. The last thing he wanted was Erik running around in Parker's mind. Never mind his friend made a good point. Parker belonged to him. His to protect. A male never allowed another to read his female's mind.

Of course, a female Draconi would be able to block any male who tried, but Parker was human and could not defend herself. At least not against mind invasions.

"All right, scout," Erik held up his hands. "You could just say no."

Jamie scrubbed a hand down his face. Did all mated males feel this way toward their females? He squeezed his eyes shut. She was not his female. Parker was human. Not Draconi. He could not bond to a human.

Right?

Goddess's toes.

"No. Read mine instead."

"I've been trying. You don't understand half of what she says either."

"I understand the words, just not the context."

"So translate for me because I understand neither."

"She wants us to go to the hospital, which is their healing ward. And yet it's nothing like our healing ward. Or the Temple. And all the healers aren't female, so I'm not sure how good the care is."

"Some care is better than none. My ankle hurts like a son of a warrior."

What kind of friend was he? So concerned about

Parker and escape he completely forgot to inquire about Erik's injuries. *Sappy idiot.* "I should have asked earlier. My apologies, friend. We will go to this hospital and have it treated."

"I will read the mind of one of the healers to learn the language."

He nodded. Much better idea than dipping into Parker's. "Parker, we need to go to the hospital. Erik's ankle needs treated."

"So does your shoulder. But I'm not sure where we are. Hold on." She reached into her purse and pulled out a glowing rectangular object. After pushing various items on the object, she showed him what looked like a map. Erik leaned forward and Parker tilted the thing so they all could see. "We're here." She pointed to a red dot. Then she touched the screen and the map moved.

Erik gasped and Jamie slanted his gaze to see if the map dropped from the side of the object. No map. What interesting magic. And yet, he did not feel a magical signature. The device felt like the hum in the air before a lightning strike. "We need to go here." Her fingernail tapped the screen. "Think you can transport us there?"

In theory. "Yes. We need a shadow to hide in so we remain unseen."

"Cast a spell, scout." Erik slapped him on the back of the head. "You learned that in first year reconnaissance lessons."

Yes, but he never needed to perform a spell until today. Well, that wasn't true. Plenty of times on their missions, spells were needed. Problem was, his spell casting ability made a hatchling seem like a mighty sorcerer. Needless to say, Erik cast all the spells.

But not in Parker's world. The dominant power

switched, thrusting him into a prime leadership role, and casting Erik into the shadows. An infusion of pride slammed through him, and he stood a little taller.

Pride goes before a tumble and makes a dragon look the fool. Words Balthor always said. Words he needed to take to heart.

Poking fun of another's calamity failed to make him powerful. Instead it made him weak and insecure. The last thing he wanted was to appear weak and insecure in front of Parker.

"Thanks for the reminder." He turned to Parker. "Are you ready to go?"

After pushing a button on the side of her device, the glow and map disappeared and she placed the object in her purse. She grabbed Jamie's hand. "Yep. Beam me up."

Why did she always say 'beam me up' when she meant transport? Something to ask later.

Jamie grasped Erik around the waist, focused on direction of the hospital, and cast them into a transport. This time they disappeared on the first try.

Chapter Nine

Parker stared at the illuminated façade of the hospital. Amazing. Even though they stood in plain sight under a light pole in the parking lot, they seemed invisible to all eyes.

She must be crazy. Her suspension, the drug, kidnappers, a heart-pounding rescue, and two hotter than hell guys clearly scrambled her circuits. Why else would she be helping two men who had enough magic tricks up their sleeves to make Houdini look like an amateur?

While she no longer thought Jamie had anything to do with her kidnapping, his insistence on being from someplace else left a sense of unease crawling across her skin. She believed him. Believed he spoke the truth. Believed he might be an alien or from another dimension. Which made no sense. Since when did she believe in aliens or other dimensions? While she might enjoy a good sci-fi flick that didn't mean she wanted to act out an episode.

How could she believe Jamie spoke the truth? Yet how could she not? Nothing else made sense. Humans did not poof from one spot to the other outside of sci-fi movies. The unbelievable situation and the fact she believed him instead of locking both men away, made her mad. Mad at herself. Mad at them.

But as the only thing she could bust them on was

being too hot to touch—and there wasn't a judge in the state who would sign an arrest warrant for smokin' hot man syndrome—she settled for anger management.

Embarrassment over one's own judgment was not a reason for anger. Really. Not. A. Reason.

She couldn't believe she was helping two men who claimed to have hopped dimensions. If anyone on the force discovered her lapse of judgment they'd never allow her to return.

Parker glanced at Jamie, at his square jaw, the lock of long brown hair he kept shoving behind his ear. So what if she jumped into the fool's pool. At least she had eye candy while experiencing her potentially fatal lack of judgment.

She gestured to the closest cars. "Squat between the cars, drop the invisibility shield, and then rise. Our appearance won't seem so sudden that way. Hopefully it will fool the cameras."

"Cameras?" Jamie's brow furrowed.

Yet another reason to believe him. His hesitancy over certain technological words. His speech pattern went beyond not being fluent in a language and entered the realm of not understanding the fundamentals of technology.

Odd, odd, odd.

More evidence to believe him.

Take that self-directed anger.

"Visual recording devices."

A deeper furrow creased his brow, but he shrugged and nodded. He turned to Erik, spoke in their language, words thick and rich as a cream based sauce. Yet they followed her directions, squatting between two cars.

"Ready?"

Jamie nodded, muttered words under his breath, and the air shimmered around them. He nodded once, and she pulled Erik's arm across her shoulders, Jamie doing the same on the opposite side. Together they walked into the emergency room entrance, blinking in the glow of white lights.

Parker directed them to the window in the ER lobby since they eyed the place like a couple of kids in a candy shop. Make that a candy shop with no candy. Two noses wrinkled in distaste as if the place reeked. Maybe they'd never smelled disinfectant before.

"My friend here fell and twisted his ankle." She gestured to Erik. "The other one has a cut on his shoulder. From a large tree branch." No use in mentioning a gunshot wound. Hospitals were required to report it, and she did not want to get her name involved with that kind of report. No telling how that would look on top of her suspension.

Her lie might buy them time or not. The doctor should be able to tell a graze from a bullet.

"Insurance?" The intake receptionist raised a brow.

"Do you have insurance?" Parker hissed at Jamie.

"Insurance?"

Why did she even ask? Although by asking she found another word having nothing to do with technology he had no idea about.

"None. We can pay cash." She hoped.

"Fill out these forms, please." The receptionist stuck multi-colored forms on a clipboard and passed it to them. "We'll call you back in a minute."

Parker took the clipboard and pointed to a set of chairs. After settling Erik in one of the chairs, she began filling out the forms, asking questions as she went.

No last name. *Seriously?* A raised brow elicited two identical confused looks. She shrugged and wrote Smith. Date of birth gave a response but how to fit thirty-second day of autumn in the five hundred and fifty-first year of the building of the Temple in MMDDYYYY format was over her head. She gave him a September 24th birthday and guessed at mid-thirties for his age, filling in the year accordingly.

Insurance, blank. *Of course.* Responsible party. Parker sighed. Leaving it blank or putting in Erik's name and a false address was stealing. And lying. Both of which tweaked her moral conscious. She wrote her name and address.

In for a dime, in for a dollar.

She continued to fill out the forms, trying to ignore the conversation between the men. The guttural cadence of their language relaxed her, easing tension from her muscles like a hot stone massage.

Or maybe that lightheaded feeling had to do with the late—or should she say early—hour.

Where was a bed when she needed one? Did she dare invite them back to her place?

Was she out of her frickin' mind? Since when did she pick up men? And two at that. Although after all they'd been through tonight, Jamie no longer seemed a stranger. She felt like she'd known him for years, and that attitude would get her in more trouble than an alcoholic partner.

Shoving the pen under the clip, she marched the paperwork back to the reception desk and passed it under the bulletproof glass protecting the intake coordinator from the sick and injured. Then she sat by

Jamie and waited.

A gentle pat on her arm and her eyes flew open. What the…? Oh, right. Emergency Room. Jamie's gray eyes peered into hers, drawing her into his gaze, casting a hypnotic spell.

"You fell asleep. They are calling our name."

"Oh. Sorry. Thanks." She rose, shot the nurse standing over them an apologetic smile and turned to see Jamie helping Erik stand.

"Put him in the chair," the nurse gestured at the wheelchair she pushed. Jamie and Erik stared at the chair, then each other, and shrugged. As if they carried on some sort of mental conversation. Which was ridiculous. They'd been talking all night in their own language.

Erik lowered himself into the chair, raising his legs as the nurse lowered the footrests. The minute she started pushing, his eyes widened, the same look from a child after sledding down a slope for the first time.

So, no wheelchairs in their hometown.

More evidence.

Okay, fine. They weren't from around here. As in not from any developed country, or third-world country for that matter. More evidence to back up her theory they spoke the truth, no matter how crazy it sounded.

Un-frickin'-believable.

The way to get back on the force was not to hang with a couple of mentally unstable men.

Parker followed Jamie into the exam room, logic becoming more of a losing proposition with each step. Like he possessed a homing beacon tuned to her frequency. She could no more walk away from him than she could take a bullet through the heart and live.

Logic be damned.

So what if he was a space alien or a visitor from a different dimension. She wanted to stay with him. When had her emotions morphed from fear and distrust to a comfortable attraction? Maybe she was the mentally unstable one.

"Are you all right, Parker?" Jamie whispered as the nurse helped Erik onto the bed.

"It's been a long night."

At the guilty look on his face, remorse sliced her heart. "It's not your fault." Not really. Most of it was Grizzly's.

"I'm sorry."

"Don't be. I'm just tired."

"You need rest."

"Yeah. After Erik's patched up."

The nurse left and returned a minute later with the doctor. They patched Jamie's shoulder first, no questions asked, and moved on to Erik. After an X-Ray and a diagnosis of a severely sprained ankle, they placed a boot on Erik's ankle, tended to the cuts on his face, and released him.

Despite the quick care, he looked grumpy. Probably due to pain. Or the sun casting pinks and oranges across an early morning sky. Parker yawned. Was it really morning already?

She wanted nothing more than to go home and crash. To crawl into her bed and sleep for days. But what would she do with the men? Rent them a motel room?

She sighed. No. No renting. They could stay with her. If she was going insane then she might as well dive into the deep end of the ocean.

An orderly rolled Erik out the door, parking the chair in front of the ER. "Where's your car?"

Good question. She guessed hers still sat in the bar's parking lot. Man, that seemed like days ago. Had it really been less than a day since her suspension?

"We came in a cab. I'll call one. You can take the chair back." Something told her Jamie would transport them away and the less people who noticed their disappearance, the better.

The orderly gave her a raised brow, but one glance to Jamie and he tapped Erik on the shoulder, motioning for him to rise. Jamie grabbed his friend around the waist, supporting him as Erik twisted his lower leg back and forth.

More evidence. Never seen an ankle boot either.

Once the orderly wheeled the chair back into the ER, doors sliding shut behind him, Jamie turned to her.

"You need rest."

"You do, too." She swallowed. "You can come over. I have a guest bed and a couch. But don't get any ideas, okay?"

His brows slammed down then released. "Ideas?"

"You know. You stay in your room, and I'll stay in mine. The invite is not into my bed."

Red splashed into his cheeks, and Erik barked a laugh. As if he understood their conversation. Which, come to think of it, he seemed to start understanding English while in the ER. Something she'd ask about later. After making Jamie realize what her invite meant.

Jamie blinked a couple of times as if waiting for the blush to disintegrate. No such luck. He cleared his throat and rubbed the back of his neck. "I would not presume such. And we thank you for the invite."

"Good. Let me tell you where I live."

After showing him the GPS map on her smartphone, he grabbed her hand and wrapped an arm around Erik's waist. A splash of jealousy punched her in the stomach. She wanted his arm around her waist. Wanted his body against hers. Wanted less hormones and more sense.

Of course, he wouldn't pull her close. He was trying to show her that he respected her boundaries. Damn boundaries. Why had she made them again?

While Jamie mumbled under his breath and the air shimmered around them, she gave herself a mental smack. What was she thinking? Hormones should not influence her logic.

Damn it.

A humming started in her feet, wrapped around her legs, her torso. The beginnings of the transport. The hospital disappeared as her thoughts disintegrated under the onslaught of her body shattering into millions of molecules.

Barking dogs sounded in the distance as they landed on her tiny front porch. The air stopped shimmering as Jamie dropped his spell. Shouts echoed down the street as neighbors hollered for their dogs to be quiet. With any luck, the neighbors missed their sudden appearance. Parker rummaged in her purse until she found her keys. "Welcome to my home."

Chapter Ten

The persistent vibration of her phone woke Parker from a dream of ruby-scaled, green-eyed dragons. She blinked in confusion, tendrils of the dream wrapping her consciousness in fog. Her bedroom ceiling came into focus, snapping her attention to the present, to the impatient dance of her vibrating phone.

She rolled onto her side, grabbed the phone and a swipe later pressed it against her ear.

"'Lo?"

"Parker?" the voice of her ex-partner, Jason Schultz, snapped her upright.

"Schultz? Where are you?"

"Home. Sobered up. Came to my senses." A long pause. She rubbed the bridge of her nose. "I owe you an apology."

"Yeah? You think?"

"You did what needed to be done. I had no right to show up drunk to work and expect you not to report me."

Her fingernails dug into her skin as she inhaled. Another long pause, this one from her. "You know they suspended me over it."

"What?" Parker yanked the phone away from her ear at Jason's shout. "You're kidding me, right?"

"Nope. Thomas and Johnson rolled on me. Claimed this had happened before and I said nothing.

I'm out on administrative leave until they can investigate."

The muffled sound of a fist hitting a wall slammed through the connection. "I'll call the captain. Get things straightened out. I didn't know…didn't realize they'd do that."

"They weren't too happy when I was promoted to detective instead of their friend, Officer Dickinson. They've been harassing me ever since."

"Why didn't you say something?"

"And be known as the complaining bitch? No thanks. I thought I was handling it until this happened."

"I didn't realize. You should have said something."

"Yeah, well. Hindsight and all that."

"I owe you a bigger apology than I thought. Don't you worry. I'll get this straightened out. I'll call the captain and speak to him about it. You'll have your job back. Don't worry."

"Thanks, Schultz. I appreciate that." She drew in a deep breath, the humiliation and unfairness of her suspension lifting as if she discarded a heavy mantle. "How are you? Have you had anything to drink today?"

"Not today. Today I decided to call AA and go to tomorrow's meeting."

A grin turned her lips. "Good, Jason. That's good. I'm glad you're finally getting help. I've worried about you." Yesterday was the first time he showed up drunk for work, but she knew how his divorce blindsided him and what brand of bottle he drank to stop his mind from spiraling out of control.

"I know. And I'm sorry. But I'm going to make it right for you. Okay?"

"Okay. And thank you."

After a few more words he cut the connection, leaving her almost giddy. Almost. She didn't really do giddy but might make an exception today.

Her phone beeped a dying battery warning. Parker set it back on her nightstand and reached for the plug. She loved her phone, but it sucked batteries dry like a vampire drank blood. Quick and with no warning.

The digital display on the phone's clock read 5:15 PM. Seriously? She'd slept all day. If it wasn't for the excitement at the possibility of getting her job back, she'd crawl back under the covers.

The sound of swooshing water from her kitchen tap drained the excitement right out. Had she really invited over two mostly-strangers to spend the day with her? Last night replayed through her mind. The good, the bad, and the eye candy. After Jamie transported them to her house, she showed them the guest bedroom and bath and locked herself into her bedroom.

Not that the lock would help against his transporting power, but it made her feel better.

Definitely a sign of insanity.

The tap water stopped running as she ran a hand down her face. Might as well get dressed and see what the men were up to. Make sure they didn't rob her blind.

She batted the thought away. Nah, they wouldn't do that. Lie about who they were and where they were from and why they came here, maybe, but steal? Nope. One look in their eyes told of their honesty.

At least when it came to home robbery.

After a quick shower and bathroom duties, Parker pulled on a pair of jeans and T-shirt and walked into the living room.

Both men sat on the couch, glasses of water on the coffee table, flipping through old issues of *Self* magazine.

"Hey. Did you sleep well?" she asked.

As one they gave her heart-stopping smiles, but Jamie spoke. "We did. Woke not long ago. What about you?"

"Yep. So, would you like dinner? What do you eat?"

"Food." Erik said, no hint of humor on his face.

She bit back the smartass response of *duh*. "What kind? Anything you don't eat, or prefer to eat?"

"We're not picky," Jamie replied. "However," he glanced to Erik before turning his gray eyes to hers, "if you have any jaba-jaba beans we'd be ever in your debt."

"Jaba-jaba beans? What's that?"

Their faces fell like children denied a sweet. "You make it into a hot drink. Wakes you up."

"You mean coffee?"

"I have not heard it called that."

"Huh. Well, follow me and I'll make you a cup and you can tell me if it's your jaba-jaba beans."

Jamie tagged behind her as she walked into the kitchen. She stuck a K-cup into the coffee maker, put a mug underneath and hit the brew button. A minute later she handed the dark coffee to an eyes-wide Jamie.

"Do you drink it with milk or sugar? I don't have cream. I like my coffee black."

He took a sip, a broad smile spreading across his lips. "Erik, it's jaba-jaba."

Erik rose from the couch, limping into the kitchen. "Truly? This, what did you call it?"

"Coffee."

"Yes, this coffee is jaba-jaba?"

While Jamie handed his mug to Erik, she pulled another one out of the cabinet, then explained how to use the coffee maker. Something told her they'd spend the rest of the evening in front of the machine if she'd let them.

Jamie tilted his head and stared at Erik who nodded, held his mug with both hands and limped back to the couch. Jamie's gaze met hers, drawing her closer as if captured by invisible strings. She took a step toward him, heat blossoming in her core, spreading through her veins.

Damn it. She wanted him. Wanted him in her bed. Wanted him in her life. But past history proved men didn't take well to female detectives who spent long hours on the job. Last thing she needed was to experience another failed relationship.

Geez, Parker, getting ahead of yourself?

Maybe. But the longer she stared into his eyes, the more she saw them together. Visions bloomed in her head, mixing with the dream she had before waking. Dragons flying. Her riding on a dragon, the wind blowing in her hair, her heart soaring with love as they dipped and flew through the mist of low lying clouds. The familiar touch of a lover. A man she could no longer live without.

Parker took another step forward, stopping a foot away from Jamie. Heat radiated from his coffee mug, warming a spot in the middle of her chest she never realized was cold. Want. Need. Desire.

This man saved her. Risked his life for hers. Came to a different city, a place foreign to him, to save her.

The least she could do was thank him properly. Parker stood up on her toes and pecked him on the cheek. Jamie's eyes widened, and she started to take a step back. She should have known kissing him would be a mistake.

Or not.

In one fluid movement, he set his mug on the counter and wrapped both arms around her waist, pulling her close. One hand rose to her neck, his head dipping toward hers. His lips brushed against hers, once, twice. Tingles exploded from where their skin touched, ricocheting through her body like a fast moving bullet, jumpstarting her heart. Heat built inside her veins as she opened her mouth, running her tongue along the seam of his lips. He opened to her, their tongues speaking where their words failed.

She might be insane for letting strangers into her home, but she wanted Jamie with a logic-defying passion. Parker melted into the kiss.

****

Jamie's arms tightened around Parker's waist, his heart a pounding drum in his chest. He could stay wrapped in her arms forever.

And then Erik turned a page, shaking the paper with more force than necessary, a gentle reminder he sat nearby.

Jamie pulled back, ignoring the cry in his blood to continue, to finish what she started, what they both craved. Parker blinked sex-glazed eyes, her body losing its languidness as a blush stole across her cheeks.

"I'm…" she drew in a breath, huffed it out. "Not really sorry, but we shouldn't have done that."

He shrugged, hoping the motion stopped his hands

from grabbing her, pulling her to him again. What could he say? While not sorry they kissed, he was sorry if it made her feel guilty, like she took advantage of his deficiency to satisfy a whim.

But then she didn't realize his lack of magic since she'd only seen him with abilities. Perhaps she kissed him for his magic and power, not out of pity.

A glance at the mix of confusion and determination written on her face obliterated that idea. She did not seem like the type of female who allowed power or lack thereof to impress her choice of lover. Did it mean she kissed him for him?

When in doubt, act like nothing happened. He picked up his cup containing the jaba-jaba, or, as Parker called it, coffee. "Your…coffee is good. How do you roast the beans?"

"It comes that way. I have no idea. What do you guys want for dinner? I can cook up some steaks."

What were steaks? At Jamie's pause, Erik spoke into his mind. *I don't care if these steaks contain more spice than your mother's cooking. I'm hungry.*

A smile turned Jamie's lips. "That sounds good. Do you need help?"

"I don't suppose you can fire up the grill?"

Fire up the grill? "If you mean light the wood, I am capable of that chore. But I see no wood."

She pressed her lips together, eyes twinkling as she tried not to laugh. "Never mind. Why don't I show you how a grill works?"

That sounds like a proposition I'd like to see. Erik turned, waggling his brows.

No, it doesn't. And you weren't invited. Jamie offered Parker a smile. "I would like to learn this grill.

What does it do?"

She opened a door in her kitchen leading outside.

The same strange flooring material inside the warehouse and where Erik was held covered a spot right outside the door. A strange metal object sat on four legs, two of which ended in wheels. Parker grabbed the handle, lifted the lid, and exposed what looked like long metal teeth. The grill.

The ensuing lesson on the intricacies of turning a switch and priming gas made him wonder on the magic in this place. No magical signature existed, and yet the wonders these people used. Amazing.

Steaks turned out to be meat sliced in thick slabs. She served the meat with diced tubers—called potatoes—mixed with rosemary and pepper and baked in a metal oven. Steamed green beans rounded out the delicious meal. When they'd eaten their fill, they sat on the couch drinking ale. Or beer as Parker called it.

"So," Parker ran her thumb across the lip of the beer bottle, "what are you going to do now? Go home?"

Did she want him to leave? He wanted nothing more than to stay by her side. To warm her on cold mornings. To see love sparkle in her eyes as she gazed upon him.

To smack his head against a convenient wall. She was human. He might want her for a mate, but Draconi did not mate with humans.

Right?

Try telling that to his heart. His soul.

"We need to stop my father." Erik's jaw tensed.

Why hadn't he asked questions yesterday when Erik first mentioned his father? Distraction while uncovering clues was never a good thing. Before he voiced his questions, Parker spoke.

"You can speak English," Parker leaned forward, gaze fixated on Erik. "You've said so little I didn't think you understood."

"He learned it," Jamie glared at his friend. *She doesn't know how you learned, and I'd like it to stay that way. Besides, we need to return to the problem. Your father.*

Erik grinned, one of those wolfish ones that meant he'd do what he wanted, despite Jamie's wishes. Goddess's toes.

"Yes, I learned it from the hospital staff."

"You picked up a language from being in the ER?" Parker's eyes flared.

"Words, but the meanings don't always hold true. Your patterns of speaking are odd. That's why we don't always understand what you say."

"How can you learn a language in a couple of hours?"

"You don't want to know," Jamie glared at his friend. Not that it was doing any good. "How did your father get here?"

"She wants to know, don't you Parker?"

Parker glanced between him and Erik. "How did you learn?"

"I tunneled around in the healers' minds. Grabbed the language from their heads."

Parker gasped, her flared eyes and open mouth the only movements in an otherwise frozen body. Then she blinked, her head tilting slightly off center as her breathing resumed. "You read minds?"

Of course. We speak in them too.

Parker slammed both hands against her temples,

squeezing her eyes closed. Jamie slapped a hand on the low wooden table. "Enough! Stay. Out. Of. Her. Head."

A low growl bounced around the room as two sets of eyes snapped to his. Delicious pain licked his fingertips, claws peeking from skin. Steam circled his face, rose in his throat, pumping up his anger.

One corner of Erik's mouth twitched. *I knew you came to her for a reason. Save her my arse. You want her for your mate.*

Air pumped in and out of Jamie's nose as he tried to diffuse a murderous rage. As if he was a male defending his mate.

You are a male defending his mate, scout. Wake up and believe it.

Nonsense. He was merely siding with a defenseless human. Right?

Adding idiocy to your list of deficiencies?

He couldn't have a mate. Until coming to Parker's aide, he possessed so little magic as to barely be considered Draconi. Taking a mate had never been on the top of his to-do list. But his current impulse to attack his friend for surprising Parker made him rethink the possibility.

Clearly he had magic even if it didn't work in Draconia. So it stood to reason if he had magic, then a mate was a possibility. Shock evaporated the steam pouring from his ears. Claws retracted into fingers as he drew in a couple of deep breaths.

Parker's gaze prickled across his skin as he turned to her frozen form. Wide eyes highlighted a pale face, the rich color of her skin leached away like dye exposed too long to sunlight.

"Don't be frightened. I won't hurt you." Die to

protect her, yes, harm her, never.

She blinked. Swallowed. Two tries later and the words escaped her mouth. "Your ears steamed."

"They do that when a Draconi gets upset."

"Draconi?"

"That is our race." Jamie gestured between him and Erik.

Parker leaned forward. "Draconi from Draconia. Isn't that Latin for dragons?"

"I do not know this Latin, but yes. Dragons."

She blinked a couple of times. "Dragons?"

"Dragons," Erik said. "Haven't you heard of them?"

"Yeah, but only as fables. So, like, what? You have dragon characteristics?"

"You could say that."

"I guess I wasn't imagining things when we rescued you." She pointed at Jamie. "I thought you roared, but then figured it was just the acoustics of the hall. You roared at Grizzly, didn't you? And it wasn't a knife that cut his throat either, huh?"

Jamie shook his head.

"Seriously? Your fingers turn into claws?"

"They can." Surprise, surprise.

She swallowed, some of the color returning to her face as she focused her gaze on him. "Huh. I wasn't imagining things. So you're like what? A werewolf?"

"Werewolves are mythological characters. Dragons aren't."

"Uh-huh. Maybe where you're from. Here both are mythological. Or they were until you came along." She sighed, pressing her fingers to the bridge of her nose. "I can't believe I actually believe you. Men do not have dragon-like abilities. I must be losing my mind."

Jamie sucked in another breath, not sure what upset him more, her thinking she was mentally unstable or the fact that dragons did not exist here. No matter where he went on reconnaissance missions, people knew dragons existed. They might think them evil or never saw one in the scales, but they believed in dragons' existence. Here, dragons were relegated to myths.

Myths.

No wonder Parker didn't believe him. Not only had she never seen magic, she'd never seen dragons and definitely didn't believe they existed.

Which meant the lack of dragons bothered him more than her coming to terms with him being a Draconi. Convincing her she saw reality shouldn't be a problem. Discovering his location in relation to his home? Problematic.

Where in Goddess's name was the city of Denver in the state of Colorado in the country of America?

"You are not losing your mind." Erik placed the flimsy book on the couch and leaned forward.

Jamie forced the beginnings of a snarl back into hiding. No reason to snarl. Erik wasn't hurting or trying to entice Parker. Holy altars, he had issues. Being stuck someplace unfamiliar was the least of things.

How was he supposed to explain to Parker she belonged to him? He'd have better luck working magic in Draconia.

"It is always hard to understand things you've always believed were myths." Jamie reached a hand toward Parker, then drew it back in case she saw it as aggressive.

"I'm a detective. I think through things logically.

Logically this makes no sense, but I know what I feel and see. I can't believe…you really had steam coming out your ears?"

He nodded.

"Okay." She rubbed her forehead. "Okay. So, not only are you not from around here, make that Earth, you have dragon-like characteristics."

"Not dragon-like," Erik offered, earning him a glare from Jamie.

"Erik," Jamie's warning growl did nothing more than elicit a wink from his friend, who continued speaking as if filled to overflowing with words.

"We are dragons. We change shapes."

Parker's eyes flared. "No fucking way, excuse my French."

Was that a curse? Judging from her shaking head he knew she once again struggled with the meeting of reality and disbelief. Why did Erik feel the need to continue adding to her shock?

"Don't be afraid." The last thing he wanted was her to fear him.

"Afraid is not the word coming to mind. Freaked out, yeah. Why don't you go outside and turn into a dragon?"

Erik barked a laugh.

Jamie pressed his palm against his thigh to keep his hand from doing something stupid like punching Erik. "I don't think that would be a good idea."

Another hand-scrubbing across her face. "Yeah. You're right. Forget I asked." Fingers pinched the bridge of her nose. "Okay. So you are men who turn into dragons. And you've come here to rescue me, right?"

Jamie nodded.

"Which you've done. Now what?"

"We need to stop my father from capturing more magically inclined humans."

Parker stopped rubbing her nose and focused her attention on Erik. "Your father?"

"You never did explain how he came here." Jamie flexed his fingers, flattening them against his thigh as he glared at his friend.

Red tinged Erik's ears. "He was banished when I was young."

"Banished?" Parker's brows furrowed then released as her head tilted.

"If a male is abusive or commits a crime against another Draconi, he can be banished or executed," Jamie said. "It's more common to banish, but even that rarely occurs. I never heard anything about your father."

Erik's fingers played with the cuffs of his shirt as he stared at his lap. "We thought it easier to say he died. But to find him here is odd. He said he fell asleep in a cave and woke up in this place."

"He spoke to you?"

"Of course." Erik stopped fiddling and shot Jamie a glare. "Once he realized who I was."

"And beat you?"

"No. This," he gestured to his face, "was due to the fight when we first found Parker. My ankle twisted when I woke and tried to fight them off. That's when he realized I was his son."

"Why was he after Parker?"

"To return to Draconia, what else?"

Parker raised a brow. "How am I supposed to help

with that? I've never heard of Draconia until today."

"He hopes by gathering humans with magical characteristics that he'll find one who can help him return. Part of his banishment was stripping him of powers."

"He told you all this?" Why was he surprised? Persuasiveness was always a strong suit of Erik's. Although it usually applied more to females and bedplay than obtaining secret motivations.

Erik shrugged, red creeping across the tops of his ears. "He hoped I'd join him in his quest."

"And?" Jamie stared at the male sitting across from him, a cold foreboding creeping down his spine. Blood trumped friendship. He'd give almost anything to see his birth father again, to feel the male's arms around his waist, to hear the tone of his voice.

Erik's gaze flashed to his, shock etched in the green depths of his eyes. "I am not a traitor. You know me better than that, Jamie."

His given name from Erik's lips hit him like a blow. Guilt mixed with the sense of foreboding, overwhelming the tingling unease. He shouldn't have doubted his friend. But something about this matter felt off, overlooked, a missing puzzle piece ruining the picture.

"I had to ask." Heat tinged his ears.

"I know. You loved your father. It's only normal you'd question my loyalties."

Jamie relaxed his fingers, uncurling them as he sucked down a breath. *Calm and in control, calm and in control.* If he didn't get control soon he was going to give himself a case of emotional whiplash.

"In case you need to hear me say it, I turned him

down. Why do you think he threw me into that locked room with no healing care?"

While he no longer doubted Erik, he couldn't shake the feeling of a missing piece, an incomplete picture. Draconi males usually cherished their offspring.

Parker cleared her throat, and Jamie's attention snapped to her as if drawn by invisible strings. Her relaxed pose failed to fool him as her sharp gaze bounced between him and Erik, eyes narrowed in thought. "Did he place a tracking device on you?"

Erik shook his head. "I said he had no magic. You can't do that without magic."

"Maybe in your world, but here they make devices small enough to fit on your shoes or under your collar that keep track of where you are."

Both Jamie and Erik blinked at her as if she sprouted a tree on her head. For a people with no magic, they sure possessed amazing items.

"Did they touch you?"

Erik raised a brow. "Of course."

Parker rose, talking as she stepped toward him. "Lean forward, let me see your shirt."

"There's nothing on there." But Erik leaned forward as Jamie joined Parker in staring at the back of his friend's shirt.

She ran her hands around the collar, pulling off a tiny metal square. "We need to leave."

"What is that?" Jamie reached for the object, but she pulled it away as Erik twisted to see.

"A transmitter. It's how they can track us." She walked into the kitchen, threw the transmitter on the hard floor and stomped on it, talking as she moved. "Damn it, I should've known better than to come home, but I thought they'd leave us alone. Stupid, stupid, stupid. Get your things, we need to get gone."

She quick-stepped back into her bedroom, leaving Jamie to stare at Erik.

"They can track with no spell?"

"Apparently. And here I thought the old male powerless."

"Never underestimate a Draconi."

A noise from the front of the house turned their attention to the door. Parker walked into the room right when Jamie started walking toward the entryway.

"What are you doing?"

"I heard something."

"What kind of something?" A click sounded as she adjusted a weapon in her hand, one that looked similar to the one wielded by the giant.

Before he could answer, the back door crashed open, two men dressed from head to boots in black swarming inside. One of them pointed a small black box at Erik, releasing a jolt of electricity similar to the weapons fired last night. Erik dropped to the ground twitching.

Jamie reached for the knife in his boot, thought better of it and hurled an energy ball at the weapon wielding intruder, the force slamming the invader against the wall. Parker aimed her weapon at the other intruder and fired. *Bam!*

Goddess's toes, that was loud. Not to mention it smelled like rotten eggs. His ears ringing from the weapon's discharge, Jamie took a step toward Erik. And got all of a foot forward as cracking sounded from behind, the front door slamming inward, bouncing against the wall.

Two more intruders ran in, pointing those electricity shooting weapons at him. The energy ball withered on his palm as a spark of electricity slammed into his already injured shoulder, dropping his seizing body onto the ground. Pain seared through his limbs as he fought to remain conscious.

Another *bam* from Parker's weapon. A yelp. A clatter of metal against tile flooring. He knew without looking she lay twitching on the floor along with him and Erik.

"Shit, this one's still awake." Black boots stepped into his line of vision.

"Hit him again."

Electricity slammed into his body carrying with it a veil of darkness.

Chapter Eleven

Parker woke to the vibrations of a rumbling engine beneath her ear. Tension laced her shoulders, stemming from cutting pain in her wrists. She tried flexing her hands. No good. Plastic ties cut into wrists tied behind her back. A cloth gag pulled at the corners of her mouth.

Damn it.

Cracking one lid, she took in her surroundings. Not much to tell. They lay lengthwise in a van, Jamie next to her, Erik on his other side, all three trussed up like Thanksgiving turkeys complete with gags. Unlike her, they still seemed out cold. They should be awake by now, provided they'd been hit by the same type of Taser she had. So why weren't they waking?

A cold shiver shot down her spine. Were they dead?

Her breath hitched as she watched Jamie's chest, watched until it expanded and contracted. The breath hissed from her nose. Thank goodness. Not dead.

Where were they being taken? Probably back to the underground tunnels. Who knew those things existed and were being used?

The van slowed, bumped over a couple of road humps and then sloped, like it drove down a hill. Instead of stiffening to keep in place, Parker forced her limbs to go limp, allowing for her to slide forward.

The van continued to roll downhill for several more seconds before leveling off. Then the engine cut.

Showtime.

Parker closed her eyes, focusing on keeping her breathing steady and even. Might as well play unconscious victim for as long as possible. She might learn something to aid in their escape.

The van door slid open. Rough hands grabbed her arms and feet, lifting her from the vehicle. Her feet dropped and the person at her arms shifted her weight around, muscled a shoulder into her stomach, and lifted with a grunt.

Carried like a backpack. How dignified. If she hadn't already been awake, the rush of blood to her face would have done the trick. She cracked open her eyes, taking in a jean-clad butt as she hung upside down. Cutting her gaze from side to side gave no input except for a long hallway. Doors on either side. Concrete floors.

Yep. Back underground in the tunnels.

How the hell was she going to get out of here?

Well, that was easy. Rescue Jamie. Then Erik. Check for bugs. Call the police.

No problem.

A crazed chuckle threatened an escape, and she swallowed to keep from making a sound. Several bounces later, the man carrying her stopped, opened a door, and flopped her onto a mattress. Then he walked back out the door, shutting it behind him, the click of a lock sealing her inside.

Great. Locked in and still trussed up like a bird.

Parker opened her eyes. This time a gasp slipped free.

A tall, dark-haired man, with a strong resemblance to Erik, leaned against the wall across from the bed. The small room shrank further until all she saw was him and the hunting knife he held.

At her gasp, he stopped picking his nails with the knife and peered at her from under heavy lids. A smile crept across his lips, his cheeks, avoiding his eyes like a thief on camera. In slow motion he straightened, slapping the knife against his thigh.

"Well, well, well. If it isn't Detective Ruby Parker." His accent slithered along her shivering nerve endings. Similar to Jamie's and yet full of what she called the creep factor. "You've proven to be more promising than I thought." He took a step toward the bed.

She would not shrink in the face of adversity. She. Would. Not. Shrink. Oh wait, too late for that. Parker stiffened, forcing her body to stop its retreat. She would not show fear.

Her heart raced a too-loud rhythm, thumping hard enough to vibrate her shirt. Each step he took echoed in her ears, the sound crawling across her nerves like a loud scream. He reached for her, knife outstretched. She failed to stop the involuntary flinch as the heavy weight of his palm grasped her shoulder. He rolled her onto her stomach while using the knife to slice through the plastic bindings cinching her wrists.

Blood flowed into numb hands, tingling zips of pain and relief darting through her veins. *See? No reason to shrink. Yet.* Parker rubbed her hands together, rolling to a sit as he stepped back to his resting place against the wall. She yanked the gag out of her mouth, twisting the cotton rag in her hands.

The man propped one leg against the wall, watching her, psychopath to her victim.

She. Would. Not. Show. Fear. A hard twist of the rag. A deep breath to fill her lungs. A slow exhale to clear her racing mind. No such luck.

Damn it.

Parker cleared her throat, projecting her voice away from the whisper it longed to speak with. "What do you want?"

One corner of his lip twitched. "You. Do you think I'd go to all this trouble of having you brought here for the hell of it?"

"Why me?"

"I think you know. I need your help."

Not likely. "Why should I help you?"

"Why should you not?"

Oh, let's see, you ordered someone to drug and kidnap me, bastard. Not that those words would come out of her mouth. She wanted to escape more than she wanted to piss off the perp. Parker forced her lips to turn. "It's not every day I find myself in this type of situation."

"Ah. So you are surprised. You probably think I mean you harm, but that is not true." As if to prove his point he sheathed the knife, then met her gaze. "Why would I want to harm the one who helps me? That makes no sense."

A dozen or so murders popped into her mind. Plenty of people helped a drug lord or crime boss and were never heard from again. Not that she would mention those cases. She blanked her mind, focusing on keeping her face devoid of thoughts. "Of course you wouldn't."

He smiled, and a frisson of fear licked through her system. "That's right. You want to help me return home. That's all I want. I'm sure you understand. Most people long for the familiarity of home."

Parker nodded. Yep, she understood. Odd thing was, she wanted to help him. Which made no sense. He tried to drug her. Succeeded in kidnapping her. Tried to harm Jamie and Erik.

Who, she reminded herself, she didn't trust at all when they first met. And now, she believed them, trusted them. Or at least she trusted Jamie and Jamie believed Erik. Which meant she trusted Erik by default. And neither of them trusted this guy, who she assumed was Erik's banished father. So why would she want to help him? Probably due to the case of begging dog eyes he wore like a fur coat.

If Jamie hadn't looked so shocked when Erik mentioned his father's banishment, she might have fallen for the dog eyes. Even knowing he drugged her. Knowing he kidnapped her, Jamie and Erik. Knowing he would undoubtedly pit them against each other to get what he wanted. She still felt an urge to help him. How effed up was that?

Usually her intuition fired when confronted with a liar, a special knowledge that helped her solve many a crime. But in this instance, her intuition remained silent. Like it did when someone told the truth. He really did want to go home. And despite knowing better, she wanted to help him achieve that goal.

Conflicted much, Parker?

Jamie's eyes flashed through her mind, a remembrance born of a desire to believe. *He lies*, Jamie's voice whispered in her head, and she white-knuckled her grip on the gag as she jerked. Did he really speak in her mind? A flashback of Erik using telepathy to talk to her earlier pinged in her memory. No freakin' way.

"What?" Tall, dark and dangerous leaned forward, concern written on his face.

Do not be fooled.

"Nothing. Just a chill."

Erik says his power is convincing others he tells the truth when he really lies.

Then stop talking and get in here! Transport me out.

A long pause. *Give me a minute. The electric weapon seems to have disrupted my magic.*

Her breath hitched. Was Jamie hurt? How had he managed to mean so much to her in such a short period of time?

"Are you talking to the Draconi hatchling?"

At the perp's words, Jamie's presence in her mind disappeared, leaving her with a strange emptiness.

Tall, dark and creepy's eyes narrowed. "I see you are, don't bother lying. You need to be careful around him and his friend. He is dangerous."

Parker swallowed, unwilling to believe Jamie was dangerous. At least not to her. "Which one?"

"The Draconi." One dark brow skimmed his hairline as he gave her a look doubting her intelligence.

Condescending creep. "Which one is that?" Two could play the ignorance game.

He sighed, shook his head. "I take it they did not bother to explain. Draconi have black-hair and green eyes." He pointed to his hair, his eyes. "I don't know what race the other male is. Definitely not a Watcher.

Looks similar to a Draconi. Would say he's a Halfling, but he's the wrong coloring. Are you surprised?"

Parker stared at him, wondering where all the air in the room went. Had Jamie lied to her when he said he was Draconi? If so, why? If not, what was this man talking about? Halflings? Watchers? "I have no idea what you are talking about."

"Never mind." He waved a hand. "I will deal with them later. What matters is that you realize they are not trustworthy."

"And you are?"

"Of course."

"Then why haven't you given me your name?"

"You haven't asked for it." His smile gave her the jitters. "My name is Kol. See, I've been nothing but truthful with you. I want to go home. I want you to help me."

"Well, Kol, we're back to the how of that help."

Another smile. Another shot of cold down her spine. "You have a power I want."

"Power?" She swallowed. How the hell did he know about her embarrassing ability to emit a blast of electromagnetic energy?

"Don't play dumb. On this you know what I mean. I saw what you did. At the bar. Come now, explain to me how this works."

Parker opened her mouth, closed it. Was she really thinking of telling him? How could a man with such a large creep factor convince her to want to help him? Her secret ability seemed weak compared to his.

See beyond his lies. Discover his truth. Play along. Sage advice given to her by her father, the original Detective Parker, when she first became a detective, shortly before he died. Words she tried to implement in her job, if only to please the ghost of the old man.

"I don't know." She shrugged. Nope, no extraneous information leaks from her. "It just happens."

"When you're stressed? Happy? Sad? When?"

Frightened was the word he wanted. Not that she'd admit it. "I'm not sure. One minute things are fine, and the next they aren't."

"Come now. Surely you've tried to experiment with this. Use the power at will."

Once. To the detriment of all involved. "Nope. It didn't seem worth the effort."

"Think you can make the effort for me?"

Not unless she learned to knock out the light bulb on purpose and fry his ass. "I can give it my best shot. But I don't see how that would help you return home."

"Think of a large puzzle. You are merely one of the pieces."

"There're others?"

"Of course. Surely you didn't think you were unique?"

Well, yeah, she kinda had. "You have others here?"

"Oh yes. Many others. All part of the puzzle. A puzzle that's almost complete. With your help we should be able to make progress." Kol moved to the door. "I'll have them send in water and a blanket. You can start helping me tomorrow. Sweet dreams, Detective Parker." The door clicked shut behind him, the bolt sliding in place with the finality of a gavel.

She sagged, resting her elbows on her thighs and her head in her hands. Now that Kol was gone, she no longer wanted to help him. But she needed to play along with him. Until Jamie came for her.

Would he come for her? Maybe she shouldn't trust Jamie either. As soon as the thought entered her mind, she rejected it. Been there, traveled that path already. The conclusion being Jamie spoke true. Unless Kol was in the room with her, trying to convince her otherwise. Well, she wouldn't let him. She hadn't let him. Not really.

She believed Jamie. End of conversation. He would get her out of here. Provided she failed to escape on her own. Even if she did get out of the room, how did she get out of the tunnels? She hadn't seen much but upside down doors on her way in.

Parker rose and walked to the door, turning the knob, proving she was indeed locked in. A quick glance around showed the bed, a nightstand, a toilet and a sink. A regular jail cell, except instead of bars, she had a door and four concrete walls.

Oh yeah. And an air vent. Not that she could fit through it. Unlike the movies with the conveniently sized and located vents. Damn it.

Now what? She sat on the bed with a huff. Waiting to be rescued sucked.

Chapter Twelve

Jamie pulled his consciousness from Parker's thoughts, unwilling to risk Erik's father knowing he, not Erik, invaded her mind. Perhaps if the banished Draconi thought of him as human, he would leave him in here without a guard on the door. Which would make his escape easier. Provided his magic started working again.

At the moment he couldn't even form enough magic to break the ties on his wrists. Ties that cut into his skin, rubbing it raw. Not ropes or metal. Some form of hardened bendable material. Yet another instance of a strange element.

Jamie spoke a spell to break the ties. Smoke wisped, the small burn stinging his skin. The ties remained intact. Goddess's toes. Why did his magic no longer work? Only last night he stood in these tunnels able to work magic, able to free Erik and kill the giant.

He shuddered at the memory. Killing had never been on his to-do list. He learned to defend himself—he had to as a reconnaissance specialist—but made an effort never to find himself in a life or death situation.

And then the giant attacked Parker. The urge to kill overwhelmed his senses, turning him into a beast, an enraged dragon protecting his mate.

Mates. Goddess's toes. How was he going to tell Parker he was her mate?

First things, first, Jamie. You need to get out of here and find her before you can tell her anything.

He tried casting the spell again. More smoke, a larger sting searing his skin. No loosening ties. Bloody dragon eggs. Why didn't his magic work? Best guess? The electrical weapon disrupted his powers. Would they return, or would he remain as powerless in this world as he was in Draconia?

No time to think on that either. Experiencing the power magic provided was a new skill. Until coming here to save Parker, his magic resembled a newly hatched young's, a far cry from the power he should possess. But that lack of magic caused him to learn a whole different set of skills. Skills more akin to a human instead of a Draconi used to relying on his magic for everything.

Like how to remove cuffs without magic.

Of course, his practice cuffs had been made of rope, not some strange material. And the escape plan only worked if his captors left his ankle knife. Which he carried despite being teased by the other reconnaissance experts. Unlike Erik, his energy balls fizzled and dissipated into smoke more often than they held form and hit true.

Practice meant his knife always hit true. Something not even Erik managed to accomplish. Not that Erik threw knives. Or that Jamie's knife throwing skills meant his friend stopped with the teasing.

If the knife remained, then escaping just became easier.

After some twisting, he determined the knife remained inside his boot. Thank Goddess. More squirming and he managed to unsheathe it without slicing himself open. *Excellent.*

A couple of sawing motions later and the ties popped off, freeing his wrists. Blood rushed into his hands, welling along the raw skin where the ties cinched his wrists. *Ouch, ouch, ouch.* He shook his fingers until the tingling stopped. At least he didn't need to worry about the shallow cuts bleeding. They appeared to have already clotted.

Now to escape. Find Erik and Parker. Leave.

But what would they do with Erik's father? Leave him behind? Return with him to Draconia? Assuming they could return to Draconia. How did they return to Draconia?

All questions for later. For now he needed to free Erik and Parker. Then they could discuss where to go.

Two strides later and he leaned against the door, the chill of the metal soaking under his skin. He shivered and pressed his ear against the door, listening.

Nothing.

Were the guards silent? Or missing?

Jamie tried the knob. Which didn't turn. Locked. Leaving his hand on the knob, he closed his eyes, picturing the internal workings of the lock, and cast a spell. Four tries later and the lock clicked, allowing him to twist the knob.

Freedom. And a possible return of his magic.

Jamie eased the door open, glancing up and down the hall, ears straining for voices.

Nothing but the hum of the ceiling lights.

Taking a deep breath, he closed his eyes and searched for the essences of Erik and Parker. Parker's spirit blinked in first. To his left. Unharmed but frustrated. Erik was to his right. Pain radiated from his essence. Not fresh pain, thankfully. Dull pain, the kind muted by medicine given to ease suffering.

His friend needed a session in the healing ward of the Temple. Not another round with his father.

Jamie took a step in Erik's direction and stopped. Should he rescue his friend first or Parker? Less chance of Parker getting hurt if she stayed in her room.

Provided she remained there and wasn't moved. Who knew what was planned for her. Or any of them, for that matter.

Jamie took another step. Stopped. Erik was hurt. In pain. Woozy. And his foot was stuck inside a healing boot, which prohibited him from walking fast. Or well.

No. If he rescued Erik first, then he'd need to carry the male. Rather hard to escape while hauling dead weight. Easier to have help carrying his friend. As much as he hated putting Parker in a position of possible conflict, things would go faster if he rescued her first and then Erik.

Even if it meant more danger for Parker. No matter what he did, danger walked her path. Just because she was unharmed sitting in her cell didn't mean she'd stay that way.

A snarl turned his lips. A male always protected his mate. Even if said mate didn't want him. Well, to be fair, he'd never asked her. Maybe she would want him.

A grin replaced the snarl. She would want him. He would ensure she wanted him. *Somehow*.

Jamie strode in the direction of Parker, knife at the ready, his gaze seeking movement, his ears searching for sounds. So far, so good.

Which, come to think of it, was worrisome. Where was everyone? Shouldn't someone be guarding their doors? Watching for signs of their escape? Or were they being allowed to escape for some nefarious purpose?

The quiet of the hall echoed in his ears, ramped his heartbeat to a loud internal thunder. His scalp prickled and he ran a hand over his head to soothe the tingles. He needed to focus on freeing Parker. Not worry about the eerie vibes reverberating through the hall.

Parker's essence shined as a bright light on his internal grid, unharmed and drawing nearer with each step. There. Behind the door on his right. A quick glance up and down the hall showed no one but him and his knife. *Excellent.*

Jamie tried turning the knob. No surprise on the lock. This time his magic flowed from his hand with a thought and the lock clicked open as if he'd used the spell his entire life. . Another glance up and down the still-empty hall and he twisted the knob, pushed open the door.

Parker stood beside the bed, one foot forward, hands loose at her sides. Her defensive posture was…attractive. What kind of male was he to find a female needing to defend herself attractive?

The kind who wanted the female. The kind who knew if she found herself in trouble, she would be able to fight instead of curl in a ball and cry for help. He still wanted to protect her. To keep her from harm. To fight to defend her. But, yes, her unflinching determination turned him on. Not that he'd tell her. Not yet anyway.

Parker relaxed her stance once she recognized him. "Thank goodness you're okay. I was worried." Red stained her cheeks, and she glanced at the ground, clearing her throat. Her gaze then met his, dropped, and met his again. "What's your plan for getting out of here? I was awake when they brought us in, but trying not to act like it so I missed seeing how to escape."

Jamie walked into her cell, closing the door to a crack. "I woke in the cell. But I can find the way out. Don't worry. We just need to get Erik. He's slow with the healing boot."

She nodded. "And apparently there're others in here."

"Others?"

"Yep. Erik's father, Kol, said he had other humans here. He wants to get home. Was that you in my mind earlier?"

"Yes. Sorry to startle you. I wanted to ensure you were all right."

"That's sweet." A smile tinged her lips. "You were right, you know. He is good at convincing. I wanted, still want, to help him return home."

"Tell me about the others."

One finely shaped brow arched. "Okay, then. He said he needed us to help him and that there were others here with abilities."

"Like yours?"

"Not exactly. At least I'm assuming not exactly. But yeah. Like mine." Another splash of red colored the rich brown of her cheeks.

What irony. She feared using the power he craved. She shouldn't. Magic was a blessing. "Don't be afraid of your power. Learn to control it. We'll work on it after we find Erik and leave."

"What about Kol? We need to call the police once we're free."

"Police?" The answer popped into his mind as soon

as he asked. The security forces. The cop. Or detective in Parker's case. "That's right. You are a police."

"Not a police. Part of the force. Or I was." Another burst of red stained her cheeks as her jaw tensed. "Never mind. How do you propose we leave?"

"What do you mean was?"

Her eyes narrowed. "How do you propose we leave?"

He should work on leaving. Instead, he wanted to learn more about her life. Jamie crossed his arms, widened his stance. "You first."

She sighed. "They accused me of something I didn't do and suspended me. I'm trying to get reinstated."

A snarl turned his lip, his blood roaring at the pain in her voice. Her protection and detection work meant a lot to her and to have that taken away made him want to claw those who upset her to shreds.

Which wasn't going to happen. *Calm, Jamie, calm.* His beast, that inner dragon he always assumed he was missing, roared a challenge. His mate hurt, and he needed to kill the ones who caused her pain.

How did mated males get anything accomplished? It took all his will not to hunt and kill the ones who hurt Parker. He closed his eyes and tried to shove his newfound beast back to its hiding place. Escaping took precedent over an irrational murderous urge. He hoped.

"What did they accuse you of?" All right. His voice sounded normal, well, mostly normal. Only a bit of a growl laced his words.

"My partner came in drunk. I reported him. They put him on leave. Then some of his friends, fellow detectives, rolled on me. Claimed he'd done it before and I hadn't reported it, which got me in trouble. Now I've explained my sorry life. Spill it on how to get us out of here."

"That's horrible. Why would they do that?" How dare they hurt his mate. He'd...sheath his claws and listen. Not turn into a demented dragon.

"You're not going to get us out of here until I spill all, are you?"

Jamie shook his head, grasped her hand with his free one. "I don't like it when you're upset."

One side of her mouth twitched. "They're jealous. I got promoted, and their friend didn't. I'm a woman and did a better job than they did. Typical misogynistic behavior. It might be the twenty-first century, but they still think women are better suited for housekeeping than police work." She shook her head. "But my ex-partner said he'd call the captain, my boss, and explain what happened. Nice gesture on his part. The captain might not listen to him, though, since Schultz was fired. In that case, I'm on my own. One way or another, I'm fighting to be reinstated."

Jamie pulled her to him, dropped her hand and wrapped his arm around her waist, keeping the knife pointed down at his side. After a brief hesitation, she returned his hug, resting her head against his shoulder.

"I'm glad you'll be getting back your position."

"Thank you for listening." She leaned back, one brow raised. "Now are you going to tell me your plan for getting out of here?"

The deep mahogany of her lips beckoned and he dipped his head, pressing his lips to hers, drinking in her essence. Heat spun through his veins, spiraling lower, until he wanted nothing more than to lay her back on the bed and claim her as his.

Right. Because bedplay ranked higher than escaping. *Idiot.*

Parker pulled back at the same time he did. "While I would love to continue…"

"I know. My apologies. We need to free Erik."

"We also need to see how many others are being held."

He shook his head. "I can't transport everyone."

"Not asking you too. We need to know so we can call the police when we've escaped. Let's move."

True words. He knew better than to lounge around while on a mission. But he enjoyed kissing Parker. Enjoyed watching a blush creep across her dark skin. Enjoyed the way her eyes glittered when she looked at him.

Sap, sap, sap.

"Erik's this way." He dropped his arm from her waist and gestured with the knife toward Erik.

"Nice knife." Parker stared at his knife like one would a prized possession.

He almost handed it over, but stopped himself halfway to her palm. Her defensive abilities might attract him, but he wanted to be the one to defend her, not give her the only weapon.

"Thanks." Jamie poked his head out the door. Still no one around. A fissure of unease skittered across his skin. "No one's around."

"That's strange." Parker's whisper caressed the skin of his neck and another set of chillbumps peppered his flesh. "Maybe they have cameras."

"Cameras?"

"You know. Devices that take pictures and then

stream them to a live video feed."

Her words bounced through his mind and he ground his teeth trying to deduce their meanings. Live video feed? Stream? If only he could see what she meant.

A quick hop into her mind and he saw what she meant. Amazing. The magic these people possessed rivaled a Draconi's. No, not magic. Technology. He saw that word inside her head too. Technology. Very few of Parker's people possessed magic. Even fewer possessed the ability for mind-speaking.

"You're in my mind." Her voice remained even, but he caught the tremor hiding behind the tone.

"I'm sorry." Not really. He wanted to know everything about her. Inside and out. But starting with invading her privacy probably wasn't the best way of going about things. "I didn't understand what you were saying."

"Don't have cameras back home, eh?"

"No. And while we have streams and rivers, that's not what you meant."

"Yeah, I suppose being here is difficult for you."

Her lips drew closer, her gaze jumping from his eyes to his lips. He closed the distance between them, pressing his lips to hers, the softness of her skin urging him to take the kiss deeper. Longer. Forever.

Jamie pulled back. *Mission, fool. Mission.*

Parker blinked. Shook her head. Pointed to the left. "Erik's this way, right?"

Jamie nodded. "Stay behind me."

No one challenged them as they walked down the hall toward Erik's cell. Shouldn't someone be around? Instead of lowering his guard, the absence of security hyped his awareness. He heard breathing, dozens of separate breaths behind the closed doors.

Parker spoke true. Others were held in these cells. Friends or foes? Innocents or guilty? Once they rescued Erik, he'd open a door and discover who lay inside.

No one stopped them as they walked to Erik's cell. No one stopped them as Jamie used his magic to unlock the door. No one stopped them when the door opened.

As soon as Jamie stepped into Erik's room he realized why.

Goddess's toes.

Chapter Thirteen

Parker froze as Kol rose from the chair, lowering the smartphone in his hand as he stood. A shit-eating grin crossed his lips as he gestured at them with the device.

"The video feed plays on this phone. I must admit, the technology almost trumps magic. Almost. But I digress. Please come in. Shut the door behind you."

Parker cut her gaze to a wide-eyed Jamie. Clearly he expected to find Erik alone in his room, not chatting it up with his long-lost father. In all fairness, she'd thought the same. And look where that got them.

Idiot. She should have known all that quiet in the hall only meant one thing. She hadn't expected the video feed to connect to Kol's phone or for Kol to be in Erik's room. Stupid, stupid, stupid.

Maybe they really suspended her for being a less than stellar detective.

Click. Dreaming idiot. Lost her thoughts, she failed to realize Jamie closed the door and stepped in front of her, shutting them in with a desperate man. Not good. Desperation made for an unstable mind, one who would do anything to get what he wanted. No matter the cost.

"My son claims you are Draconi." Kol's gaze raked Jamie from head to foot, a quick raise and lower of his brow indicating he doubted the fact.

Erik's eyes widened, his head jerking once—

startled or in denial?

Jamie tightened his grip on the knife, stillness descending upon him, predator to Kol's prey. Tattoos like red scales scurried along the nape of his neck.

Parker blinked and the scales disappeared. Was she seeing things?

"Do you doubt your son?" The warning tone in Jamie's voice prickled her skin.

Kol stopped a foot from Jamie, apparently oblivious to the waves of predation surrounding him like an ambush. Or maybe he didn't care.

"Draconi don't have your coloring. Nor do Halflings. What are you?"

Interesting. Something Jamie never mentioned. But why should he? He just met her. The knowledge failed to stop an ache from setting up residence in her chest. Damn it. She just met him. Well, yesterday, but still. Close enough. No way she should be upset he didn't tell her everything about himself in the short period of time they'd known each other.

And yet. She was. So much for logic. Look what happened the last time she fell like a gavel for a man. Someone else's long legs wrapped around his waist. No thank you. Not again. She learned her lesson.

Damn stupid chest ache. Her internal conversation only made it worse.

"Leave him alone, Father." Erik stood, swayed, and took a stumbling step forward. Kol steadied him with an arm around his waist.

"He needs to explain himself, son. Stop defending him."

Erik's eyes narrowed, but before he could speak, Jamie countered, ignoring Kol's question. "Why were you banished?"

Kol gritted his teeth, dropped his arm from Erik's waist, and sniffed the air around Jamie. "You smell Draconi. Magic. A scent I miss." Sorrow laced his voice. "Do you know how hard it is to be away from that smell? To live among humans? Won't you help me return home?"

Help him return home. Yes, she needed to help him. She needed to send him home. She wanted to send him home.

Jamie reached for her hand.

The instant his skin made contact with hers, her rush to help Kol faded. Parker shook her head. *He lies, he lies, he lies.* Convincingly, but lies nonetheless. She could not believe him. Could not. Would not. Jamie tightened his grip on her hand as he spoke, the warmth from his touch an imprint sinking through her skin into her heart. "Your magic doesn't work on me."

"Don't be ridiculous," Kol said. "My magic does not exist in this world."

"Or in mine."

Kol chuckled. "You think the High Priestess stripped me of my powers before banishing me, do you not? That is true. But stripping powers isn't permanent. Only temporary."

"How would you know? Your magic shouldn't work here."

"It doesn't. But how do you think Fasolt returned to Draconia all those years ago? Luck?"

Erik and Jamie gasped as if given coal for a Christmas present. Clearly whoever Kol referred to was bad news.

"So why kidnap humans?" Jamie asked.

Her exact thoughts. Did Jamie read her mind?

No, I didn't.

Parker jerked as his words drifted through her thoughts. At her movement, he squeezed her palm, a small show of support.

"I need the humans to return home." Kol thrummed his fingers against his thigh. "Some of them have powers. Granted, they refuse to admit it, but with enough humans, I can cobble together their powers and use them all to return home."

"Father!"

"That's crazy." Jamie gasped. "Do you mean to bring back the humans?"

"You call me crazy? What kind of thought is that?"

Jamie tilted his head.

Kol took a step back. "No. The humans would stay behind. They would use their powers to send me home. I have no desire to unleash humans on Draconia."

He spoke *humans* with the same tone one used to describe rotten trash. Parker bristled. She opened her mouth. Closed it. *Don't let him get to you.* She knew better. Knew to let a perp's words flow like water across her nerves.

But sometimes she couldn't help herself. She wanted to smack him one.

"Let us go."

Kol shook his head, a grin turning his lips with malevolent glee. "After all these years, I finally get to see my son. You truly expect me to release you? Ah, I see you do. Whoever you are, you came here. You can get me home."

"I have no idea how we got here or how to get home."

Kol's eyes narrowed. "Well, then, that creates a small problem. I want you to return me home."

"Want in one hand, magic in the other. Which gets you farther?"

A growl slammed against the concrete walls, the echo sending reverberating chills across her flesh. Parker tugged her palm out of Jamie's grasp and took a step back, hand reaching for the door knob. A quick turn and she breathed a sigh of relief. Not locked.

Kol turned his gaze to her. "Step away from the door. Please," he tacked on. Not that the pleasantry changed her mind.

His growl had snapped something inside her. Made her realize he kept them in the room for a purpose. And not to hear them talk.

Was his crew waiting outside the door? Waiting to capture them? Return them to their rooms?

"Father. Leave him alone."

"I said, stop defending him!"

"No!" Erik snapped. "He doesn't know how to get home. I brought us here."

"What do you mean you brought us here?" Jamie's brows furrowed. "I touched the cave wall."

"And I touched you."

"But your magic wasn't working right in the cave."

"Neither was yours."

"So why do you think it was you?"

Kol's eyes flared as he turned to Erik. "Smart lad. I should have realized."

"Realized what?" Jamie growled.

"Traveling dimensions apparently runs in the family. See, Father, you need me, not them. Let them go."

"Dimensions?" Jamie asked simultaneously with Kol's sharp, "No!"

"Why not? Father."

With Kol's attention on his son, Parker once again reached for the doorknob. A twist and she eased the door open a crack. If she turned around, Kol might notice so she forced herself to remain still as she strained her ears listening for incoming backup.

Which was a little hard to do with the loud voices several feet in front of her.

Dimension hopping. Who would have thought that possible? Sure, TV shows and movies explored the issue, but really, who believed those for truth.

What was Jamie's world like? Magic played a huge part, and technology was next to non-existent. What about women? Judging from his behavior, they were considered weak, in need of protecting. Maybe she wouldn't enjoy his Draconia. She had enough of egotistical males at her job.

Make that former job. Nope. Make that going to be reclaimed job.

At any rate, she didn't need men calling her little lady and thinking she couldn't tell the business end of a gun from a hole in the ground.

On the other hand she wanted to explore a relationship with Jamie. How crazy was that? From distrust to relationship status in less than a day.

She should have stayed in the hospital for a brain scan.

Clearly she needed to meet more people. Hang out with her girlfriends. Do things on the weekend that didn't involve beer and sports. Stop being so damn lonely.

Loneliness was a lot like desperation. One tended to make really stupid mistakes to remedy the problem.

Was Jamie a stupid mistake? Or a true gift? If he returned to his home, how would she discover the truth? Easy. She wouldn't. She'd be left here. In Denver. Pining for her job. No, damn it, pining was for sissies. And she would get her job back. Job equals life. Or at least it had until she met Jamie.

What was wrong with her? Daydreaming while she should be paying attention to what was going on around her.

"There's something off about him, that's why."

Parker startled at Kol's words. Daydreaming idiot. What were they talking about? Oh, yeah, Kol's refusal to release them. Of course he wanted to keep them. He lacked one hundred percent certainty that Erik told the truth.

And his curiosity about Jamie sealed their fate. No way would he let them go until he satisfied that curiosity. Which meant they needed to move their asses instead of gabbing like gossipy old ladies.

"Would you stop chatting him up and get the lead out?"

Three sets of eyes focused on her. What? Could they not feel the urgency of escape? Someone needed to take the lead, and since neither of the men stepped up, she would do the deed.

Parker yanked the door wide, stepping so she leaned against the frame, able to see both the hall and the room. No one in the hall, but the room exploded into movement.

Kol reached into his back pocket, withdrawing a Taser he aimed at her. Jamie knocked Kol's arm up, grabbed the Taser out of his hand, and threw it to the ground. Erik shoved Kol into the chair as Jamie stretched an empty hand toward their struggling captor.

A rope appeared from nowhere wrapping around Kol's torso, pinning him to the chair. Jamie took a step back and slid his knife into his boot as he watched Kol try to get free.

Shouts echoed from the hall, and Parker whipped her head toward the noise.

Damn it. Six incoming. A veritable wall of muscle.

"Come on! Get a move on!" She reached for her Glock out of habit, hand falling to her side as it hit air.

The men darted toward her, Jamie grabbing her hand.

"Erik! Don't leave me here! Take me with you! Please!" Chair legs cracked against concrete as Kol struggled to free himself from the rope.

Erik paused, but Jamie grabbed his arm. "Leave him."

"He's my father."

Damn it. No time for second thoughts. Parker took off in a jog, running away from the inbound wall of muscle, her hand wrapped around Jamie's, who in turn tugged a hobbling Erik. A roar bellowed from the room seconds before a plume of fire shot across the hall, singeing the walls with soot. Holy shit, what the hell was that?

"Holy altars," Jamie stopped, yanking Parker out of her dash. "Did he change?"

"We should take him."

"Snap out of it, Erik. We can't take him. He's banished. Now come on, let's go!" Jamie started moving again, taking the lead, Erik limping along as fast as possible.

How far until they reached…what? The exit? An elevator? The garage? She should have paid better attention.

"Can't you transport us out?"

"I don't know if we're underground or not."

"What about transport to the exit? Then we could run out or whatever." Parker glanced over her shoulder as thundering steps filled the hall.

Wall of Muscle was gaining. Damn it.

They scurried around a corner, then another one, coming to a quick stop as the corridor ended with a door. The way out? Or a trap?

Not much of a choice at this point.

Jamie shoved open the metal door. Warm air slapped her in the face, and Parker drew in a shaky breath.

The parking garage. Freedom.

Heavy steps and loud voices echoed down the corridor as the guards sprinted toward them.

Erik hobbled through the door, slammed it closed, and leaned against it seconds before the thing rattled in its frame as if smacked by a volley of bullets. Yeah, right. One body against a wall of muscle.

"Can you get us out of here?"

Jamie nodded. "I need a second. We're going to try to get us back home."

"My house has been compromised. They know where I live."

"Not your house. Mine."

Parker blinked, her veins turning to ice. Oh hell no. He thought to…to…she couldn't go, right? Just because she'd wondered what his home was like didn't mean she wanted to visit. Right?

Pounding on the door jarred Erik, but he managed to keep it shut. Parker threw her weight beside him. As if that would help stop the forward momentum of six oversized men.

Jamie grabbed Erik's forearm, reaching out a hand to her, palm up.

Breath hitched in her chest. If she took his hand, her life would change. Was he worth it?

A pounding *bam-bam* shuddered the door, echoing a response in her bones. Was he worth it? The door burst open, knocking her to her knees, Jamie and Erik remaining upright by luck alone.

Screw this. She was not going back in a cell. Parker leapt forward, grabbing Jamie's hand. At the same time, Kol darted into the parking garage, his cry of 'No!' echoing through the concrete structure.

A fog descended over her vision, the room fading, colors muting. Kol jumped as a shot of electricity sparked a path into their circle. The room disappeared, swallowed by the fog. Air slapped her skin as if she fell from a distance. Air?

Parker smacked against concrete, rolling on impact, breath escaping her lungs in a burst. She lay stunned, body aching like she'd been hit by an eighteen wheeler. Grunts and groans sounded nearby, as if the men mirrored her aching body on concrete position.

What happened?

"Parker?" Jamie's voice cut through the pain, and she forced her eyes open. Darkness surrounded her, interspersed by metal lumps and tall shelving. A warehouse. What were they doing in a warehouse? Weren't they supposed to be in Draconia?

"Parker?"

Maybe she needed to answer Jamie and alleviate the concern she heard in his voice. "Over here."

She flexed her hands and feet, arms and legs as the rasp of clothes against concrete indicated Jamie's scramble to her side. No broken bones, thank goodness, just aches and bruises. By the time Jamie found her, she was sitting, trying to catch her breath.

"Are you all right?" he asked simultaneously with her, "Are you okay?"

She grabbed his outstretched hand. Damn lack of lighting. Was he okay? Only his shape showed in the darkness.

"Are you hurt?"

"No," she shook her head, "just some bumps and bruises, that's all. Where's Erik?"

"I do not know. I sought you first."

And didn't that make her heart soar. A smile crept across her lips. He cared. For her.

She squeezed his hand. "Why are we here?"

"I don't know. Erik? Erik, can you hear me?"

A distinct groan from the opposite side of the room answered his question. Jamie pulled Parker to her feet, formed a blue light in his palm and together they hurried toward the noise. Erik lay on his side, eyes blinking a slow up-down as if he woke from the land of nod.

Or the land of unconsciousness.

Jamie knelt by his friend, running his hands down Erik's arms, clearly feeling for broken bones. Erik grunted and shoved off Jamie's hands.

"Scout, I like you, but not that way."

Jamie bit back a laugh. "Glad you are all right."

"Did Father come through?"

Parker shrugged. "I don't know. He jumped at us, then there was this bolt of electricity, and we landed here. I should call the police. Let them know about the others being held. Do you have…" *a phone* died on her lips. Right. They didn't know what a phone was, let alone have one. And since hers was sitting at home, so much for reporting the kidnapping.

Unless this building had a landline.

"Have what?" Jamie stood and helped Erik to his feet.

"A phone. I need to file a report." Shouldn't there be an office up front with a phone? Parker turned in place. Which direction was up front?

"We need to leave before Kol finds us."

So much for finding a phone. Wait a minute. Was she really going to return with them to Draconia?

"That's what I meant to do." Erik shoved a hand through his hair. "I tried to take us home."

"Perhaps we have to leave through the same portal from which we came."

"That makes sense." As much sense as possible considering the circumstances. A couple of days ago she would never have considered the possibility of dimensional jumping as normal. Now? Sci-fi flicks had nothing on her experiences.

"We came through over here," Jamie pointed toward shelving. How he could discern one shelf from the other in the dark was beyond her understanding. They all looked identical to her eyes.

"What about Father?" Erik hobbled after Jamie, Parker bringing up the rear.

"He's been banished. We can't return with him."

Was she really following them to Draconia? Was she really going to leave her world, her job, her friends—what few of them she had—behind?

Parker stopped a few feet away from where Jamie circled in place, a human homing beacon. Erik stepped beside him, grasping forearms like they had earlier in the tunnels. Was she going to go? Or stay?

Stay for what? The possibility of getting her job back? Of more lonely nights, wishing for a man while working on her latest case?

Or go. To what? What was his land like? What if this budding sense of attraction for Jamie melted? What if he stopped caring for her? If things went sour? Then she'd be stuck in a strange land. Or would she be stuck? Maybe she should give him a chance. If she didn't like his land, she could return.

Hopefully.

Shuffling sounds echoed from her left, the scratching of a downed person trying to rise. Parker turned to the sound as a shadow rose from the concrete. Her eyes popped wide. Kol. Lack of lighting didn't deter her from knowing the shadow belonged to him. He lurched toward her.

Stay or go?

Light surrounded Jamie and Erik as Jamie stretched out a hand toward her. Stay or go? Kol took another step, gaining speed as he rushed toward her. Parker ran toward Jamie. So much for staying. She'd rather face the unknown than return to that cell underground and be used as a lab rat.

Parker leapt, grabbing Jamie's hand at the same time a large body slammed into her back. She stumbled, but the light surrounded her, pulling her into its gravitational field, carrying her across time and space.

Pain ripped at her bones, through her flesh, a sharp edged dagger tearing into her soul. Hard rock slammed against her soles and she toppled, collapsing on rough stone.

Breath tore jagged holes through her lungs. But at least she could breathe. Meant her ribs weren't broken. Her brain still functioned. Grunts sounded as heavy bodies landed next to hers.

Clothing rustled. More grunts indicated shifts in position. Blue light lit the darkness, hurting her eyes. Parker blinked several times, trying to stop the dance of dots against her retinas. Jamie held a small flickering blue flame in one palm, his other hand outstretched to pull up Erik. Neither noticed as Kol pushed up to a sit, a smile lighting his face.

"Home."

"Hey!" Jamie dropped his palm from Erik's, but before he could reach Kol, the man popped to his feet and took several steps back.

"Father. Wait." Erik started to rise, his injured ankle slowing the attempt.

"Thank you, son, thank you. And I'm sorry." Bright light formed in his palms, eclipsing Jamie's blue flame, illuminating the glee in his expression.

"No!" Jamie and Erik yelled. But Kol moved faster, pitching the light their direction, a racing explosion of color.

Another burst of pain slammed into her, through her, baking her bones in a fiery agony. Her mind clicked closed, thrusting her into welcoming darkness.

Chapter Fourteen

Hard stone pressed against Jamie's side, a damp chill seeped through his skin. Where was he? And then the last moments before everything went dark slammed into his mind. Transporting. Kol latching on to Erik, his presence almost throwing them out of the transport except they managed to compensate for the extra weight. A rough landing. Kol's escape.

Bloody dragon bones. He'd returned a banished male to Draconia.

Jamie pushed to a sit. Dark spots danced whirling winds across his vision, dizziness an unwelcome remnant of the energy ball. Damp air clogged his nose with rot. Water dripped in the distance. A feminine moan sent a cold chill chasing across sweat drenched skin.

Parker.

"Jamie?" Erik's voice grated like metal hinges.

"Here." Jamie formed a flame. A puny flame. He sighed. So much for keeping his magic.

The light flickered across Erik as he struggled to rise, the healing boot hampering his movements. Jamie gathered his feet under him and offered Erik a hand. Where was Parker?

A quick turn and splash of light illuminated her sprawled on her back, eyes fluttering behind closed lids. An ache ran through his chest, a dull pain speeding his breathing. Jamie knelt and touched her arm only to release it as a burst of blue light exploded into view.

"Praise the Goddess," Erik muttered. "My magic works."

Ignoring a streak of jealousy, Jamie focused on Parker, his touch gentle as he grasped her arm.

"Parker?"

He shook her arm, and her eyes rolled open.

"Jamie?" her voice squeaked and she cleared her throat.

At the sound of her voice, the ache in his chest flowed away, and he slumped forward. "Hey." He offered her a slow smile. "Glad to see you awake."

"What the hell was that light ball?"

"An energy ball set to render us unconscious." Good thing it hadn't been set for kill.

"Like a stun gun?"

Stun gun? Jamie made a non-committal noise and held out his hand.

"Thank you."

Parker grasped his palm, allowing him to pull her to a sit.

Jamie placed a hand behind her back. Heat from her skin flowed through her shirt into his palm, and he stroked his fingers against the thin material. Touching her felt right, as if her skin was made for him and him alone. He should stop, drop his hand, offer to help her rise. But he left his palm where it rested. As Keara always said, just because you can doesn't always mean you should.

Of course she wasn't referring to the present circumstances, but advice was meant to be used, right?

Erik cleared his throat. "Are you going to lounge

around all day, scout, or are we going to inform the Council of Father's return?"

Parker's brow wrinkled as Erik spoke in Draconi.

Use her language.

Teach her ours.

"Parker," Jamie ran his fingers along the ridges of her spine as he spoke in her language. "We need to inform the Council of Kol's return. And your arrival."

"I'd think twice about that, scout," Erik said. In Draconi.

Jamie snarled. *Use. Her. Language.*

Erik chuckled. *Think. Do you really want the Council to know we returned with a human?*

I'm half human, dumbarse. What difference does it make? Alviss no longer sits on the Council.

Have it your way. But you might want to explain things to her.

Jamie opened his mouth. Closed it. Goddess's toes. Would Parker's arrival bother the Council? What about his parents? She belonged to him. And if they rejected her, then they rejected him. He swallowed. Could he leave Draconia, his family, his people? Throw it away like an unused gift? Return to Parker's world and experience using magic at will instead of struggling to cast a small spell?

Was magic worth abandoning his home, his family? He'd already lost his birth parents. Could he bear to lose his adoptive parents too?

He wanted Parker, yes, but to leave all he knew behind and live in her world?

Assuming she wanted him to live in her world.

Did she feel the same about him? How did a male convince a female she was his mate?

Scout?

Erik's voice slammed into his mind, jolting him back to the present.

Right. Cave. Kol escaped. Parker's presence needed to be explained to the Council. No time for musing.

"You're talking to each other again in your mind." Parker clicked her tongue several times in rapid succession. "Which I would say is rude, but, wow. I'm no longer in Kansas, Toto."

Kansas? Toto? "My apologies. But I thought you said you lived in Denver? What is Kansas?"

"Oh, sorry. It's from a movie."

"Movie?"

"A motion picture?"

Jamie cut his gaze to Erik, who shrugged, his face mirroring Jamie's confusion. So much for understanding her speech. When in doubt, ignore and redirect.

"Erik thinks the Council will not react well to your presence."

Parker's eyes narrowed. "What? Humans aren't welcome?"

"Something like that," Erik said.

Parker stiffened.

A growl gurgled in the back of Jamie's throat, his lip curled into a snarl as he fought not to attack Erik. *Stop scaring her.*

Erik held his hands palms out, his eyes popped wide. *Whoa, scout. She needs to know what to expect.*

Jamie sucked down a breath and hoped the extra air doused the urge to attack simmering beneath his skin. Maybe he should get busy growling at himself. Instead of saving Parker, did he bring her into danger? Were things really as bad as Erik claimed?

"If I'm not wanted here, why didn't you leave me behind?"

"I couldn't leave you behind." *You belong to me. You're my mate.* As if she wanted to hear fate decreed her mate was a magically deficient Draconi. "Things aren't as bad as Erik says."

"Trust me," Erik huffed. "You refuse to see the bad."

"Alviss is dead. Halflings comprise a good deal of the population. Goddess's toes, Erik, I'm a Halfling. That's half human. In case you forgot."

"Yes, but it's also half Draconi. That's the important half."

"Thanks a lot." Parker glared at Erik, who had the decency to look remorseful.

"No offense."

"It will be all right, Parker." Jamie stroked her back. "I won't let anyone hurt you."

Her eyes narrowed as her gaze raked over his face, sharpened claws of insight. She drew in a deep breath and nodded once. "You do realize Kol escaped, right? Instead of discussing the welcoming committee or lack thereof, shouldn't we be trying to catch him?"

Probably. But concern over Parker outweighed capturing Kol. He owned that excuse, but why did Erik not chase after his father?

As if he mind-spoke the thought, Erik's eyes narrowed, white lines forming around his lips. So much for hearing an answer to that question any time soon. His friend's face turned into a shuttered mask, a smooth avoidance of truth.

Jamie shrugged and focused on Parker. "I can find him again." He hoped. "That's what I do, you know. Find people."

"You mentioned that before." One side of her lips twitched into a grin.

"Do you feel like traveling?"

"Yep. Where are we going? To this Council you keep mentioning?"

Jamie stood and helped her to her feet, the touch of her palm a lightning strike through his blood. Her gaze met his as if she felt the same. Maybe convincing her she belonged to him would be easy, simple, like most Draconi weaved magic.

He was not most Draconi.

Either way, the end result was Parker as his mate. He hoped.

Blue light faded, blurring her expression yet highlighting her lips. Soft lips. Plump lips. Lips he wanted to kiss. Again.

Her gaze drew him closer, wrapped him in a heated embrace, tempting him with things to come, pleasures to experience. Moist breath brushed against his lips, heat from her skin slid against his, sending a jolt of awareness straight to his shaft.

"Stop staring and start moving."

Erik's voice snapped shut the budding sexual heat. How close he came to kissing her. Inches. Maybe he should have charcoaled his friend earlier. Would have saved him from his current aching shaft condition.

Parker's eyes flared. Despite the dim light, Jamie swore red tinged her cheekbones. Her gaze darted to Erik and back. "He's right." She sidestepped him, following a retreating Erik.

Jamie gripped her hand, as if his grasp held the fragile ties weaving between their souls. She laced her fingers through his and squeezed, which elicited a corresponding pressure in his chest. Or maybe that was his heart pounding a hello-beautiful rhythm.

"You'll be summoned with us once we cross the ward lines." Erik spoke her language over his shoulder, as he limped toward the cave entrance, his voice echoing against the stone walls.

Parker stiffened, and Jamie squeezed her hand. Why did Erik insist on speaking words he knew would upset her? As a test of her strength? To prove a point?

"Do you get off on trying to scare me?"

Erik stopped and turned, his brows furrowed. "Do you imply I derive pleasure from your fear?"

"Exactly."

"No, I do not." He turned and started walking.

Then what are you trying prove?

For a Draconi who crossed worlds to find a female, you can be dense.

Dense? You scare my female on purpose and then accuse me of being dense?

Exactly.

And that's supposed to mean what?

Erik's sigh drifted through his mind. *Goddess, you are dense.*

Good thing he didn't need his mouth to talk. He doubted words could escape a jaw locked as tight as a dragon's treasure chest. What demon possessed his friend? Giving Erik a tongue-lashing might ease his ire, but he refused for Parker to see him lose his temper. Which began to leak out his ears as steam.

Jamie sucked in a breath. If he breathed in then the

steam couldn't come out. In theory.

Parker made a non-committal noise and glanced over her shoulder. Her eyes widened. So much for breathing in dissipating steam.

"And here I thought steaming ears was an expression of speech."

"Sorry."

She held a hand out by his ear. "Nothing to be sorry for. Draconi ears steam often?"

"Only when we become mad."

"Interesting. And he," she jerked her thumb over her shoulder in Erik's direction, "upsets you when he needles me, eh?"

"Something like that."

She smiled. "That's sweet. You're...protecting me."

Busted. Did she realize his protective nature meant he'd recognized her as his mate? That the longer he stayed around her, the less likely he could leave her?

"Hurry up. We don't have all day."

Yes. He really should have charcoaled his friend while he had the chance.

"You're starting to sound like a broken record, Erik." Parker tugged Jamie's hand as she walked into the main room of the cave. Erik stood at the cave's entrance, hands on his waist, the light behind him casting his face into shadows.

"A broken record? How do you break what you record?"

Jamie wondered the same thing, but refused to let Erik know he was equally clueless. No more fodder for those dense comments.

"Never mind." Parker shook her head. "Where are

we going?"

"Back to Draconia." Jamie stepped beside Erik, water from the fall wetting his back. "We're right outside the border."

"It might hurt when we cross the ward line."

"Why? What kind of hurt?"

"The wards are designed to keep out humans," Jamie explained. "They'll pull on you a bit, but you are with us so it should be all right."

"Should be?"

"As long as you're with us, you'll be fine."

Erik held out a hand to Parker. "Don't let go of me."

"I didn't think your magic worked."

"It doesn't work well in your world. Here, it's normal. His," Erik tilted his head toward Jamie, "doesn't work. Now take my hand."

Parker placed her palm in Erik's outstretched one, and Jamie swallowed a ball of steam threatening an appearance. Erik was not making a move on Parker, he needed to touch her to transport. The same as putting his hand on Jamie's forearm, forming a circle. No need to attack.

Goddess, how did male Draconi live with all these crazy attack-what-hurts-my-mate emotions pinging through their system?

And then all thoughts hummed to background noise as Erik threw them into a transport. A transport almost as slow as his. The wards tugged at his particles, holding on as long as possible before throwing him to land in a heap of limbs. At least he landed in Draconia.

What in the name of the Goddess happened?

His eyes shot open as he scrambled to all fours.

Where was Parker?

Right next to him. Thank the Goddess.

Her eyes opened, saw him and narrowed. "You guys need to work on your landing."

"Are you hurt?"

"No. But I'm sick and tired of falling out of the sky to land on hard ground."

"Me too. I'm not sure what happened." Had traveling through the cave injured Erik's magic?

Erik sat upright, several feet away from them. "I've never had that happen before. What went wrong?"

"You're the one powering the transport." Jamie glared at his friend. "You tell me."

"Must be remnants of that energy ball Father threw." His eyes flared. "You realize we returned to Draconia without the Halfling."

"Isn't it more important that we inform the Council of Kol's return? We can always complete the mission later."

"Do you want to explain to them why they shouldn't fry our arses for failing a mission?"

What was wrong with his friend? Why didn't he understand Kol's return posed a security threat?

Blood means more than societal rules.

Was Erik trying to hide Kol?

Jamie dismissed the idea as soon as it appeared. Erik would never betray Draconia. Right?

"What are you two talking about now?" Parker crossed her arms.

Jamie gave himself a mental smack. Hypocrite. Being angry at Erik for speaking Draconi in front of Parker when he did the same. "Sorry. Erik says we need to complete our mission before returning to the

Council. I say we need to report Kol."

"I agree." Parker nodded.

"I don't." Erik shook his head. "I for one do not relish the thought of having my arse fried."

"Your father is a security threat. He was banished for a reason."

"What if that reason was wrong? What if he made a mistake?"

"Are you taking his side?" Jamie's eyes widened.

"Of course not." Erik swallowed, ran a hand down his face. Drew in a breath. A strange expression crossed his face, leaving Jamie unsettled. Then he spoke, and the moment vanished. "I'll inform the Council about Father, and you two can find the Halfling."

"Are you jesting?" Did Erik's common sense disappear with the hard landing? "Informing them about Kol is more important. We can find the Halfling later."

"I'll handle it. Don't worry. I'll transport you to the south border and return."

Parker shook her head. "A possible security threat trumps completing a mission any day."

"You don't understand," Erik's words ran together as if he couldn't wait to set them free. "I will tell the Council about Father after taking you to the border. You two can find the Halfling, and I will inform the Council we let Father escape."

"They'll char you. We'll stay."

"They'll char us all then. No, I'll take you to the border."

Jamie opened his mouth to protest, but Erik grasped his shoulder, grabbed Parker's arm and threw them into a transport. If only he possessed full powers,

Erik would never be able to transport him against his will.

Anger burst through his veins. Anger at his measly powers. Anger over Erik's stupidity. Anger, fueled by shame, coalesced into a ball of energy, releasing as a flash of light.

Pop! Pop! Pop!

Jamie hit the ground hard, knees collapsing under his weight, body rolling several feet before stopping face down. Not again. What was Erik's problem?

A moan sounded, and he lifted his head. Parker laid a stone's throw from him, moaning. Erik sat legs crossed, his head in his hands. Jamie scrambled toward Parker, muscles aching each time a hand or foot struck the ground. Ignoring the pain, he forced limbs to move, to stretch, until he reached where Parker lay curled on her side.

Goddess, how badly was she hurt?

"Parker? Can you hear me? Are you all right?"

"I've…been…worse." Her voice rasped an ache inside his chest.

"Did you break a bone?" Jamie ran his hands over her arms, her legs. Thank Goddess. Nothing was broken.

"She all right?" Erik spoke in his ear, and Jamie started. "Sorry. I don't understand what went wrong. Again."

"You have problems." He'd never heard of anyone dropping out of a transport. Except for his earliest attempts at transporting. Even then he never landed like this, rolled on the ground like a sausage. Last he remembered, anger seized his scattered particles into a vise, a potent mix of ire and power.

Plenty of Draconi transported angry. None of them dropped from the air like a hailstone. Which meant it wasn't his anger issues. Something was wrong with Erik's magic.

Parker rolled to her back, wiggling her arms, legs and fingers, testing for breaks and bruises. No breaks, thank the Goddess.

"What's wrong with my magic?" Erik formed a flame in his palm. "It seems to work fine. Feels normal, not like in her city. Maybe it's you."

"Maybe you need to stop dragging us around Draconia and report to the Council on your father's return."

Erik shook his head, his eyes sad. "Sorry, scout. No can do. You find that Halfling, and we'll meet up at the Council later."

Between one blink and the next, he disappeared. Jamie punched the ground. Why did Erik insist upon leaving them to find a Halfling they could find later? He couldn't stay here, nor could he leave Parker behind while he tried to chase Erik.

Holy altars.

"Can't you go after him?"

"Not with you. I can't leave you here either."

"That sucks."

Sucks? The expression didn't match the definition, but he understood it all the same. Sucks. Yes, that summed things up well.

Parker cleared her throat. "I think it's my fault we fell out of that transport. I felt this surge of anger and got scared."

"What do you mean you got scared?" Jamie felt his brow rise.

"When I get scared, I produce a burst of energy. Like when they drugged me and I couldn't move and was lying on the sidewalk, all the streetlamps exploded. Right before you showed up. That's not the only instance." Her gaze clouded as if lost in memories. "It's a horrible ability. It's why Kol targeted me."

Jamie touched her arm, running his fingers up and down her tanned flesh, trying to ease the fear shivering through her limbs. Why would she hate her power? "You transformed my anger into a burst of energy?" Amazing.

"I think." Her gaze fell to her hands. "Maybe. Yes." Her lids raised, dove gray eyes shining. "Sorry."

Jamie gave her arm a squeeze. "We'll teach you to use it." *We'll?* He wished. "Well, I won't because I don't have much magic."

"You used magic a lot in my world."

"That was a fluke. It was like your world was filled with titanium."

"Titanium? What does that have to do with anything?"

Was he going to tell her the bane of Draconi? Give her power over him? Apparently he was, seeing how his mouth started moving of its own volition. So much for keeping a secret. "A Draconi's magic is inhibited by titanium. Right before we came to your world, we were in the cave, and Erik said the titanium deposit interfered with his magic. But when it would interfere with his, mine would activate."

"Didn't you learn when you were a kid that titanium affected your magic?"

"We ban the substance as much as possible. I'd never been exposed to it."

"Titanium is in a lot of things back home. Maybe that's why you were able to work magic in my world and Erik couldn't."

"Yes. That's what we thought." Jamie stood and held out a hand. "We need to find Erik. He can't leave us here while he reports to the Council."

"You actually think he's going back to the Council to tattle on his dad?" Parker grasped his hand and let him pull her to her feet while she spoke. "Because it seems to me he's going to find his father and needed a convenient way of getting rid of us without harming us."

Jamie blinked. And again. And one more time. Did he hear her correctly? Did she just accuse Erik of aiding a banished male? Clearly she didn't realize how insane that proposition was. No male in his right mind would aid a male who'd been banished. Not even for a blood relative.

He could say a lot about Erik's attitude, but his constitution did not include aiding and abetting a known criminal.

"Of course he is. You don't understand our society. We would never help a banished male."

"And yet you refused to chase after Kol when you landed in the cave."

"That was because I was concerned about you. And I can find people with ease."

"Or he messed with our minds. Didn't Erik say that's what he did? So, if he messed with our minds, to what end? What's he want?"

The answer slammed into his mind. Impossible.

"Why was he banished?"

"I don't know. I always thought he was dead. Erik

never talked about his father. It was just him and his mother." His mother. Jamie gave himself a mental smack. A mated male would return for his mate. But Erik helping a banished male made no sense.

"Perhaps he returned for his wife. Were they in love?"

In love? If Kol felt for his mate anything close to the strings binding Jamie to Parker, then love was a poor word for the overpowering emotion. A male separated from his mate became crazed, prone to irrational behavior. At least until he learned to control the pain of separation. Some never learned. Would rather join their mates in death than live alone.

"A bonded male is a fierce beast. Protective of his mate, even to death. Living apart, knowing the other existed and being unable to reach them would be torture."

Her eyes narrowed, flecks of jealousy darting through their depths. "Do you have a mate?"

Now would be the perfect time to tell her his suspicion. To inform her of the bond trying to grow between them.

To overwhelm her with too much information at one time. Passing through a portal into a different realm and confronting a different species was shock enough. Learning a defective shape-shifting dragon identified her as a mate might push her over the insanity cliff.

"It was assumed because of my lack of magic that I do not have one," he hedged, hoping she missed the delay in his answer.

Her expression relaxed, jealousy giving way to curiosity. A soul-piercing gaze latched onto him, breaking down his resistance, until he lay bare before her.

Jamie swallowed.

"Only a Draconi with magic can have a mate?"

"I'm a Halfling. I'm not a full breed. Not all Halflings have mates. That doesn't mean they can't love, but a mate is a sacred bond. Only one mate per Draconi."

"How do you find your mate? Date around?"

"Date around?"

"Just the two of you going out. For dinner. Drinks. Other things."

Other things? His mind tripped into a fantasy featuring Parker splayed on his bed, eyes shining with desire. Shaking off the vision, he focused on her question. "We take bed partners. Meet to talk and eat. If we find a female we like, then we can test for mating compatibility."

"How?"

"Put one of the pair in a dangerous situation and see if the other transports to them. If the non-endangered one transports against their will, then the couple are mates."

"That is the strangest thing I've ever heard of. I don't even know where to start with the questions."

"It is a little odd, I admit. But it works." Or so he'd heard.

"It isn't any more odd than some mating practices in different countries of my world." A pause. "What are we going to do about Kol and Erik?"

"I'll try to contact Thoren to come get us."

"Can we walk back?"

"I'm not certain where we are."

"Perhaps you can transport us. When I was shot, I

broke my arm. The doctors fixed it by putting in a screw. A titanium screw. Touch me. See if it helps."

"Your healers use titanium to repair bones?" Hope and surprise warred within him. What was more shocking? The fact her healers could not repair a broken bone without using metal or by carrying a small amount of titanium within her body, she became his personal power source?

"Yes. Try it." Parker held out an arm, presumably the one she had broken.

Jamie grabbed her bicep, the muscle firm under his fingers, her skin soft to his touch. Before attempting a transport, he tried to form an energy ball, to start small and increase his magic. Provided his magic worked.

With only a thought, an energy ball appeared in his upturned palm. Jamie blinked. Extinguished the ball. Imagined transporting to the nearest tree, several feet in front of them. The familiar feel of his body pulling apart slammed through him, the tree appearing as they materialized.

Jamie turned Parker to face him, grasping her other arm. "Thank you!" He lowered his head and pressed his lips against hers.

Her body stiffened then relaxed, her arms circling his neck, pulling him closer. Her lips softened, mouth opening, tongue tangling with his as he dropped his grip and wrapped his arms around her waist.

Heat flooded his veins, stiffened his shaft, his thoughts returning to the vision of Parker naked, lying on his bed. Tingles started in his legs, circling upward, a transport in slow motion. Transport?

Before he could take a step backward, his body split apart, flying over the ground as scattered particles to land in his bedroom. His. Bedroom. Goddess's bloody toes.

Parker took a step back, her gaze flitting around his room.

What an idiot. But how was he supposed to know that thinking of a place meant an imminent transport? He needed to explain before she thought he was pulling a fast one. Not that he minded pulling a fast one, but a couple of kisses did not mean she wanted him for bedplay.

"Guess the transport needs a bit of work. At least we didn't fall out of the sky."

She grinned, her lips swollen from his kiss. "Good job. I'm going to be sore for a week from all that falling out of transport." She shook her head. "Never thought I'd hear myself say anything like that."

Did she regret meeting him? "Changes are difficult."

"Especially when they strike without warning."

"Sometimes, though, they're for the better." *You, for instance.*

Her eyes flared like she heard his internal thoughts. As if that could happen without him projecting them to her. "True. Sometimes."

He held out his hand. "Come. I'll take you to the Council. We need to tell them about Kol." And Erik. The thought churned his stomach into a ball of wiggling worms. What was Erik thinking?

He was afraid he knew the answer. No, no, no. He refused to go there. Erik was loyal to the Council, to Draconia. He would never betray either, not even for his father.

Parker ignored his outstretched palm and ran her

fingers across his dresser. "I've got to admit, I'm a little nervous about meeting this Council." She picked up a large ruby. "Is this your room?"

"Yes." He dropped his hand. "Don't let Erik's words trouble you. I'll be with you. The Council won't hurt you." He hoped. What if they refused to allow her to live with him?

Would he like living in her city? Jamie shuddered.

"I know. It still makes me nervous." She swallowed and held out the ruby. "You found all these?"

"Yes. I like jewels."

"I can tell. You seem to like rubies."

"They're my favorite."

Parker chuckled. "Seriously? That's my first name. Ruby."

First name? "What is a first name? You said your name was Parker."

"Ruby is my first name, like Jamie is yours. But most people call me by my last name, Parker. A last name is a family name. You said at the hospital that you don't have a last name. Then how do you tell who belongs to which family?"

"We refer to ourselves as sons or daughters of whoever is the most powerful in the family."

"Like the Vikings did."

"Vikings?"

"Sorry. They were ancient warriors. Whose son are you?"

Jamie swallowed as his father's face flashed in his mind. "Bjorn was my father. But I am the adopted son of Thoren and that's how I'm known."

Chapter Fifteen

A wave of sympathy crashed into Parker. Whatever happened to his parents left an indelible mark upon his soul. She understood the emptiness that came from losing a parent at an early age.

"I'm so sorry. I lost my mom to cancer when I was young. What happened your parents?"

Jamie grimaced, pain etching lines in his face. "They were killed in front of me. I ran and hid when a group of soldiers came and only by the Goddess's hand did they not find me. They wanted me, not my parents, but Father tried to fight them off. The soldiers possessed a titanium sword, which prohibited him from using his magic. They killed him before he could turn into a dragon. Sometimes I wonder if my parents would still be alive if they hadn't resisted. If they had handed me over."

"Oh, Jamie. I'm so sorry. Were the killers caught?"

The grin curving his lips sent a shiver down her spine. "Oh yes. Thoren and Enar killed them."

"That's good." Detectives arrested suspects, leaving sentencing to judge and jury. But in her mind, Parker tried the perps herself, no jury necessary, sentenced them to a few years, life or death depending upon their crimes. And in her book, killing parents in front of their children ranked as one of the most heinous crimes. "You must have had a hard time growing up without your parents."

"I was lucky to be adopted by Keara and Thoren."

"Tell me about the first time you met them."

"Keara found me after my parents," he swallowed, "died. She was an apothecary and was out hunting herbs and found me instead. I lived with her a few months until Thoren rescued us."

"Rescued?"

"We weren't born in Draconia. Keara and I. We were both Halflings, but she didn't realize it. We lived in Caustasia, in River's Run. The townsfolk hated anything different, and she stood out like a jewel in a case of rocks. Thoren rescued her and by extension, me."

"And he brought you both back to Draconia?"

"Yes. She was his mate, and after their mating ceremony they adopted me." Jamie ran his hand over a ruby the size of a grapefruit, his gaze caught on his moving fingers. "They're my family. My father's Draconi relatives want nothing to do with me. Halflings are usually prized, but not by all Draconi." He cleared his throat, his gaze rising to meet hers. "What about you? Your mother died when you were young?"

"Yeah. My dad never remarried. He threw himself into his work as a detective in an effort to forget about her. He died shortly after I was promoted to detective." Parker forced her jaw to relax as childhood memories snuck past overused barriers. "He was the one who encouraged me to go to the Police Academy."

"Police Academy?"

"Classes that teach you to be a cop. You have to be a patrol cop before you can become a detective."

"A detective belongs to a security force, right?"

"Yep. A couple of years on patrol and then I put in for a transfer to be a detective. Just like Dad." Her fingers clenched into a fist. So much for believing in the adage forgive and forget. Words burst from her lips like a cleansing deluge. "I wanted to please him. I liked helping people, so I followed in his footsteps. Tried to impress him. But grief can obliterate everything else in someone's life." Make a father forget he had a daughter. Make a daughter put aside her dreams to impress her father. Make life seem dull and gray.

Jamie's touch on her arm snapped her out of the miasma of memories. "At least I knew my parents were dead. It must have been hard to live with both a dead ghost and a living one."

"Yeah. It was. Anyway, enough of being morose. In case you think I regret my job, I don't. I love it. Loved it." Her captain's voice slammed into her mind. Administrative leave.

"What will you do if your ex-partner cannot convince your boss to reinstate you?"

"I need my job. It's my life." Rather like her father, come to think of it. And how effed up was that? Turned out she was more like her old man than she thought.

Damn it.

She would get her job back. Not if. Would. House payments didn't grow on vines. "So, what about this Council?"

Not that she wanted to see this mysterious, and apparently fear-inducing, Council, but it beat discussing the past and her sorry state of affairs. And Kol needed to be brought to justice. As in slap his happy ass in jail and see how he liked being locked up. Would serve him right.

And then there was the problem of what to do about Erik.

"Right. The Council." Jamie slid his hand down her arm to grab her hand.

Devil take her, but she liked the way his large palm gripped hers. Liked the heat licking up her arm. Liked how the heat filled her veins with giddiness.

She must be losing her damn mind.

Stay on topic, Parker. "What will you tell them about Erik?"

"He should already be there."

"He won't be."

Dark brows knotted together. "Yes. He will."

"Jamie, think this though. Blood runs thicker than society rules."

"Not this rule. And not Erik."

"Okay. If you say so." Erik ran off to help his father. No other explanation existed. And something told her that little tidbit of news wouldn't go over so well with this esteemed and frightening Council.

Why was this her problem? She barely knew Erik, and his teasing made Jamie ear-steaming mad. All evidence pointed to her ignoring this issue, letting Jamie sort things out, this being his society and laws. But Erik was Jamie's friend, and she hated to see Jamie hurt.

Which was something she learned early in her career. You can't free everyone from hurt. Without pain, there can be no growth.

"This angers you?"

How perceptive of him. "I disagree with you, that's all. It's your people. You know them better than I do."

Dread crept across her skin as she thought of

meeting this Council. Meeting strange people should not bother her, heaven only knew she met enough strangers working a case.

But the thought of Jamie's countrymen gave her a case of the willies no gang member ever inspired. Probably since she lacked her metal friend.

Relying on her Glock instead of her wits only led to trouble.

"Yes. And no Draconi would help one who is banished."

"Not even their father?"

"Of—" He paused, a faraway look in his eyes, a remembrance of his childhood, or what he'd do to see his father again? "I...No. Of course not. Not even for their father."

"Well, then." *You'll be in for a big surprise.*

One eyebrow cocked a query as if he heard her snide remark. Impossible. Wait, he read minds. Damn it. How embarrassing.

Thank goodness her darker skin hid the heat splashing her cheeks. Or so she hoped. "What about that Council?"

Jamie's lips twitched. "We'll go see...no wait. You need to learn the language."

"Unlike you I can't pull it out of someone's mind, and there's no way in hell I can learn a language in a day."

"I will give it to you."

"You'll what?"

The words no sooner left her lips than a sound like a thousand fluttering butterfly wings filled her mind. Images of runes coupled with sounds spilled into her brain like too many papers in a case file. Pain stabbed, and Parker clapped her hands against her head. As if that would keep the file from expanding.

And then the pain receded.

"Sorry. Are you all right?" Concern bled from the edges of his eyes as he knelt in front of her.

Knelt? Oh. Right. Sometime during the language download she'd dropped to her knees. And, she might want to remove her palms from her head lest she give the impression of addled wits.

Had he really given her an entire language like a file downloaded off the internet? How was that even possible?

"Parker?"

Yeah. Definitely needed to drop her hands. Drop. Her. Hands.

Right when she feared learning a language shorted out her ability to move, her hands dropped. Parker blinked and focused on the small specks of yellow dotting Jamie's gray eyes. She drew in a breath and then another one for good measure.

"Fine. What did you just do?" The fact she asked a question to which she already knew the answer did not bode well for her mental functioning.

"Gave you my language."

"Did it work?"

"You're speaking it."

"I am?" *Way to look intelligent, Parker.* Of course she was speaking it. New words swirled in her mouth, lingered on her tongue, clouded her ears. A thick language, like a sausage-and-cream based soup.

A grin played along the corners of his lips. "You are. Do you feel all right?"

"My head hurts a bit." Amazing. She spoke a new

language. Now that she was aware of her new ability, she heard the different sounds in her speech. The way the words rolled off her tongue. Or stuck there as the case may be.

"It will improve. I didn't want to hurt you, but you needed to be able to speak before the Council if they request without me translating. They will see you more as their equal if you speak their language."

Maybe. Or maybe not. A nervous energy surrounded him like a cloud, leaving little drops on her skin. A shiver snuck down her spine. No use huddling on the floor like a scared child. Being a sissy never did her an ounce of good.

Using Jamie's broad shoulders as leverage, Parker pushed to her feet. "Ready." She really needed to stop lying to herself.

"It will be fine. Do not worry."

Why did she feel she wasn't the only liar in his room?

Parker looked down at Jamie kneeling at her feet and had a sudden memory of her ex-finance in the same position, proposing. Not a memory she wanted. Especially now. In Jamie's room. Standing among his things. Breathing a scent distinctly his. A scent that reminded her of strength. Dependability. Love.

Love? *Get a grip on reality, Parker.*

Attraction was not love. But something about Jamie drew her in, made her long for more, for that elusive L word she had sworn never to feel again. She wanted to move in with him. To raise a family. To love.

Clearly, by transporting to a different dimension, she lost her mind.

And then she had no more time to think of it as

Jamie stood, grabbed her hand and threw them into a transport. They arrived in front of a circular stone building. Imposing gray stone rose toward the sky. Tall, wooden doors outfitted with iron hinges barred the way inside.

Parker tensed. She'd faced worse. Like administrative leave. But not even those two words compared to the strum of power surrounding this building. She swallowed and rubbed her palms across her hips.

Jamie paused in front of the doors. Straightened his shirt. Sucked in a deep breath.

Great. How reassuring.

"Nothing to worry about." For whose benefit was he saying that? "Ready?" He grabbed the iron door ring and gave a tug.

Not really. But seeing as she had no choice in the matter, Parker followed him through the entrance.

The chill of the building struck her like a falling icicle. She forced her arms to remain at her sides instead of crossing. But the chill didn't so much come from the ambient temperature as from the forces of power working within.

A semi-circle of thirteen carved wooden chairs sat against one rounded wall as if presiding over an execution. Balls of light hung in candelabras around the room, casting a harsh glow across the stone walls and marble floors. If the place was built to creep people out, it succeeded.

Off to one side a group of thirteen men huddled around a table. At the click of the doors, all heads swiveled toward them. A punch of energy hit her in the chest, her heart tripped an uneven rhythm. Jamie stepped in front of her, blocking her with his body.

"I'm following up with Erik's report."

One of the men, tall with shoulder length black hair who looked no more than ten years older than Jamie, stood. "What report from Erik? Why are you separated?" The man shifted a bit to the side, cutting her with his glare. "And why did you bring a human into the Chamber? Where's the Halfling?"

Oh, yeah. This interview was not off to a good start.

Jamie shifted. "What do you mean Erik did not return?"

All the men stood, the one speaking moved forward. "Why are you separated?" He again moved to look at her, but Jamie moved with him, blocking her from view. Or protecting her.

Parker swallowed.

Jamie drew in a deep breath, releasing it on a heavy exhale. "We were separated when we returned. You know what trouble I have transporting, so it took me awhile to make it here. I assumed he'd already given his report."

"Why don't you give it for him? And start by explaining why there's a human hiding behind you instead of a Halfling."

"I had dreams about her. We decided to go find her before finding the Halfling."

The man raised a brow.

"We fell through a portal into her world and discovered Kol—"

"Kol? Erik's father?"

"You know him?"

Another man stepped beside the first. Silver

highlighted his long black hair. "We banished him. Of course we know him."

"He returned with us."

"What? How?"

Jamie explained how Kol grabbed them when they transported. "His powers returned and—"

"Nonsense. Powers don't return once they've been stripped."

The first man turned to the one who spoke. "It's happened before."

The man shook his head. "Impossible."

"He said powers grew back over time."

"And he returned with you?"

"Yes." Jamie paused. "That's how we became separated. We thought it prudent to return to the Council and inform them of this matter before we hunted for the Halfling."

"Wise choice. He worked with a male bent on Draconi destruction. Who's to say he doesn't still want revenge? More so since his banishment."

"You still haven't explained the human female's presence."

Jamie glanced over his shoulder at her, apology written in his eyes. For what? Bringing her here? While power emanated from the men like an aura, they had yet to make a threatening move toward her. Maybe they were about to?

When he turned back to the men, he straightened his shoulders and drew in a breath. "She returned with me because I believe she's my mate."

Mate? What the hell? Maybe she misunderstood. New language and all. Or not, judging by the males' reactions. Wide eyes followed by pitying looks.

Pitying? What? Did they not find her a worthy match for Jamie? Or did they believe him addled for the suggestion? Either way, heat rushed up her spine, her jaw tightening.

"Son," said the first man, whom she assumed to be Thoren given his address to Jamie, "I mean you no disrespect, but we've discussed this before."

"I know what we've discussed, and we were wrong. She is my mate."

The older man with the silver streaks glanced at Thoren and shrugged.

Thoren nodded.

In the blink of an eye Thoren vanished, only to reappear next to her. Strong arms banded around her waist, and before she could push him away or scream, he transported them out of the circular building. A roar like an enraged elephant filled her ears, cut off as she disappeared.

Air pulled at her molecules, as if she swam through a lake of molasses. An ear-pressurizing pop sounded as they materialized in the middle of a grassy field. Thoren released her before she could smash his instep, and she stumbled forward, off balance.

Parker caught her balance and turned, one foot back, hands held loose and ready, but Thoren had already taken several steps away from her. His black brows slashed over his eyes, hands shaking like he grabbed electricity and disliked the burn. With a quick shake of his head, the expression vanished.

"Sorry. We had to prove to Jamie—" His words hung dying in the air as a roar slammed through the clearing.

Jamie appeared near her, steam circling his head,

tiny red scales rippling up his arms, across his neck. Claws tipped the ends of his fingers, long knives flexing.

Parker froze. What the hell? Maybe she should have taken him seriously when he said he belonged to a race that turned into dragons.

"Leave my mate alone." A growl tinged his words, warping them into a deep menace.

Thoren raised both hands, palms facing his son. "Jamie, calm down. We had to perform the test. I'm not going to hurt her."

Jamie paused, his gaze raking Parker from head to toe to head. A couple of blinks and he drew in a deep breath, a full body shiver cascaded down his limbs, eradicating the scales. He crossed the few feet dividing them and wrapped her in his arms. The tension holding her upright relaxed at his touch.

"Don't ever do that again."

"Don't worry, son. I won't." Thoren cleared his throat. "Are you going to introduce us?"

Do you want to speak to him? Jamie's voice drifted through her mind, a stroke of velvet against skin.

Did she have a choice? She rather liked being held. Having a man's arms wrapped around her in a caring embrace hadn't happened for a while. And what a surprise to discover being protected instead of doing the protecting felt like a warm bath on a cold day. A girl could get used to being held.

A girl also needed to make her own way instead of relying on a man.

Parker placed her hands against the firm muscles of Jamie's chest and pushed until he loosened his grip. She needed answers to a plethora of questions. Might as well start with chatting up his father.

"Sure."

Once Jamie released her, she turned and stuck out her hand, speaking over his introduction attempt. "I'm Detective Parker." As she failed to find a Draconi word for detective, she used the English one.

After a brief glance to Jamie, Thoren grasped and released her offered palm, then rubbed his hand on his pants. His brows drew together and relaxed as he gave her a nod.

"Detective," he stumbled over the unfamiliar word, "Parker, it is a pleasure to meet you. Perhaps you will care to join my mate and me for the evening meal?"

Food sounded wonderful. When was the last time she ate? Scratch that. When was the last time she slept? Not since her capture, which was how many hours ago? Shouldn't it be the middle of the night or early morning? Instead, afternoon sun shone warm on her face. Either she was held in that cell for longer than she thought or time ran differently here.

Something she should have paid more attention to upon landing in this world.

And she might want to pull her thoughts out of introspection and focus on her surroundings. Along with answer Thoren's question.

"I would love to."

"Good. Are you," he gestured to Jamie, "able to return to the Chamber for further questioning?"

"As long as you don't disappear with Parker."

The tips of Thoren's ears reddened. "I apologize. We did not expect these results."

Jamie shrugged. "Neither did I." He glanced at her, a grin tingeing his lips. "But I'm glad it happened."

"What do you mean, you didn't expect the results? What results? Him to come after me?" Parker asked.

"You mean you haven't told her?"

Now it was Jamie's turn for red ears. "Until now, I only suspected she was my mate. And it doesn't seem to work the same in her world."

"What are you talking about?" She had a sneaking suspicion their conversation had something to do with Jamie's announcement she was his mate.

"Oh, ho," Thoren barked a laugh. "Good luck with that explanation."

Jamie snorted, then turned to Parker. "I'll explain later. We need to return and answer questions. Then we can eat. All right?"

"All right." The delay would give her time to add more questions to her almost overflowing list. What did he mean by mate? She assumed that meant spouse, but without her consent, how could he say she was his?

Wait a minute. What did she know about their wedding rituals? Nothing. Maybe she unknowingly made some gesture or mentioned something that caused them to become wedded.

Damn it.

Although to be fair, if she had to marry someone, Jamie would top her list. Nicer and more caring than her ex-finance, she doubted she'd find him in her bed with another woman's legs in the air. She hadn't known him long, but at least he listened to her.

On the negative side, he apparently possessed the ability to set the bed on fire. Literally.

Now, metaphorically. Yep, she could get with some metaphorical setting of a bed aflame.

Jamie raised a brow, his lips twitching.

Damn it. Did he read her mind? Heat splashed into her cheeks. His head bent, lips whispering against her ear.

"We can try that later. If you want."

Embarrassment and sexual heat took turns assaulting her. Yeah. He heard her. Damn it. She needed to learn to keep things to herself. Or maybe he needed to learn not to read her mind.

Yet another thing to discuss.

"Ready to go back?" Thoren's eyes twinkled as his gaze bounced between them.

Jamie nodded. "Might as well get it over with."

"I used to feel the same way." Thoren placed one hand on Jamie's shoulder and the other on Parker's.

"Ready?" Jamie grabbed Parker's hand, and they transported back to the Chamber.

This time they landed inside before the same gawking men. Direct path to the firing squad. And, yep, they all stared at Jamie as if he grew a third arm. Even Thoren, who waggled his fingers like they stung.

From the titanium in her arm? Did titanium sting when touched by a Draconi? And if titanium was their bane, how could he touch her and still transport?

Maybe that's why he'd given her a bunch of puzzled looks. And why Erik's transports ended with them falling from the sky.

The tall man with silver streaks in his dark hair cleared his throat. "You said Kol returned with you, and you and Erik were separated. Where is Erik now?"

"I don't know. I thought he returned here."

"Do you think Kol captured him?"

"No. Kol disappeared some time before Erik left."

"Where do you think Erik is?"

Jamie swallowed. "I do not know where either of them are."

Good answer. She didn't know where Erik and Kol were either, but that didn't mean she couldn't take a fair guess. The two were together. Someplace.

"We need to find them. Thoren, you and Enar go with Jamie to search for Erik, while the rest of us will organize a search and find party for Kol. Where did you last see him?"

Jamie told him where the cave was located.

Parker glanced up at the ceiling far above her head as the others organized a search party. Windows framed the upper reaches of the circular room, allowing light to filter down through floating dust motes. Besides the thirteen carved chairs and the large table with what appeared to be a deck of cards spread across the top, the room boasted multiple candelabras with round pale balls in the holders instead of candles. What odd lights.

"Jamie," Silver Streaks spoke, snapping her attention back to the wall of men, "you and your mate are dismissed. Wait for Thoren and Enar outside, please."

Jamie nodded, grabbed her hand and led her out the double wooden doors. Outside the air felt muggy as if hours before a storm.

"That wasn't too bad, was it?"

Parker raised a brow. "What's your definition of too bad?"

"Answering questions with questions is an evasive technique."

"Thank you, Dr. Phil."

"Who?"

"Never mind." What harm would it be to tell him?

"It wasn't as bad as I thought."

"Good."

On to more important things. "What's this talk about us being mates?"

Huh. Looked like a man really could become as still as a statue. Jamie swallowed as his ears and cheeks reddened.

"We need to talk."

"Yeah, you think?"

Pop! Parker started as Thoren and a tall man in his mid-fifties with blond hair going silver appeared before them. The man tilted his head her direction.

"I'm Enar."

"He's Thoren's best friend and like an uncle to me," Jamie said as he gave the older man a one armed male hug complete with back slapping.

"We'll drop your mate off with Keara," Thoren said, "and then search for Erik."

"Thank you, but no." Raised brows greeted her statement. What? They didn't think a woman could track a missing coworker? Some things remained the same no matter where she went. "Back home my job involves tracking clues and finding criminals. I can be of assistance."

"You are allowed to go on missions?"

"They aren't missions, they're cases. And yes. I track criminals."

"That's what her title, Detective, means," Jamie grinned at her. "She's part of her town's security and tracks law breakers."

At least he didn't seem to mind her occupation.

Thoren exchanged a look with Enar, and both men shrugged. "Very well. You can come with us."

How generous of him. "Thank you."

"Where do you think he is, Jamie?"

Jamie glanced at her. A tickling, like butterflies brushing her skin, fluttered across her mind. *You were right. Just don't tell them. I want to get to him first.*

Parker's eyes flared. Nice to know he had the guts to admit he was wrong. *Okay.*

Does okay mean all right?

A grin twitched her lips. *Yes.*

Good. Thank you. He spoke aloud to the men. "I don't know. Maybe he thought I would reach the Council first and decided to go hunt for the Halfling. We didn't think it wise to appear with Parker and no Halfling. But Kol's return meant we had to."

"I find it unlikely that he would try to find the Halfling alone. But if you believe he might, then we'll travel to the border and try to obtain clues."

"Then we'll travel to where we came through the wards and see if we can follow his trail from there."

"Tell me where, and I'll take you there."

Jamie smiled and wrapped his arm around Parker's shoulders. "I can take us."

"Are you sure?"

"Of course."

"How?"

"It's complicated. I'll explain over dinner."

Thoren raised a brow. "Very well. I look forward to hearing this complication." He touched Jamie's shoulder. "May the Goddess go with you."

"And also with you."

Jamie transported them to where they first entered Draconia.

"So where is Erik?"

"Not here."

"Really? Never would've guessed. So why did you bring us here?"

"In case they followed. Thoren has that look in his eye, the one he always got when I'd try to get away with something as a child."

"You don't think he believed you."

"Oh, he'll go check the way out of Draconia toward the Halfling, but it won't take long. Erik's not there." He glanced away from her. "I should have listened to you."

"You live and learn." Parker smiled. "Where is Erik?"

Jamie closed his eyes, his body becoming still. Then his eyes opened, and he gripped her palm. "Hold on."

A moment later, they stood in front of a stone house, late afternoon sunlight shining through trees, dappling shadows across the ground. Light shone from the windows, a welcoming beacon for weary travelers.

"Is this his house?"

"His mother's, but he spends a portion of his time here too."

"What's the plan?"

"Convince him to explain why he appears to be working for Kol."

"You think he's a traitor?"

"I think he's confused."

Chapter Sixteen

Parker cocked a brow. "Confused?"

Jamie drummed his fingers against his leg. Maybe he was the confused one. Erik clearly believed in blood over society. Something Jamie had never understood. Something he was now beginning to understand.

Erik could no more turn his father over for execution than Jamie could admit to the Council his friend's duplicity. At least not until he heard how far that duplicity went.

"I have a hard time believing he means harm to Draconia. But we don't banish others unless they harm Draconi. Which means Kol caused harm to another. Erik shouldn't want to help a banished male, but you appear to be correct," as much as he hated to say it, "that he chose blood over societal rules. Did Kol convince him to do something he wouldn't normally do, or is there another reason?"

"Maybe Kol returned for his wife."

"His mate? You said that before." And he ignored it before. One thing he'd learned in the last few hours was to listen to Parker. Her suspicions proved correct. "Maybe he did. Let's go ask."

When they reached the house, Jamie knocked on the door. Footsteps sounded, and then Erik pulled the door open, his surprised expression freezing on his face. Then he blinked, and the moment passed.

"Jamie? What are you doing here?"

"What do you think? I went to the Council and discovered you hadn't."

Erik licked his lips. "Did you tell them where I was?"

"No. I told them we were separated and you were supposed to return and give report. And that Kol returned with us. We're all looking for you. It won't take them long to come here."

"Kol's not here. He never crossed into Draconia."

Jamie closed his eyes, searching for Kol, learning the truth of Erik's words.

"You see I'm telling the truth."

Jamie nodded. He located Kol's presence a distance from the borders of Draconia. "Good. But that doesn't explain why you lied."

Erik ran a hand through his hair, his eyes staring at a spot over Jamie's head. He released a noisy exhale. "He wanted to see Mother. I came here to ask her, but she already knew he was close. She felt him through their mating bond. When I arrived, she'd already packed. I took her to him. That's it. They wouldn't let her go with him when he was banished all those years ago. They watched her for years to ensure she remained."

"Since she wanted to go with him, he wasn't banished for harm to her?"

"Of course not. They were the sun in the other's sky. He could no more harm her than he could harm himself."

"Then why was he banished?"

Erik looked at his shoe, at his toe twisting into the floor, as if it could dig a hole and swallow his body.

But he was saved from answering by a series of *pops*, the Council members arriving.

Erik's gaze snapped to Jamie. *Don't tell them where Mother is.*

I won't.

Even if it meant lying to his father. Not really lying. More like withholding the truth.

Something he'd done a lot of, especially when younger. No sense in his parents knowing how he spent a good deal of his youth.

"Erik," Balthor's voice rumbled across the grass, a deep roll of thunder. "Explain yourself."

Erik paled, licking his lips before swallowing. "I apologize. I needed to let my mother know of Father's return."

"And?"

"She was not here."

"Why did you linger?"

"I tried to find where she went."

"And Kol?"

"I do not know."

"Do not know or will not tell?"

"Do not know."

"Do you know his plan?"

Erik shook his head, a bead of sweat rolling down his cheek.

"Does he plot revenge?"

"No. I'm not sure."

"Do you know where he crossed into Draconia?"

"He didn't. At least not that I saw."

"Then we need to search and see." Balthor pointed to three males. "Go search the caves and all possible entry points. Check the wards."

The males nodded and disappeared.

"Erik, I am disappointed you did not return to us earlier, forcing us to find you."

"I'm sorry, sir. It won't happen again."

"These were unusual circumstances. You will let us know if Kol attempts contact."

Erik nodded, his pulse visible as a rapid beat in his throat.

Balthor cleared his throat. "We are done here. You two will leave tomorrow and complete your mission. Understand?"

"Yes, sir," Jamie echoed Erik.

Balthor gestured to the Council members and as one, they transported away.

Don't forget dinner, floated through Jamie's mind as Thoren disappeared.

Jamie exhaled. For a second there, he thought they saw through his deception. Through Erik's.

Erik ran a hand through his hair as he stepped inside. He gestured for them to follow. Once Parker was inside, Jamie shut the door and leaned against the wooden panels. His heart pounded a rapid beat and he focused on sucking in deep breaths. In and out. In and out.

How long had it been since he experienced this rush of adrenaline, the lightning strike of energy from a risky adventure? Years. Hunting Halflings was exciting, but far from a risky adventure.

The child inside clamored for more adventure. The adult breathed a sigh of relief the questioning ended at the door.

"Why would they forbid your mother from following your father when he was banished?" Parker asked.

"Further punishment."

"It's painful for mates to be separated." The thought of Parker abandoning him replaced his heart with an aching hollow.

"But it backfired." Erik's lips flattened. "Mother was equally punished and had to suffer in silence."

"That wasn't their intention." He hoped.

"But it was the outcome."

"Now what?" Parker's gaze bounced between them.

"We have dinner with my parents and meet up with Erik tomorrow to find the Halfling."

"Try to breathe." Erik sank into a chair and propped his injured foot on a stool.

"While you're breathing, remember how not to get us into this mess. And go to the Temple to have your ankle healed."

"It's not my fault your 'find the dying female' campaign led to my father. And trust me, it won't happen again. Go have your dinner. I'll see you tomorrow. After my trip to the healing ward."

Jamie took another deep breath and uncurled his hands. He made the decision to obscure truth. And he'd do it again to protect Erik. No need to step on his tail over the matter.

"Good night."

He held the door open for Parker and followed her outside. Insects chirped in the late afternoon light, a symphony of beating wings.

"He had no right to ask you to lie." Parker crossed her arms, eyes glaring fire.

"I would have done it without him asking. And how did you know?"

"I didn't fall off the turnip truck yesterday, you know."

"Turnip truck?"

"I wasn't born yesterday. The saying? I've been around and seen things?"

"Right." What strange expressions she used. "I try not to lie."

"But he's your friend."

"Yes. And Kol really isn't in Draconia. If I had been thinking clearer, I would have known that. There isn't a threat. At least I hope there isn't one. So it's just a matter of falsifying timelines. The Council wants things done in their timeline, not ours. What difference does it make as long as they were informed?"

"Good rationalization. But sometimes it can come back and bite you in the butt."

"True. Which is why I try not to obscure the truth." He grinned at her. "Are you ready for dinner?"

"I'm starved. But I need a shower. It was bad enough meeting the Council looking like I'd been drug backward through the bushes, but I refuse to meet your mother with grass stains on my clothes and leaves in my hair."

"You look fine. There aren't leaves in your hair." Green stained her blue trousers, starting at her hip and traveling down to her ankle.

Maybe she had a point. Another thought crossed his mind. Parker. In a bath. In his house. Oh yes. A male could get used to that thought in a hurry.

"And I need another change of clothes."

"I only have my own. They'll be too big on you." Although he liked the idea of her wearing his clothing, his scent covering her like he longed to do with his body.

"Do you have a washer? We can wash them. Not sure if that would give them enough time to dry before dinner. When is the evening meal?"

"In an hour or so. When the sun sets. And I don't have a washer." He grinned. "But I do have magic. Perhaps I can clean them that way. Or you can scrub them in your bath."

"Is that how you clean clothes? With magic?"

"Yes, with either magic or with water."

"All right. I'll bathe, and you can clean my jeans. If you don't mind?"

"Not at all." He grabbed her hand. "Ready?"

At her nod, he transported them to his house, explained how to use the bathing room since it did not contain a shower and stepped outside the door. After a moment, Parker pitched out her shirt and trousers, the door closing with a click.

He longed to open the door, undress, and slide into the pool of water. Take her into his arms. Make love to her.

Instead, he picked up her clothing, took it to the large room and flopped into a chair. Several tries later, he sighed. Her clothing remained grass stained. Apparently he needed to touch Parker in order to work magic.

Jamie walked into his bedroom and sat by the bathing room door. "Parker? I'm sorry, but I'll need to touch you in order to cast the spell to clean your clothes."

A long pause. "All right. I'm coming."

The door cracked open a moment later, her hand reaching through the crack. He grabbed it, held his other hand over her stained clothes, and cast the spell. This time it worked, the stains dissolving, her clothes returning to a clean state. He passed them through the crack in the door, and a few minutes later she emerged.

"I feel better. Thank you. What about you? Bath time?"

Females preferred clean males to dirty ones. "Be right out."

Parker was observing his ruby collection when he finished bathing, running her fingers over the jewels, picking them up and turning them so the facets caught the light.

Ruby. A sign from the Goddess she belonged to him. Rubies were his favorite jewels. Would she let him call her Ruby? Should he ask? She seemed to prefer the name Parker.

When she saw him, her lips turned, her gaze raking his body, a sexual heat he felt to his soul. She clearly found him attractive. But did that translate into acceptance of him as her mate?

He stepped forward and grabbed her hand. "Ready to meet my parents?"

"As ready as I'll ever be." Her voice remained smooth, but the dampness of her palm betrayed her nervousness. Or maybe the damp came from his palm. What if Keara didn't like her? What if Parker didn't like Keara? Did all males worry about their families meeting their mates?

"Jamie?"

"Sorry. You're the first female I've had them meet." And she'd be the last. Something he needed to tell her. Something she probably already knew from his outburst at the Council Chambers.

"Good to know you're nervous too."

His lips twitched. "Glad that makes you feel better."

"You know." She shrugged.

"I do. Come on. No sense in delaying the inevitable."

A quick squeeze of her hand, and he transported them to his childhood home. The stone house sat in the middle of a gently rolling field, trees as windbreaks standing sentry around the periphery. Smoke circled the chimney, evaporating into the evening air. Insects chirped a welcome melody as they walked to the front porch.

"Nice. You grew up here?"

"Since I was ten." He stepped up to the door and sucked in a breath. This case of the knee-knocks and sweaty palms needed to end.

A cool chill from the doorknob pressed into his palm. He twisted the knob and stumbled forward as the door swung open. Keara caught him by wrapping her arms around his waist.

"There you are! Thoren said you would be coming to dinner."

Her scent of herbs and cinnamon encircled him, a relaxing combination. Home. Tension flowed out his pores, replaced by a calming sense of peace. Everything was all right. No need for nerves.

Jamie stepped back, keeping a hand on Keara's shoulder. "Keara, this is Parker. Parker, this is Keara."

Parker's eyes flared. "She hardly looks older than you." She clamped a hand over her mouth as Keara's lips twitched. "Sorry. I tend to speak before I think. But you look so young."

"Thank you, love. I can tell we're going to get along just fine." Keara patted Parker's arm. "Didn't he tell you? Draconi, including Halflings, age slowly so we look much younger than we are."

A stillness swept across Parker's face. "How slowly?"

"Draconi usually live around five hundred years."

A pale green crept under the bronze of Parker's skin.

"Parker? Parker?" Keara gestured at Jamie. "Grab her before she drops."

Jamie wrapped both arms around his mate as she slumped against him.

One hand slapped a weak thump against his chest. "Buddy," she muttered. "We gotta talk."

Jamie swung her into his arms and placed her on the couch in the family room, Keara following behind.

"Thoren mentioned you had neglected to tell her some things, but I didn't believe him. I thought you knew better."

Heat rushed into his ears, his face. Criticism from Keara always made him feel like a child caught pilfering the jewel chest. "It's been a crazy last few days."

Keara grabbed Parker's wrist, taking her pulse. "She'll be fine. Parker, you are awake, yes?"

Parker's head bobbed. "Dizzy."

"Yes. I seem to recall having a similar reaction when I first arrived in Draconia. But I'd rather be here than anywhere else and it didn't take me long to realize that either. Maybe a week. Or less." She patted Parker's arm as she rose to her feet. "You'll like it too. Well, I need to check on dinner. I'll just leave you two alone to chat. Thoren should be here shortly. Council business, no worries. But you already know that."

Seeing Thoren was the least of his worries. Telling Parker she was his mate and all that involved ranked at the top of the worry list.

Parker groaned, both hands clasped against her head. She tried to sit, but Jamie pushed her down.

"Don't try getting up yet."

"I need to get up and redeem myself. How embarrassing to pass out in front of your mother."

"It's all right. She's a healer. She gets that all the time."

"Yeah, but not from me." Parker pushed off his hands and sat, leaning forward, elbows on knees, head in hands. "You have some explaining to do. Start with our visit to the Council. What did Thoren mean by calling me your mate?"

"Exactly what he said."

"How? We haven't dated or married."

His tongue sat thick and dry in his mouth. Useless. Blocking his throat. Prohibiting air from being inhaled. "As I said earlier, Draconi mating habits are different."

"I didn't think they applied to me."

"Well, see. That's what Thoren proved. He gave us the mating test and you were shown to be my mate."

"Mating test?"

"Yes, remember? Put a possible mate in danger and if the other can transport to them, then they are mates."

"So what you're saying is that I have no choice in the matter? We're mated no matter what I think?"

"Is that bad?"

"Are you clueless?"

"I do not recall being given clues."

"This isn't the way things happen in my world. The woman has a choice."

"But you don't have true mates."

"We fall in love. We get married."

"There is only one male for each female in your world?"

"No. There can be many people you would fall in love with."

"And you? Do you have this love?"

"Once. But we broke it off."

"Why?"

"He cheated. I found him in our bed with another woman."

Jamie hissed. "That would never happen in Draconia. A Draconi male cannot leave his mate for another female. Once they are bonded, they remain that way for life. Mating is the highest form of love."

"Even when you barely know the other?"

"Once you know who your mate is, the feelings are there. They are there before you know"—even if the dumbarse male denies the emotions—"and grow stronger with time. You cannot tell me you do not feel a bond between us."

She ran her hands through her hair and turned to glare at him. "It's happening too fast."

Did that mean she felt no bond? His breath hitched, his stomach formed an empty hollow of panic and shoved his body into the dark maw. Perhaps she felt the same, but had no experience with the bonding. Of course she didn't. How could she if males in her world could take a mate, yet have a bedromp with another female not their mate?

Jamie's chest relaxed, and he drew in air. Her

world was not his own. He should not expect her to feel the same, to want the same, to need the same. But he wanted her to. He wanted her to crave him the same as he craved her. Her body, her soul, her being.

Perhaps she would never feel the same about him. Perhaps he should let her go. His body reacted as if hit by a blow. He curled forward, wrapping his arms around his stomach as if the action could protect him from her words. He could never let her go. What male refused his mate?

The front door swung open and Thoren strode inside. "Hello, there, son. Glad to see you and Detective Parker are already here." He took a couple of steps forward and stopped, clearly picking up the distress written into the emotional layer of the room. "Am I interrupting something?"

"No."

"Yes," Jamie spoke simultaneously with Parker.

"Oh. Well. I'm sure your mother needs me in the kitchen." He turned as Parker stood.

"We're all right. I, um, felt a little ill when we arrived so we stayed in here, but I'm better now."

"That's good," Thoren looked over her head to Jamie. *She didn't take the mating talk well, eh?*

Jamie narrowed his eyes. *I'm handling it.*

Thoren's lips twitched. *You couldn't do worse than I did, and look how things turned out.* "Come along, then, and we'll see what Keara stirred up for dinner."

Parker scurried after Thoren as if the room was ablaze and he was her only means of escape. Jamie sighed and ran a hand through his hair. Thoren's optimism about his mating predicament gnawed his stomach, a writhing of tiny carnivorous worms.

Optimism should encourage him, lend strength to his abilities, but instead it left him empty, fearful. What if he failed? What if he couldn't live up to Thoren's expectations?

Quit being morose, Jamie. Parker will understand. It will be all right.

Or would it? Jamie smacked a hand against his head as if the hit would knock out the negative thoughts. He had no choice but to win Parker over. A male was nothing without his mate.

Chapter Seventeen

Parker stalked after Thoren, her head a roar of ire, her jaw clenched tighter than a thief's grip. If the choice was left up to her, she would be happy with getting to know Jamie better, following through on the insane attraction, seeing where things led. But to be told she was his mate, end of discussion, stuck in her chest like a festering splinter. She worked all her life to prove she was equal to a man and now she found out she has no choice about her spouse?

Where were her gun and a firing range when she needed one?

And then her thoughts and body froze as they came to the kitchen. The room was large, with counters, a table and a cluster of sofas, a combination of kitchen and living room, but the size wasn't what stopped her feet.

Nope, the complete halt was due to spoons in three pots on the fire-burning cook stove stirring without hands. As if she stood on a fantasy movie set.

Okay, Parker, no more sissy moves. Breathe, damn it, breathe.

Seeing Jamie work magic, being transported, and jumping into a different world like a character in a sci-fi TV show should have prepared her for spoons stirring independent of a hand. Apparently not.

Jamie placed a hand on her lower back, startling

her into movement.

And damn it, but she liked the warmth spreading from his hand to her core. Damn it, damn it, damn it. Maybe being mated wouldn't be so bad.

A state of conflict was not where she wanted to be.

"Feeling better, Parker?" Keara paused from chopping vegetables, her knife inches from the cutting board.

Parker nodded, swallowed, pulled her voice out of its hiding place. "Yes, thank you. May I help?"

Keara shook her head as she peered at the pots. "No, I'm—" Her voice pitched into a giggle as Thoren grabbed her around the waist, planting a kiss on her cheek.

Jamie cleared his throat and gestured to the table. "Would you like to sit?"

Good idea. Sitting might help with the lightheadedness playing havoc with her vision. Parker sat and rested her head upon the cool wood. Chair legs squeaked as Jamie lowered himself into the seat next to hers.

"It takes awhile to adjust."

"How would you know? You were born this way."

"Not really. I mean, I always knew of Draconi magic, but I wasn't born here."

"That's right. Sorry. I knew that." Idiot. Listening and retaining information used to be valued characteristics. *Concentrate, Parker.* She raised her head and met Jamie's gaze. "How long does it take to adjust?"

"It took Keara about a week. She didn't believe in magic. Me, only a couple of days." A shadow passed through his eyes, a remembrance of shock upon arrival or how his lack of magic placed him always as an outsider? No wonder he wanted to mate her. Her titanium screw made him normal.

One glance at him, and she realized the inaccuracy of that thought. A mixture of concern, kindness, and lust reflected in his gaze. No, she meant more to him than an ability to work magic.

Which failed to make her lack of choice any better.

Behind Jamie, Keara and Thoren gave her long glances under lowered lids, questions vibrating in the surrounding air. Parker swallowed. Parents always had a thousand questions, no matter where they lived.

At least she was a clean sissy instead of a grass stained one. That had to help. Right?

"Your parents would like to talk to us." Her whisper was meant for Jamie's ears only, but Keara and Thoren turned their heads as if they heard. And why not. Sharp hearing, steaming ears, self-stirring spoons. What other magic would she see?

Jamie turned around, head cocked as he stared at his parents. Keara flushed red and the tips of Thoren's ears colored.

"Well, do you blame us for having questions?" Keara raised a brow, the curve of her lips betraying the harshness of her voice.

"This is not a Council inquisition." Jamie stood and crossed his arms.

"Don't be so defensive, son. You know we mean her no harm."

"It's fine, Jamie," Parker placed a hand on his arm as she stood, "They can ask me questions."

"That sounds so cold," Keara grinned. "We're simply curious. You are different. It's in the energy that sparks around you. We want to know you better. Welcome you to the family. Not quiz you endlessly."

And yep, the feeling was mutual. Did everybody stir pots handlessly? Could they snap a finger and clean up the kitchen? Because she was down with that skill.

Parker pointed to the stirring spoons. "How did you get them to stir like that?"

"A simple spell. I can…" Keara pursed her lips. "No, I can't." She sighed and one corner of her mouth twitched. Then she waggled her brows. "I can teach Jamie the spell so he can help you out."

"Thanks, Keara." Jamie made a face.

"It never hurts to help your mate around the house, you know."

"Hey," Thoren crossed his arms, his face set in stern lines, his eyes twinkling. "No jabs about my housekeeping skills."

Keara pecked his cheek. "None intended. I was merely telling Jamie how to act."

"He's a grown male now, in case you haven't noticed."

Red splashed into Jamie's cheeks as he gave her a sidelong glance.

Parker tried and failed to stop the grin turning her lips at their banter. She edged closer to the stove and leaned against the counter, trepidation flowing away as she relaxed. The same unwinding she felt with her partner before his wife left him and he turned to the bottle as his friend. Something she missed with her father once her mother died.

Listening to their teasing, watching the men help Keara set the table and place the dirty dishes in the sink, awoke a longing in her she forgot existed. A longing for family. A wish to belong. To not have to worry about every move, every behavior. To just be oneself. And that sense of belonging would be hers if she accepted Jamie as her mate.

Besides the obvious, what did being his mate involve? Where would they live? What would she do with her life? Love might conquer all, but whoever invented that saying did not have her situation in mind.

Jamie touched her arm, and her thoughts snapped to the present, to the kitchen, to three sets of eyes staring at her. Right. She must have been asked a question.

"I'm sorry. What did you say?"

"Does your village not have magic?" Keara smiled and Parker wanted to tell the woman her entire life, which was crazy. And probably not what Keara wanted to hear.

"It's a city and no, we don't."

Keara's eyes flared. "A city? I've never been to a city. Tell me about it. How many people? Where do they all live? Does it stink?"

Parker chuckled and told her about Denver, while the men took dishes full of food to the table. A twinge of guilt snapped her, but no one seemed to need her help. Despite how comfortable she felt, she knew the real reason she was here. Quiz the mate. Some rituals crossed nationalities or, in this case, worlds.

She continued talking about her hometown until they sat at the table. And it might have been rude of her to dominate the conversation, but since they continued to pepper her with questions about city life and her world and—to Jamie's delight—technology, she continued to talk.

Keara was a delight. Everything she asked had the ability to wrap around Parker, drawing her closer, marking her family. Energy buzzed around Thoren, a storm of invisible power, keeping her at a distance. His welcoming banter and smiles belied an aura of danger. If given a choice of Thoren in a dark alley or a man-eating tiger, she'd take her chances with the tiger.

The man might give her the willies—not that she'd admit it—but love shone in his eyes when he glanced at Jamie. And especially when he looked at Keara. The heat sparking between those two made her wish she carried a fan.

Or had her own man.

Something that could be easily remedied. If she would agree to be mated. Married without dating. Married and barely knowing the person.

Love at first sight never sat well with her. How could someone want to marry when they barely knew the person? She knew her fiancé for years, never thought he'd cheat and look how that turned out.

Despite her reluctance, she felt drawn to Jamie, as if bonds tightened between their souls, inseparable, forever. But was he worth leaving her job, her life, her friends?

"Parker?" Jamie touched her hand, snapping her back to the present.

"Sorry. Lost in thought."

Thoren leaned forward. "Jamie mentioned you possessed an unusual talent. Do you care to demonstrate?"

Seriously? He wanted her to demonstrate a surge of power with the ability to knock out light bulbs and fry electrical outlets? Not that the house appeared to have either, but still. Parker licked her lips. It could be worse. He could have asked her to do something hard like play the piano or darn socks.

"It's not something I can do by thinking about it. I need to be under a lot of stress and scared."

Jamie's lips curled. "You will not frighten her."

"Of course not. Most humans possess no magic. I'm curious as to hers." Thoren smiled, his teeth flashing white against his tan. "Did your parents possess powers?"

"Not to my knowledge."

"Interesting. Usually they are passed down and, if traced back far enough, can be attributed to Draconi blood."

"Until Jamie and Erik appeared, I'd never heard of Draconia."

Thoren drummed his fingers against the table, a rolling thump-thump-thump of a busy mind. "You must have Draconi blood somewhere in your ancestry."

"Maybe powers work differently in my world. Magic isn't thought to exist outside of fairy tales and fantasy novels."

"Perhaps." Judging by his expression, he didn't think much of her theory.

"What difference does it make?" Jamie leaned forward as if to shield her from Thoren's view.

Parker pressed her lips together to keep the grin off her face. Damn her for a sissy, but she liked Jamie's protective streak.

"Just curious is all. Don't get your tail in a kink."

Jamie relaxed, his shoulders dropping, his posture remaining straight as an edge. Protective.

"Just ignore them, love." Keara tilted her head at

Thoren. "You never did tell me what a detective is."

"I track criminals who commit crimes."

Keara's eyes flared. "It sounds dangerous."

"Keara," Jamie glared, "leave her be."

"It can be. It's also rewarding. Especially when the perps are caught."

"Perps?"

"Perpetrators. You know. The criminals."

"Ah. You have different words. And a good grasp of our language. Which if she never heard of Draconia is rather amazing, don't you think?" Keara's eyes narrowed at her husband. Or should she say mate?

"Good point." Thoren looked at Jamie, brows raised as if waiting for his answer.

Jamie cleared his throat, his ears a bright shade of tomato.

Embarrassed in front of his puzzled parents.

"Is giving me your language against the law or what?" Parker gave herself a mental smack as Jamie reddened even more. Maybe she should have kept her mouth shut. Too late. As usual.

"No," Thoren answered and Parker breathed a sigh of relief. Last thing she wanted was to get Jamie in trouble.

Jamie shoved his chair back, grabbing his plate. "Look at the time. We need to clean the kitchen if we want to have enough time to play Marble Jump before going to bed."

"Wait just a minute." Keara's voice stopped him halfway out of his chair. "You gave her our language?"

"Sorry," Parker muttered. She needed to learn to keep her mouth shut.

Jamie's jaw tensed. "How else was she supposed to

speak before the Council?"

"You put our language in her head."

"How else are we supposed to learn languages when we go on missions?"

"Taking a language is different than giving one."

"It's the same concept."

"Concept, yes. But for someone who has difficulty getting dressed using magic, interjecting a language into another's head should be impossible."

Jamie met Keara's gaze, eyes wide, the secret of his power written in the lines of his face.

Apparently Keara's surprise had nothing to do with the illegality of placing the Draconi language in her head and everything to do with Jamie's newfound ability to work magic.

Parker swallowed. Would they be upset to learn the small titanium screw in her arm gave Jamie the ability to work magic?

"Maybe my magic is manifesting itself. Maybe I'm no longer as deficient as everyone thinks."

"Oh, I didn't mean it like that. I think it's wonderful you have the ability to give her our language. I just meant you've never been able to do anything like that before. I want to know why."

"That's why we're asking these questions," Thoren gestured to Parker. "Parker can do more than produce energy. She seems to give you the ability to work magic."

Jamie white-knuckled the chair and plate as his parents watched him like he might explode. Parker watched Keara and Thoren. Watched the small tells of their body language. Knew they spoke the truth. They loved Jamie. And like he protected her, they protected him. From her.

Put into their position, could she blame them? What did they know about her? Next to nothing. If her parents were still alive, they would react the same way. Quiz the potential spouse for criminal traits, bad behavior, violent tendencies. Yep, parents were the same no matter where one lived.

"Is that a problem?"

"It's true then. She gives you powers."

"What difference does it make?"

"Do you really need us to spell that out?" Thoren crossed his arms.

The chair back creaked as Jamie tightened his fingers. "Thank you for dinner. It was good. We'll be leaving now."

He set his plate down and reached for her hand as Keara's mouth opened.

"No, no. Don't leave. I've enjoyed talking to Parker. Thoren didn't mean it the way it sounded."

Thoren raised a brow, a silent contradiction.

Jamie gripped her hand tight enough to pop the joints. Parker opened her mouth to protest when the kitchen vanished in a blur of whirling darkness, her vision clearing to different surroundings. A small kitchen stood to one side of the room, the other held a couch, chair and table. The short hall ended in a door, which led, she assumed to the bedroom.

Jamie's house.

"You can't keep running from them. They only have your best intentions at heart."

"They insulted you."

"Oh." Clearly she didn't read their body language as well as she thought. "I thought they liked me." Was that a petulant whine in her tone?

"Yes. They like you. They don't understand how we could be mates, though, and it scares them a little."

"I thought you said mates were chosen by fate, not parents. Surely that means some people find mates their parents hate."

"They can't hate another Draconi."

"But they can humans?"

Jamie shrugged, avoiding her eyes. "I'm sure not all parents are happy with their children's mates. But my parents are not all parents."

"They're just worried."

"Stop defending them. They insulted you. They insulted me. They don't think you're good enough for me because you're human, and they are trying to find a way to show you aren't my mate."

"Are you sure that's what they think? Keara seemed so friendly."

"All right. Maybe not Keara, but that is what Thoren thinks. I could read his mind. He thinks you are a security risk."

"Because I'm human?"

"Because you're different. He senses the difference but can't yet identify it."

"I take it telling him about my arm is a bad idea."

"I hoped he wouldn't care."

Parker squeezed his hand and tugged him closer. "I don't care." Not here standing next to Jamie. Her job, her few friends, her life. Nothing mattered except for Jamie. Standing before him, she wanted to give comfort, to prove she cared, to wrap her arms around him and never let go.

His gaze met hers, pupils dilating before he

focused on her lips. The rough pads of his fingers grazed her cheek, stroking along her jaw, behind her ear. In a fluid move, he ran his hand across her nape, tugging her to his lips. Soft. Firm. Parting.

Parker thrust her tongue between his lips, his tongue meeting hers in a twisting slide of pleasure. He dropped her hand, wrapping his arm around her waist, pressing her against his hard length, entwining them as one. Her body throbbed to the beat of his heart, ached with each pulse of her core. As if he was her other half, a soul mate she never believed existed.

Nothing she had experienced in her life prepared her for kissing Jamie, for the strength of his arms around her waist, for the emotions pinging through her veins like a richocheting wild shot.

He dropped his hand from her nape, placed his arms around her waist and lifted, never breaking the kiss. Parker wrapped her legs around his waist, the hard length of him hitting her right where she needed. Jamie headed toward the bedroom, his hands a firm heat on her ass.

Bam, bam, bam! Parker started as whoever stood at the front door knocked harder. Jamie pulled his head back as she released him, her legs slowly lowering to the ground.

"We don't have to answer."

"Oh, yes, we do. That's Thoren."

Heat splashed into her cheeks. Great. Thirty-two years old and she reacted the same way she had when eighteen and caught naked with her high school boyfriend. Some things never change.

Chapter Eighteen

Releasing Parker ranked as one of the hardest things he'd ever done. Jamie wanted nothing more than to crawl into bed with her and never leave. To join them as mates, their souls entwined for eternity.

But no, he had to answer the door before Thoren transported inside and caught them in the act, so to speak. Knocking was Thoren's way of apologizing for his earlier insults. Normally he transported into the living room.

After all, normally Jamie never had company of the female variety.

Red colored Parker's cheeks. Embarrassment over Thoren or did she regret kissing him? Probably the former. He hoped.

"Go on, now. So we can finish what we started."

Definitely embarrassment.

A grin turned his lips as he winked at her before opening the door.

Thoren glanced over Jamie's shoulder at Parker, his eyes flaring as the tips of his ears turned red. Looked like Parker wasn't the only one embarrassed.

"Sorry to interrupt." His gaze snapped to Jamie. "I came to apologize for insulting you. That was not my intent."

"I know." But it hurt when his father admitted finding him magically defective. Knowing Thoren loved him despite his deficiency only partially eased the ache in his chest.

"I would never hurt you. You know that, right?"

"I know. But you insulted Parker."

Thoren glanced at Parker and back to Jamie as he slipped into mind-speak. *She has a peculiar energy about her. I'm concerned she might hurt you.*

I'm aware. That doesn't excuse the insults.

She might be a security threat.

Jamie crossed his arms. *She is not a security threat. She's human.*

I'm half human.

Thoren ran a hand through his hair. *I forget that sometimes.*

A bud of pride and love unfurled in his chest obliterating the ache. To have Thoren, one of the most powerful Draconi, forget he was a Halfling was like being given a large, polished ruby.

Thank you.

One side of Thoren's mouth curled. *I'm still not convinced she's not a threat.*

I know she's not. She never heard of Draconia until we told her. Why would she mean us harm? She's my mate.

At the risk of picking an open wound, it seems odd to me that with her appearance you take on typical Draconi traits. No offense.

It's complicated. Heat flooded his cheeks. So much for Thoren not noticing.

Thoren's eyes narrowed and Jamie swallowed. *What other abilities have you manifested?*

I've always had abilities. They were just hidden.

Hidden? Thoren's brows dropped.

Jamie paused. How much to tell him without exposing Parker? How much to hide? He scratched the back of his neck. *I could work magic in her land as freely as you wield it here.*

Thoren's eyes widened. *How? What is different about her land?*

They have no magic and use technology. The materials used to build many things are derived from titanium. That's when I discovered, unlike you, titanium is not a bane to me. Being around the substance is the only way I can work magic.

Thoren blinked. And again. *Are you sure?*

Positive.

And titanium doesn't hurt you?

Just the opposite.

Amazing. Wait until I tell the Council. They'll be awestruck.

I wish you wouldn't.

Why not?

Come on, Thoren. I'd go from one oddity to the next. It's bad enough people think I'm magically deficient. Can you imagine what they'd do if they knew how I derived my powers?

Thoren ran a hand through his hair and glanced at the eave of the roof, his gaze bouncing back to Jamie. *Point taken. I'm sorry, son. I knew it was hard—*

Don't bother. It doesn't change anything.

I suppose you're right. But I'm sorry anyway.

Apology accepted. He couldn't live his entire life angry at Thoren. Living that way only harmed him, not the object of his ire.

Parker cleared her throat. "Are you going to invite him in or not?"

Jamie looked over his shoulder. "Give us a minute."

She nodded, leaned against the wall, her eyes narrowed as if in concentration.

Thoren glanced at Parker. *Does she carry titanium on her person? Is that the oddity I sense?*

Jamie froze, the loud boom-boom of his heart echoing in his ears. How could he tell Thoren if it meant harm to Parker? Would it mean harm to Parker? How could he take that risk?

I'm correct, aren't I? It must be a very tiny amount of titanium since I was able to transport her. I would assume a Draconi with less powerful magic would lose their powers if she was around.

Like Erik falling out of transport. Fear morphed into aggression as his lip pulled into a snarl. *You will not hurt her.*

I do not intend to. But I do need to assess the threat she presents to others.

By what means?

A simple spell to determine the distance of her titanium's reach. I'm assuming she cannot set the metal aside?

It's a part of her.

Interesting. How?

It's how her healers fix bad bone breaks. By using titanium screws.

Intriguing. Don't tell Keara. She'll never leave your mate alone.

I'd prefer you leave her be.

You know I cannot. But I can perform the spell here. It will not take long.

And it will not harm her?

No. I promise.

Then what? Do you have to report this to the Council?

I cannot answer that.

Then I cannot allow you to proceed. You promised no harm would come to her. I am not convinced telling the Council would keep her safe.

Thoren sighed. *We're not that bad, you know.*

Jamie shrugged.

Very well. Unless her titanium's reach is found to be a threat to Draconi I will not inform the Council. And I don't think it will be. If I didn't know she carried the metal, I would not realize it was in your house. And as you well know, even a small piece of titanium has a large reach.

Jamie glanced at Parker, who leaned against the wall, arms crossed, staring at them as if reading their minds.

Which was impossible. Draconi could project their thoughts into a human's mind to mind-speak, but a human didn't have the ability to eavesdrop on a Draconi mind-speak conversation. Right?

"Have you finished determining my fate? Is he," her chin tilted toward Thoren, "here to," she swallowed, "arrest me or something?"

"He wants to perform a spell to determine the reach of your titanium screw. You don't have to let him."

Her gaze shot over his shoulder and back as she released a nervous chuckle. "Uh-huh. He's not on board with that idea."

"I won't let him if you don't want to."

"Why don't you just send me back? Then you won't think I'm a security threat."

An ache exploded in his chest as his breath caught in his throat. She couldn't mean that. She was his. She couldn't leave him and return to her world.

"I do not have that ability." Thoren placed a hand on Jamie's shoulder. "Will you consent to the testing?"

"Do I have a choice?"

"Yes." Jamie shrugged off Thoren's hand. "You do not have to."

"Jamie," she pushed off the wall, took a step toward him. "I think I do. All right, I consent. What does this involve?" She swallowed, her bronze skin paling.

"Sit." Thoren pointed to a chair. Parker sat. "Are you going to let me in, Jamie?"

Jamie paused, his gaze locked on Parker. *You don't have to do this.*

Yes, I do. Now, let him in.

Stepping aside to give Thoren entrance physically hurt. While he believed Thoren thought the spell was harmless, he did not want to take the chance with his mate. His mate. Now that he found her, discovered he possessed a mate like other Draconi, the last thing he wanted was for her to hurt. In any way. Physically. Mentally. Emotionally.

And watching Thoren stand beside her, hands held above her head, a spell twisting words on his lips, sent a vibration through Jamie. The same vibration experienced in the underground tunnels. The same vibration that shook him when his hands changed into claws, his skin into scales.

Protect his mate at all costs.

Parker smiled at him. "It doesn't hurt. I can't even feel what he's doing."

The vibration slowed, the frantic buzzing in his ears calming into a gentle sway. He unclenched his fists. Stepped inside. Closed the door.

Golden threads like large raindrops twisted around Parker's head in a slow drift toward her feet until she sat entombed in light. Her eyes sparkled, wide and bright, her hands loose in her lap.

No, she wasn't in pain. Jamie released a breath. Sucked in another one.

Thoren dropped his hands, the golden threads of the spell fading into the air. He touched Parker's upper arm and held his other hand palm up. Sweat beaded his forehead as a small flame ignited in his outstretched hand. Closing his fingers, he extinguished the flame.

"I will keep your secret. Make sure she doesn't touch those with lesser magic. And keep her away from the Temple. She might interfere with healings."

Jamie nodded, relief rendering him mute.

"And, son? You can't use your magic in front of others."

"Wh—" The answer slammed into his thoughts, snapping the words off his lips. To protect Parker. Jamie nodded. Proving he possessed magic was nothing compared to ensuring Parker's safety.

"So that's it? I'm no longer a threat?"

Thoren shook his head. "I'm sorry I upset you."

"You should be apologizing to Jamie."

"I already have."

"Then I accept your apology."

Thoren nodded. Turned to Jamie. "Keara said that if I apologized correctly and you didn't throw me out on my arse that I'm to invite you back to dinner tomorrow." He turned to Parker. "I promise, no more questions."

Jamie shrugged, one corner of his mouth kicking into a grin. "We'll see."

Forgiveness did not mean he wanted a repeat of tonight's disastrous ending to dinner. Although, in all fairness, since Thoren uncovered the information he wanted about Parker, he probably wouldn't question her relentlessly again.

Probably.

"Oh, and I'm also supposed to give Parker this." He held out his hands and a cloth-wrapped package appeared. Parker grabbed the bundle, untying the string. Female clothing fell out.

"Tell Keara thanks."

Thoren nodded. "Well, then, I'll leave you two alone." From one blink to the next, he disappeared.

Parker sagged in the chair.

"Are you sure you're all right?" Jamie hurried to her side, resting a hand against her shoulder.

"It really didn't hurt. For a minute there, though, I thought he wanted to splice me open like a bug under a microscope."

Microscope? He could imagine what that word meant. "He's like that. Very security oriented. A lot happened to make him that way, but he's a good male. I wouldn't have let him hurt you."

"I know." She straightened, offering him a grin. "That's why I agreed. You said I didn't have to, but I knew you wouldn't have let him offer if he meant me harm."

Warmth spread through his limbs. He held out a hand. "Do you care to pick up where we left off?"

****

Jamie's hand beckoned, sturdy, warm, dependable. She saw the way his lip curled when he talked to his father, how his body grew as if to prevent Thoren entrance, to prevent her from harm. She never thought she'd like a man to be protective of her. In her line of work, she'd seen protectiveness lead to jealousy which in turn led to abuse.

But she liked how Jamie's protectiveness bolstered her sense of wellbeing. He made her feel cared for, cherished, loved.

And while Thoren sent her spine into full shiver mode—not that she'd admit it—she understood his questions, his desire to protect his family, his son, his people, from mysterious strangers.

She felt the same about Jamie when she first met him. Calling out the kettle when she was a pot made no sense.

Neither did replaying the last few minutes when a hot man stood in front of her, offering her sexual relief.

Parker placed her hand in Jamie's large one, their skin a contrast in colors, and let him pull her to her feet. Holding her gaze, he lowered his head until their lips met, one arm encircling her waist, the other placing their joined hands over his heart. She ran her fingers through his hair, her mouth opening for the thrust of his tongue.

Heat crashed through her, small streaks of fire filling her veins, pooling in her core. A shot of lust mixed with an emotion she'd rather not admit, not even to herself, slammed into her chest, powering her heart, her mind. She wanted nothing more than to give herself to Jamie, to allow him inside the darkest chambers of her heart, to erase fleeting memories of her fiancé and replace those memories with a more substantial relationship. She wanted him forever. And the thought scared the hell out of her.

Thoughts she'd rather forget. Forever might never happen. So she'd settle for tonight.

Tingling started around her legs, spread upward as if she transported. The thought of which snapped her eyes open. Yep. Transported. Right into Jamie's bedroom. A handy skill.

Jamie stepped back, his face the color of sun-kissed skin. "Sorry. I'm a little new to transporting."

"You've got to admit, beaming us in here has its advantages." She grabbed him by the shirt and pulled him toward her. "Less distance to travel."

And then her lips found his, seeking the comfort of his touch, the kindness in his embrace. He walked her backward until her legs hit the bed.

"Looks like you're trying to tell me something."

He grinned. "You think?"

"I'm smart like that."

His hands grabbed her waist, lifting her up and back, pitching her so she landed on his bed. He followed, crawling up her body like a cat until his elbows rested by her arms. Parker spread her legs as he settled into the cradle of her body, his hard length rubbing where she needed.

A thought jolted her from the moment, a thought unwelcomed and invasive.

He paused, his lips almost to hers. "What?" His breath brushed across her parted lips.

"This is silly," and embarrassing, "but this works the same way it does at home, my home, right?"

He cocked a brow, and Parker stumbled over more

words. "I mean, you said you turned into a dragon. So…"

"No worries. Dragons do not experience bedplay."

Good to know. She breathed a sigh of relief. "Sorry. That thought just popped into my head."

"Understandable." A grin spread across his face. "I'd ask if you have any bedplay rituals, but we'll learn together."

"Sounds like a winner."

His lips brushed along her jaw, down her throat, sending tingles shooting across her skin. She ran her hands down his back to his hips, then pushed up his shirt to feel the play of muscles under his skin.

"This needs to come off."

"True." The material she held vanished.

Parker sucked in a breath. Right. Magic. Expedient magic. A girl could learn to like that talent of his. "Wow."

Jamie grinned. "You like that, eh?"

"Can you disappear my shirt?"

A blink later and her shirt vanished. Heat from Jamie's skin bathed her in warmth, and she reached to pull him toward her. But he resisted, one finger tracing the lace on her black bra.

"I like this. What do you call it?"

"My bra?"

"One day you can walk around in just the bra."

"It comes with matching panties." She pointed.

He raised a brow. A second later her jeans vanished. His eyes flared as he sat back on his knees, running his gaze from her bra to her panties and back.

"Wow."

"You like?"

His hand splayed against her stomach, traced the curve of her hip. Warmth spread outward, tracings of heat twining through her limbs.

"You are beautiful."

"You are way overdressed."

He winked, and his trousers disappeared. Then he lay on top of her, fitting against her as if formed from a mold of her body. Hard muscles rubbed against her sensitive skin while his lips and tongue tempted her with pleasure. The lace of her bra rasped against the calluses on his palms as he cupped her breast.

"Why don't you take it off? I can model it later."

He shrugged, and air touched the bare skin of her breasts.

"Nice magic show."

"I try." One corner of his mouth kicked up before he lowered his head to pay some attention to her breasts.

Parker sighed, her hands running through the coarse strands of his hair, across the muscular planes of his back. Part of her wanted to crawl inside his embrace and stay forever. The draw of his presence, of his touch, cocooned her in warmth, in—dare she think it—love.

Jamie kissed down her stomach until he reached her panties. "Raise your bottom for me."

"No magic?" She did as he asked.

"This puts you right where I want you." He slid her panties off and positioned his arms under her legs, raising her to his mouth.

"Oh, yeah."

His tongue sent shivers of pleasure roiling across her skin, over and over again until she screamed her release. When she opened her eyes, Jamie wore an expression of pride, as if he single-handedly brought down a drug cartel. He lowered his body over hers one slow inch at a time.

As soon as his thick head pressed against her core, her mind snapped out of its post-orgasmic haze, and she shoved at his shoulder.

"Wait a second." Jamie gritted his teeth, his eyes closing as he sucked in a breath. "Sorry, but we need a condom."

His eyes popped open as his brows furrowed. "A condom?"

"Birth control? You put it on over your penis."

"Draconi are not very fertile. We don't use birth control."

"I'm not Draconi. And you're half human. Besides, don't your males get non-Draconi women pregnant? Isn't that your job to find their offspring?"

Jamie sat back on his heels. "You're right. It's not something I've ever had to think about." He glanced at his dresser. "Erik, though, found something like what you're talking about in a village on our last mission." He walked to the dresser and pulled open a drawer. After rummaging around, he returned with a small cloth bag, closed with a drawstring.

He sat on the edge of the bed and Parker rolled toward him, her hand resting on his thigh. "I'm sorry. I always take precautions."

"Do you not want children?"

Did she not want his, is what he meant. His eyes broadcast the thought as if a movie screen. "Not now. Maybe someday. Is that a problem?"

"No. I'm not so sure I want them either." He pulled the string on the bag and took out a small object, which he handed to her.

A red ribbon tied the smooth casing into a flat package. Parker held it up to her nose. Not latex. She untied the ribbon and the material expanded to the size of a penis. Jamie pulled out a jar.

"An apothecary gave Erik this. Said to apply the cream to the male-parts and cover with the fitted sock before bedplay and no children will result."

"Are you sure it will work?"

"Apothecaries give good medicine."

"What about diseases?"

"Draconi are not susceptible to those types of diseases. Is this questioning common before bedplay in your land?"

"Yeah. If we're smart about it." Parker held the strange condom. Was she willing to take a chance? The invisible strings tying them together tightened. Jamie wasn't a one night stand. He was forever. As crazy as that sounded. "Do you mind wearing it?"

"No." No hesitation.

Her heart swelled.

He held out his hand and she dropped the condom into it.

She dipped her hand into the jar and spread the cream over his stiff length, stroking as she rubbed it in.

Jamie moaned, his head falling back.

Parker pushed him against the mattress, scooting with him until she straddled his legs.

Jamie put on the condom and Parker positioned the head of his length at her opening. A couple of shifts and she eased him inside. Filling her. Completing her.

A moan escaped her lips, found a twin in his sigh. She moved along his length, building a rhythm, stroking against him where she ached. When she exploded into pleasure, he held her, joining her in bliss.

After he removed the condom and drew her into his arms, she lay with her ear against his chest, the beat of his heart a rapid thud-thud of life. She fell asleep wrapped in his embrace, as if their souls entwined them for eternity.

Chapter Nineteen

Parker woke to the steady thump of fists against the front door. Jamie untangled his legs from hers, rolled off the bed and walked out of the room, leaving her skin chilled without his warmth. As soon as she heard the squeak of hinges, Erik's voice boomed through the house.

"Are you trying to get us killed? We were supposed to have left half an hour ago. Why don't you have on clothes?" A pause. "Oh." Another pause. "I'll sit out here and hope the Council doesn't decide to check up on our progress. Or lack thereof."

A click indicated a closed door. Jamie appeared in the doorway a few seconds later, running his hand through his hair until it stood straight and frizzy.

"I forgot about having to search for the Halfling."

"Me too." She threw off the covers and sat. "I can help you if you'd like." Judging by the raised brow, he might not want her help.

"I should stop being shocked over anything you ask. The village where we're going is outside Draconia borders. Females rarely leave Draconia, so I'm surprised you want to go."

"What?" What kind of backward place was this? "What do you mean females don't leave? Do you men keep them chained up or something?"

"No, no, nothing like that. Females carry a bit of

the Goddess inside them, and they must be protected. They are free within Draconia, but they don't leave."

"And none of them have a problem with that?"

"Danger exists outside our borders. They understand and prefer the safety of Draconia."

"So you're saying if I live here…"

"If?"

"If I live here, you'd expect me to stay put and clean house?"

"Of course not. Females don't clean the house. That's a male's job."

Okay, she could live with that. But not with staying put. "Then what do you expect me to do while you're off running around?"

"You are angry."

"You are observant." Parker stood. No sense in having a fight while sitting. Standing put her on equal footing. Even if she stood nude.

Thick carpet cushioned her feet, carpet like the grass in her yard, lush and soft. Homesickness slammed into her, stealing her breath, sending a dose of dizziness. Parker leaned against the bed. So much for being on equal footing.

Would she ever see home again?

"Parker?" Jamie rushed to her side, wrapping an arm around her waist.

Breath sawed in and out of her lungs as if she ran a mile. Could she return home? Why did it take her until now to realize how far away from home she was?

"What's wrong?"

She focused on the concern in Jamie's voice, on the touch of his arm against her skin, the warmth radiating from his body, draping her like a security blanket. *Breathe, Parker, deep breath in.* The dizziness subsided, while the empty hole in her stomach grew, a depository of ice. *Get a grip, it could be worse.* Shivers shook her limbs, rattling her bones like a box of loose bullets.

So much for self talk.

"I can't go home." Her voice escaped small and trembling. Embarrassing. *Get a grip.*

Jamie rubbed her back, drew her into his embrace. The thump of his heart, the powerful thud-thud, failed to calm her. Damn it. She needed to stop acting like a sissy, crying over the matter would get her nowhere.

But chills continued a relentless slide down her spine, paying her attempt at self talk no attention.

"You'll be all right." A couple of pats. "We can try to go back with Erik's help. Not sure if he'll help or if we'll be able to do it again, but we can try." Uncertainty crept through his words, a thief on a mission.

"Don't leave me here alone." Did those cry-baby words actually come out of her mouth? Apparently Draconia brought out her inner sissy.

Get a grip, damn it.

"You can come with us."

"You just said it wasn't done."

"Draconi females don't leave. You're human."

Yeah, and humans were frowned upon here. Yet another reason to go home. So why did the thought of leaving Jamie bring such an ache to her chest? Probably due to remaining panic particles floating through her veins.

"And that's bad."

"Not to me it isn't. It's just different."

"If I stay here, I won't be accepted."

Jamie stiffened. "Once Thoren tells them you aren't a threat, they'll accept you. I'll make sure of it."

"You can't force people to believe a certain way."

"No, but you can persuade them the error of their beliefs." He inhaled a raspy breath. "I can return with you. To your world. If we are able to return."

Force him to leave his family, his home, just so she would feel at ease? Being a selfish bitch was not in her playbook.

"Maybe we should go our separate ways."

Jamie's breath hitched, his panic wrapping her in a blast of suffocating fog. "Let's not make a hasty decision. We can find the Halfling and stop by the caves on the way home. All right?"

Hurting Jamie was not her wish. Although, if she returned home and left him behind, hurting him would be the outcome. Everything inside her resisted, a ball of pain formed behind her sternum, spread outward, cold and clammy. No, she couldn't leave him.

But how could she stay in a place that didn't want her?

****

Jamie tried sucking in deep breaths on the off chance the air would stop the pulsing ache in his chest. How could he let his mate go? How could he force her to stay if there was a way for her to return to her home? He wanted to tie her to the bed, to chain her in his house, to refuse her request to leave.

A male was nothing without his mate.

But he knew better than to deny her request even if it meant losing her.

Parker nodded. "I'm sorry."

231

"Nothing to be sorry for. Finding yourself in a different realm with different customs is bound to be disorienting."

"To put it mildly." A deep breath in. A noisy release. "All right. Let's go get this Halfling. Then we can figure out what to do about us."

After a quick bath, they met an impatient Erik outside.

"Finally. My arse was going numb." Erik stood and rubbed his arse as he raised a brow at Parker.

"Better than other parts." Jamie slapped him on his arm. "How are you?"

"Better. Went to the Temple and they healed my ankle." His voice lowered. "Why's she here?"

"Parker is coming with us to find the Halfling."

"Can she do that?"

"Of course I can." Parker crossed her arms. "You have a problem with it?"

Erik threw up his hands, palms out. "No, no. No problem. It's just unusual is all. Never been on a mission with a female."

"We want to stop by the caves on the way back. See if Parker can return to her home. Would you return her home?"

Erik's brows furrowed as his gaze darted from Jamie to Parker and back. *Are you sure about that?*

She needs to try. Even if he wanted to deny her the ability.

She's your mate.

She needs to decide.

Erik shrugged. "We'll stop by the caves if that's what you want. As long as we find the Halfling. The Council will have our hides if we don't."

Jamie grabbed Parker's hand. "Point taken. I'll meet you outside Hogsbreath. That's where the Council said the Halfling lived."

"What do you mean meet me? You need me to transport."

"You weren't doing such a good job of it yesterday." Jamie grinned at his friend. "We'll meet you there. Ready?"

Parker nodded, and Jamie threw them into a transport, Erik following behind. They appeared on the outskirts of Hogsbreath to the south of the Draconia border, hidden in the trees that lined the edges of the road, protective sentries marching toward the village.

Parker dropped to her knees, gagging as tremors wracked her body.

Jamie knelt beside her, pressing a hand to her back. "Ward lines suck."

"It'll get better." He hoped. Maybe he should ask Thoren about it when they returned.

If they returned.

What would he do if Parker left him? Or if she insisted he return with her? Of course he'd go, but would he ever see his parents again? His land? His friends?

The magnitude of Parker's sacrifice punched him in the gut like an enraged boar. Who was he to demand she stay here? If he went with her, if he abandoned all he knew and loved, he could use his magic without constraint. Without hiding. Without seeing pity in others' eyes.

The thought tempted him, luring him in, a bright jewel for a treasure chest.

Maybe he would offer to return with her. Maybe.

Parker wiped the back of her wrist across her mouth. "It's better." She sat back on her heels. "How do we find the Halfling?"

"The Council heard of the existence of a child Halfling in this village." Erik leaned against a tree. "We're sent to see if the intelligence is correct."

"You mean you were sent out here on a rumor?"

"That's usually the way it works."

"But don't you," she turned to Jamie, "find people?"

"Yes. But it helps to know something besides rumor about a person."

She sighed and slapped her palms against her thighs. "Then we need to ask. Unless you have a magical way of getting information?"

"None that we're allowed to use."

She grinned. "I'll keep that in mind."

Jamie offered her a hand, pulling her to her feet. For a long moment, she stared into his eyes, a meeting of souls pulling him deeper into the pool of, dare he say it, love. Love. An emotion he never thought to feel for a female. Much less have a chance at that love being returned.

He assumed she felt the same. What if she didn't? What if he was the only male to find his mate and then lose her?

Jamie closed his eyes, breaking the connection to Parker, as he drew in a breath. *Pull it together. Focus on the mission.*

Parker squeezed his hand when he opened his eyes. As if she knew his thoughts.

Impossible. Right?

Parker dropped his hand as they walked toward

Hogsbreath, her strides in step with his, her body close enough to brush against his arm. As if they walked as one. One mind. One body. One heart.

Sap, sap, sap.

Were all Draconi males this crazy about their mates? If so, how did they get anything done?

Focus on the mission, idiot. You can worry about Parker later.

Parker turned to him. "Did you say something?"

"No." She couldn't hear him. Humans did not mind-speak.

"I thought I heard my name."

Goddess's toes. Maybe humans could mind-speak.

"I didn't say anything."

"Would you look at that?" Thank Goddess for Erik's interruption. With any luck Parker wouldn't notice the heat splashing his cheeks.

"What?" Parker stopped before she ran into Erik, who stood still in the road.

Jamie glanced at his friend and followed the direction of Erik's point. He blinked. And again. Why did Hogsbreath have a stone wall twice his height surrounding it?

"Have they been attacked?" Who would attack a village known primarily for cloth, spices and herbal medicines? Most villages didn't bother with walls, leaving those fortifications to larger towns.

"Do I look like I know?"

"You commented on it."

"And that makes me privy to their secret meetings?" Erik grinned.

"Does it matter whether or not they have a wall?" Parker tilted her head, one brow raised.

"It might. If they are expecting raiders, then we'll be under suspicion as outsiders."

"Do they not have travelers?"

"They used to."

"Spices and cloth and whatnot." Erik waved a hand.

"So we pretend to be merchants."

"We don't look like merchants."

"We look Draconi. Well, I do. He," Erik gestured to him, a grin turning his lips, "always confuses them as to his race. Is he Draconi? Is he human?"

Jamie shook his head. Being accustomed to his friend's teasing and liking it were two different beasts. "It's better than thinking I'm the arse-end of a dragon."

Erik slapped a hand over his heart. "I'm wounded."

"You'll live." A grin twitched Jamie's lips. Erik's teasing pricked his pride at times, but living without it would be akin to sleeping without a blanket on a cold night, doable, but not comfortable.

"Now that we have that settled," Parker cleared her throat, "Why don't you magic some merchant-looking clothes. You can do that, right?"

Jamie suspected Erik's flared eyes mirrored his own. Use costumes to find a Halfling? Clearly Erik wasn't the only one full of humor this morning. "That's not how we operate."

"Everyone should know that we are Draconi. It generates respect."

Parker raised a brow like she thought them addled. Which they weren't. At least not on this matter.

"All right. Then what do you suggest?"

"What we usually do." Erik crossed his arms.

"Go in and ask around. Find out what the

townsfolk know."

"Tell me again why you can't just use your ability to hone in on the Halfling's location?"

"It doesn't work like that." Although he'd give half his rubies to be able to find people that quickly. "I can only get close. In this case, I can feel that there is a Halfling inside, but can't tell you the exact place."

"Do you feel closer to one area than another?"

"No. Just inside." And the young one's energy field felt odd, like it split into two different fields.

"What's wrong?" Parker touched his arm. "You look puzzled."

"He's just thinking." Erik shrugged.

"The energy field is different for the Halfling. Split in two."

"That makes no sense." Erik's eyes narrowed. "It's probably just the wall. It's throwing us off and making us worry about nothing. Let's get on with it."

"Should we split up?"

Jamie shook his head at Parker. "We are supposed to stay together."

"Fine. Lead on."

Once they walked through the village gates, past the guards who waved them inside, a cold prickle of caution raised the hair on his nape. The usual brisk bustle of a market village remained in direct opposition to the unwelcoming stares and fear darting in the depths of the merchants' eyes.

Fear? Perhaps they had been attacked. Perhaps the market drew a bigger business than he thought and as such attracted raiders and thieves. Or they hated others different from them, much like River's Run, the town where he lived with Keara before coming to Draconia.

Jamie shook the prickle away. Or was it a memory?

"I don't like this place," Parker whispered.

He nodded, reaching out to give her hand a quick squeeze and release.

Erik led them to the main market, a stone lined street with small wooden booths displaying merchants' goods. No sign of the Halfling. No sense of where the youngster was either.

Why would a gift from the Goddess let him get close, but not allow him to pinpoint the exact location of a person? Jewels he understood. To have a gift where one could amass large amounts of treasure with little effort would lead to greed. But what would be the harm in finding people with a thought, with ease, especially abandoned Halflings?

Erik stopped at the first booth on the right. "We're looking for a red-haired child. Have you seen one?"

The merchant's eyes flared as his gaze darted between the three of them then to either side. He shook his head. "Can't say that I have. Could I interest you in spices from the Southlands? No?" His small eyes performed another sweep to the left and right as he leaned forward. "Three stalls down. They might know something, but you didn't hear that from me."

Jamie reached into his purse hanging around his waist and flipped a coin to the merchant. The man caught it and slipped it into his own purse, his gaze moving to the crowded street.

Why didn't he want to tell them the youngster's location? Who could overhear and care? Most villagers treated their bastard children like outcasts and were eager to give them away. Which was why they never needed disguises. Let all know they were Draconi coming to collect their own.

As Erik said, it generated respect, not to mention a bit of awe and a touch of fear.

A respectful kind of fear. Not the fright wafting through the air of the village like the stench of malfunctioning sewers.

A lady sat on a tall stool behind the counter of the third booth, the voluminous folds of her dress hanging in mounds around her feet. Cloths of different fabrics, textures and colors spread across the counter like plumes from a bird. Blue eyes topping flushed cheeks narrowed at their approach.

"Cloths?"

"We're looking for a red-haired child—"

"Didn't think you wanted no cloths. You ain't dressed the type."

Parker gave him a sideways glance, a look of I-told-you-so making a run across her face.

"Have you seen the child?"

"Rumors, rumors. You should leave 'em be and scat." She leaned forward. "You ain't wantin' to stick around. Don't care who you think you are. You ain't wantin' the man to see you here."

"We'll leave once we have the child." Parker placed both hands on the counter and leaned forward, her voice lowering to a whisper. "Tell us where he is so we can avoid the man."

The merchant swallowed. She whispered something into Parker's ear, her words a low murmur even his sensitive hearing couldn't understand. Parker nodded, thanked the woman, met Jamie's gaze and jerked her head in the direction of the gates. After a quick touch on his arm, she turned and dodged her way through the crowd.

Jamie glanced at Erik's wide eyes as he started to follow Parker, who darted around buyers congregating like chattering birds. Where was she going? What did the merchant say? Parker ducked into an alley, disappearing from view.

A quick thud of his heart sped up his breath as a loud group of people walked between him and the last place he saw Parker. He shoved through the group, ignored their voiced complaints and turned into the alley, Erik following.

Parker stood at the end of the alley, a slow turn of her head indicating she looked for something. But what?

"Don't rush off like that." He stalked toward her, fear and relief mixing his tone into a low rumble.

"You were right behind me." She gestured at the brick wall to the left, while he tried to stop inhaling air like a dragon about to spit a fireball. "Third door on the left. Did I miss one? There're only two."

Doors? Doors? "I'm serious. Don't run off like that."

Parker turned to face him. "I didn't mean to upset you."

Of course she didn't. But what if something happened before he got to her? What if she was harmed? He released his clenched fists and got busy sucking in air. No sense in letting fear morph into anger.

"I know. But I don't like thinking something bad might happen to you."

"I'll wait for you next time, all right?"

"Thank you." He stepped next to her, showing with a touch on her hand all was forgiven.

"How sweet." Erik stepped beside Jamie, shaking his head. "Kiss and make up, will you, so we can continue on our mission."

Jamie glared at Erik until the tips of his friend's ears turned red and he dropped his gaze. Enough was enough.

Parker cleared her throat. "The merchant said second alley and third door on the left and that's where we'd find the children. Did you know there are more than one?"

Jamie blinked as Erik's eyes flared. "There's another Halfling?" If so, it would explain the strange split energy he felt when trying to find the Halfling's location.

"She didn't use that term. She said the children we wanted were here. But I don't see the door." She turned to the brick wall. "One door." She pointed at the door. "Two doors." Another point. "Big stretch of…" Her brow furrowed and she walked closer to the wall, running her hand over it. "Oh."

Oh was right. Instead of the wooden panels demarking a door, someone had painted bricks across the wood, blending the door into the wall. Upon first glance the door was indistinguishable from the wall.

Clever trick.

"Should we go in?"

Erik stepped forward. "I'll go first. Close the door behind you." Grabbing the doorknob, he twisted and shoved. Hinges squeaked, silenced by a murmured spell. Erik stepped into the dim light.

Parker glanced at Jamie. "Ready?"

He placed a hand on her lower back, encouraging her forward. "You first."

"Don't let go of me." A corner of her mouth kicked up. "You want to work magic if need be."

"Maybe I just want to touch you." He whispered in her ear, giving her a peck on the cheek. Definitely wanted to touch her. More than touch her. Cover her body with his. Mark her as his for all to see.

Bloody mission.

Upon which he needed to focus.

"Maybe I want to touch you too." Parker placed her hand against his face. "But now isn't the time."

"After you, my mate."

She stepped through the door, and Jamie pulled it closed behind him, the thud of wood against brick a finality that sent a shudder down his spine.

Chapter Twenty

Dim light filtered from an inner door, enough light to make out shapes, but not much else. Parker swallowed. Dark didn't bother her, but stepping into the unknown did. And this definitely qualified as unknown. Strange country. Strange town. Strange door in the wall leading to a strange room.

Warmth spread from where Jamie's hand rested against her shoulder. Close to her titanium screw. Close to her heart.

Would she be able to leave him at the end of this mission? Would she be able to return home, to return to a job she loved, to a life consumed by her work?

Would she be happier in a land where the residents thought her odd for her humanity, but where she found a man she could love?

Could love? More like did love. *Oh my gosh, did I actually use the word love?* Yep. Definitely pulled out the L word and threw it at a guy. Not just any guy. Jamie.

She glanced at her shoulder where the heat from his palm soaked into her skin. Who would've thought she'd ever fall in love again?

A crash sounded, shaking the ceiling, as if a heavy object fell in a room above them. Parker jumped. So much for love thoughts. She needed to concentrate on where she was and what was going on, not daydream about Jamie.

Damn it.

Erik reached the door, light shining around the frame, and plastered himself against the wall. Parker mirrored his position, Jamie tucking in behind her. Erik cracked open the door, stuck his head out, then slipped through the opening.

Breath rasped through her lungs as her hand slapped against her hip. Damn it. When would she learn? No Glock. No weapon. Nothing but her wits.

And Jamie. Who, as long as he touched her, could count as a weapon.

See, Parker? Safer than you thought.

Tension wove through her muscles as she reached for the door, the same tension twisting her gut whenever she worked a case. Before she darted through the opening, Jamie squeezed her shoulder.

"Let me go first."

For once a man's protective streak didn't bother her. Jamie cared about her safety. Unlike other men who only cared about their pride.

She nodded, and Jamie slipped through the door. Taking a breath, she started to follow when shouts erupted on the other side of the door. Grunts followed by two thuds. A body slammed against the door, swinging it open. Which she managed to avoid by a quick jerk of her head. Air rushed past her face from the slammed-open door, and she scrambled further into the shadows to avoid being hit. Not to mention remaining concealed.

The door bounced off the wall as she scurried into the nearest corner. Rough stone pressed against her back as she squatted against the wall, hoping the shadows buried her in darkness, her breath a ragged series of gasps.

Was Jamie okay? How bad was he hurt? Why the hell did she not insist on a weapon? *Idiot, idiot, idiot.*

"Check and make sure no one else is there." A high-pitched male voice oozed through the room.

"These are Draconi. They come in pairs. Always pairs." Another male voice, this one low and raspy, like a long-time smoker.

One of the men grabbed the half-open door and pulled it shut. Footsteps grew softer, their voices disappearing. Did they leave Erik and Jamie where they fell? What caused two magical beings to drop like a hammer? The real question was how the hell was she going to rescue them?

Cowering in the corner like a sissy got her nowhere.

Move, Parker. Now.

Heart pounding, she rose, plastering herself against the wall as she eased toward the closed door. A deep inhale and she darted to the other side of the door, back against the wall. The knob chilled her palm as she twisted it, cracking the door enough to see into a brightly lit room.

Parker blinked until her eyes adjusted to the brightness. Jamie lay in front of the door, Erik several feet away. No sign of the men. Or the Halfling. Not that she could see far. The only sounds coming from the room were the soft snores of Jamie and Erik, as if they had fallen asleep. At least there wasn't blood.

So what felled them?

Parker opened the door wider, poking her head out, eyes searching for the men. No strange men. Just the two she came with. She darted through the door and dropped to her knees, her fingers finding the steady pulse in Jamie's neck. Her breath released on a welcome sigh. Steady. Alive. No blood.

What knocked him out?

She stepped over Jamie, knelt by Erik. Same steady pulse, but her fingers knocked loose a small stick in the side of his neck. What the hell?

Muffled cries echoed down the stairs, snapping her attention to the sound. Stairs ran down the right side of the room, wooden slats allowing a clear view of the steps. No one hiding. Where were the men? Upstairs? Outside?

Parker glanced around the room. What to use as a weapon. The lamp? How clichéd. She darted to the side table that held the lamp, her gaze cutting to the stairs. What kind of a lamp was this? It looked more like a kerosene lantern. She picked it up. Make that a full kerosene lantern.

Not happening. What else?

Her gaze landed on the fireplace, a poker leaning against the hearth.

It's the butler in the living room with a poker.

Right. Nothing else in the almost bare room lent itself to weapon qualities. She lifted the poker, twisting it in her hands. Yep, it would work.

A quick glance showed no one on the stairs, but the murmured cries meant someone was in the house. Who? Jamie and Erik remained still, their deep breathing the only indication they lived. Damn it. She could use a little help. If only she had her Glock.

Too damn bad, Parker. Deal with the poker.

Taking a breath, she started for the stairs, the metal

of the iron poker rough against her hands. At least she could swing it, unlike the lantern.

Brandishing the poker like a bat, she started up the stairs, trying to tread with no noise. Her heart pounded an uneven beat in her chest. Two steps gone. Four steps. Two more left.

Squeak!

Parker froze as the noise echoed, quieting the muffled cries to small hiccups of fright. Nothing moved. She released her held breath, avoided the squeaking stair and stepped onto the landing.

Light streamed from a window set over the stairs, illuminating the landing in an airy brightness. Shadows populated corners with a chill damp. A shiver shot down her spine. Her grip tightened on the poker.

Doors marched down the hallway running off the landing, sentries of impending doom. Parker glanced over her shoulder. No one coming up the stairs. She turned. Nothing but a door behind her. A deep breath in. Should she check the door or head toward the childlike sniffles coming from the hallway?

Free the children. Provided the sniffles belonged to kids.

She swallowed. Another glance at the door. Still shut. Sweat dampened under her arms, pooling in her bra. She stepped forward, coming down on her heel, slowing the shift to the ball of her foot. Another step. Followed by another. She exhaled in relief when she made it to the door. The locked door.

At least the lock wasn't keyed. A simple latch, but it kept the victims inside. Her quick glance up and down the hallway showed nothing but light and shadows. She lowered the poker and slipped the latch unlocked. A turn of the knob and the door swung silently open.

Anger chased away fear as she peered into the dim room. A covered window gave little light, but let in enough for her to see two children tied with ankle chains to a bed. Thin, with stringy red hair and brown rags for clothes, they shrank from her, as far as the chain would allow.

The iron poker cut into her palm. Energy beat through her veins, energy she normally tried to suppress, energy she now wished to throw like an explosion on the men who chained these children like livestock.

She hated working children cases. Hated it. Give her an armed robbery gone bad over crimes against children any day.

Heat washed through her as she walked toward the children, holding out a hand. "It's all right. I'm going to help you."

Halfway to the bed, the children's eyes stopped focusing on her and darted to the space between her and the door. A whoosh of air swept past her ear. She ducked, bringing the poker up to deflect the hit.

A medium-sized man dressed in a decorated red tunic swung another sucker punch. Easy to block. Thank god for martial arts training. The wave of energy beat harder inside her chest, wanting to escape, wanting to harm. Instead of hiding the power, she released it as a concentrated beam right at her attacker.

He flew straight up as if attached to guidelines, slamming into the ceiling before crashing to the floor.

Parker blinked, her heart a racing drum behind her ribs, her muscles trembling with adrenaline. Since when did her energy rush cause a person to take flight? Exploding light bulbs, sure, but flying people? *Interesting.*

And no time to ponder. She needed to get the kids out before the other man came or the downed one woke.

Two pairs of wide eyes watched her careful approach. Thank goodness they no longer shrank from her.

"It's all right. Let me see. Do these need a key?" Her fingers ran around the edge of the shackle. Yep. Needed a key.

"He carries it." The boy pointed toward behind her, and Parker twisted around.

Whew. No new man. Clearly the boy meant the unconscious creep.

Parker darted to the downed man. She patted along the front of his tunic and down the sides of his legs. Cool metal met her questing fingers on his right side. A quick tug pulled the key free from where it hung on his belt.

Then she ran back to the children, her fingers fumbling to twist the key in the shackle's lock. The girl drew the back of her arm under her nose as she sniffed, her gaze never leaving Parker's fingers.

"Where are you taking us?" The boy's voice trembled as he yanked his leg free.

Parker grabbed both of the chains and pulled them toward the man. "Draconia."

"I want to go home," the girl sniffled.

Parker snapped a shackle on each of the man's meaty wrists.

"You can't go home," the boy said. "Mother's

249

dead."

Whimpering filled the room.

Parker held a hand out to the girl. "We'll find you a new home with nice people, all right?"

The girl looked at her brother who shrugged. She drew a hand under her eyes, her wary gaze upon Parker's palm-up hand.

Come on, take it. Come on.

The boy grabbed his sister's hand and pulled her toward Parker. His grip tightened on hers, a silent entreaty for care. Parker returned the squeeze and rose slowly to her feet. She led the kids to the door, tossed the key down the hall and picked up the poker.

Hefting it over her shoulder, she dropped the boy's hand and peered both ways up and down the hall. "Stay behind me."

After a quick glance to show they obeyed, she tip-toed toward the stairs.

"Sigmund!"

Parker froze, her grip tightening on the poker. The voice was the same as who spoke downstairs. The same voice who harmed Jamie. Who knocked out her man. Who knowingly kept two children chained to a bed in rags. Fury exploded like a grenade.

And the two small bodies pressed against her back, trembling hard enough to shake the material of her trousers only ignited the rage.

The door next to the stairs swung open. "How long does it…" A tall, blond man stepped onto the landing, his eyes flaring as he caught sight of Parker. Then they narrowed as he stepped toward her. "You're going to be sorry." The trembling of the children against her legs turned into a metronome of distress.

Anger fueled her strength, the iron poker becoming an extension of her arm. Parker screamed and ran forward, her momentum yanking free of the children's grasp. She swung the poker at the man's head, but he caught the thing and used her forward force to throw her into the wall.

Omph. The air blew out of her lungs on a hard exhale. The man turned with her, his back to the stairs, one arm lifted in a punch. Adrenaline lent strength to her limbs, beat back the pain in her shoulder, fueled her kick.

Her foot landed on his groin. His eyes widened. His hands dropped to cover his 'nads.

Didn't expect that, did you, jackwagon?

A kick to the chin sent him tumbling head over feet down the stairs. Breath heaved in and out of her lungs, her captain's words echoing in her mind as the man landed in a broken heap at the bottom, his neck at an angle.

Conduct unbecoming of a police officer.

Yeah, but sometimes the bad guy needs to die.

A loud intake of breath ending on a whimper had her turning to the children. *Good job, Parker. Kill a man in front of kids, why don't you.*

She held both hands in front of her, dropping the poker to the floor. "It's all right. He won't hurt you again."

Two sets of wide eyes returned her stare. Then the girl moved forward. "All right," she whispered.

"Don't look at him as we pass. You don't need to see him." She grabbed both their hands and led them down the stairs.

The man's wide blue eyes stared unseeing as they

passed, and Parker used her body to block the children from the sight. She led them to Erik and Jamie.

"Who's that?" The boy pointed to Jamie and Erik.

"My friends. The bad men knocked them out."

"With the darts." The boy nodded.

"You know about that?"

"He used them on us. When we were bad."

Was it possible to resurrect the blond and kill him again?

"That won't happen again. I won't let it. All right?"

"Why are you taking us to Draconia?"

"You are Draconi. You belong there. These men were sent to take you home."

"But that's not home." The girl shook her head.

"It wasn't his home either," Parker pointed to Jamie, "but he was rescued and grew up there and loves it."

He loved his home. Could she ask him to leave it to go to her world? What was home? A physical place? A building with rooms? Or where the man she loved lived?

The boy looked at Jamie, the girl remaining focused on Parker.

"How do you know we'll like it? Why can't we go home?"

"I told you," the boy turned to his sister, "Mother died."

The girl sniffed. "I know that. But why can't we go home?"

"We have no home. It's them or the bad men."

Her eyes narrowed on Parker, her thoughts as readable as a page: *How do we know they aren't bad too?*

Yep. Would cheerfully kick the blond down the stairs again.

"What are your names? I'm Det—" No, she wasn't. Not any longer. Parker cleared her throat. "I'm Ruby Parker."

The girl's eyes widened. "Like the stone," she breathed. "I love rubies."

A Draconi trait? Jamie certainly had a fascination for the jewel. Not that she was complaining. A man could do worse than giving her rubies.

Provided he planned to give her one.

"Me too."

Both sets of green gazes fastened on her with a thief's scrutiny. The fine hairs on the back of her neck stood at attention. Which was an odd reaction to children.

And she still didn't have their names. "You're right. It's a pretty jewel. What is your name?"

"Jathan." Jathan gestured at his sister. "She's…"

His sister stepped forward. "I'm Flanna."

"It's nice to meet you both. We'll leave as soon as they wake."

"It could be some time." Jathan nodded as if everyone knew how long the drug took to wear off.

Damn it. Time was not on her side.

Thud, thud, thud! Parker glanced to the shaking ceiling. Clearly, the unconscious creep woke and decided he hated being chained. Poor baby. Served him right.

Jathan wrapped his arms around Flanna, trying to protect while his arms trembled in time to her body.

"He's not going to hurt you ever again. I promise. All right?"

They nodded, continuing to shake. Poor babies. Her nails cut into her palms. Conduct unbecoming of an officer would be storming up the stairs and permanently knocking out the chained man.

But damn if it wasn't tempting.

She knelt by Jamie, pressing her fingers against his wrist. The steady, thump, thump of his heart soothed a thread of tension.

"Jamie," she whispered in his ear, brushing a stray lock of hair off his forehead, "wake up."

His even breathing continued, unmarred by her request.

Damn it.

Parker sat back on her heels. Ran her hands through her hair. Stared at the ceiling. *Thud, thud, thud*, followed by garbled shouts. Tension coiled in her belly. The children huddled against the stone wall, a quivering mass of limbs.

What she needed was a car. But those seemed to be in short supply here. Why would you need a car when transporting would get you there in a fraction of the time? Maybe a cart?

"Did the bad men have a cart?"

Jathan shook his head, following it with a shrug. "Don't know."

Okay. She could leave the kids in the house with two unconscious men, one dead man, and a chained creep, to search the premises for a possibly existing cart in a town where she didn't know a soul.

Yeah, right. She blew out a breath. Sure, they could wait for Jamie and Erik to wake, but who knew how long that would take and Mr. Awake and Pissed Off could rouse help. Heaven only knew his shouts were loud enough to wake the dead.

A quick glance proved the dead man remained dead. As if he'd turn into a zombie or something. *Get it together, Parker.*

"If they had a cart, where would it be?"

"Outside."

Smart alec. "Would you like to show me?"

"We're not supposed to leave."

"Who's going to tell?"

A couple of blinks later their arms unwrapped from each other and Flanna took a hesitant step forward. "I'll go with you."

"Me too." Jathan glared.

"Right, then. Let's go out front."

When she opened the front door and stepped into a small garden, both kids stopped as if an invisible wall barred their exit.

"Come on. It's all right." Parker held out her hand.

But neither saw it. Jathan stepped out first, both hands turned palms up. Flanna followed, raising her face to the sun. Unlike the shadows in the house, the sun illuminated their stringy, unwashed hair and soot smudged faces. Parker curled her fingers hard against her palm, dropping her hand to her side.

How long had it been since they'd been outside? How many months had they lived in that house chained like animals?

The sharp scent of herbs snapped her attention to the garden. A rock-lined path led to a wall about head-high that ran the perimeter of the garden, disappearing on either side of the house. A barred iron gate sat in the middle of the wall.

So much for getting friendly with the neighbors.

Clearly the owners didn't want anyone to see what went on inside. Creeps.

And of course, no cart. Where would there be one? Along the sides of the house?

She stomped through the garden, stepping over plants, trying to walk on the stones weaving a convoluted path. Neither child paid her any mind, too busy touching plants and staring at the sky.

No cart on that side. Parker turned and headed for the opposite side. She peered around the house, a smile twitching her lips. Yes! A cart. If one could call it that. More like an oversized wheelbarrow. Which might be a good thing seeing how no horse stood around to pull it.

The cart rested next to a pile of manure complete with flies. Parker shoved the tarp off the flat cart, grabbed the handles and lifted the cart to balance on its one wheel. Okay, she had the cart. Now how was she supposed to lift two tall men and hide them in a space the size of two large dog crates?

Carefully.

The wheel left the rock border, crushing several small plants before she stopped at the front door. Jathan and Flanna watched with wide eyes.

"You found one."

"I did. But I need help getting the men inside."

"I'll help you carry them," Jathan volunteered.

"Me too!"

"Great! Let's go." Before chained creep's shouts notified a neighbor.

The children grabbed Erik's feet and she took his shoulders. After some finagling, they managed to shove him into the cart, twisting him to the side so his legs fit. Then they lifted Jamie, tucking him with more care into the cart.

Should she cover the two? What about the kids?

The noon sun beat upon her scalp as a thin stream of sweat ran between her breasts. She wiped a hand across her forehead.

Think, Parker, think. Cover or not?

Probably needed a cover. Like a tarp. With some manure sprinkled around the edges. Less likely to have the gate guards lifting the tarp if the cart stank.

Jamie's handsome face caught her glance. She couldn't dump manure on him. But she could on Erik.

Conduct unbecoming of a police officer.

Parker's lips twitched as she walked to the side of the house, grabbed a shovel and carried back a load of manure. She dumped the manure against Erik's back, mounding it in a way that with a bit of luck would conceal the two. Then she grabbed the tarp.

"What about us?"

"What about you?"

"Should we hide too?"

The 'no' froze on her lips. Maybe the kids should hide. After all, the merchants hesitated to acknowledge their presence to the point where they feared mentioning their existence. What would the townsfolk do if she tried to walk out the gates with two ragged children?

Capture them all?

But where would she hide them? The cart was full. Overfull.

She ran a hand through her hair. "Can you squeeze in between them? You will have to remain motionless. Can you do that?"

Flanna climbed onto the cart, huddling in the small

space between the men. Jathan curled into a ball at their feet.

"All right then."

Parker tossed the tarp over the four and tied it to the sides of the cart. Using the shovel, she sprinkled manure on top of the tarp, hoping the look gave the load authenticity.

Here goes nothing. She grasped the handles and with a grunt lifted the cart. How the hell was she supposed to push this load out of town? Luckily the board-high footrest kept the men from falling off the front.

Leaving the cart in the garden, she pushed open the gate to the yard and looked both ways. The main street lay to her right, busy with throngs of people jostling for the merchants' attentions. A few people walked the opposite end of the street, dodging wagons parked in front of homes. No one walked in front of the house.

Time to move.

She propped the gate open with a rock, walked back to the cart, took a breath and lifted. Only to have the cart tip to the side, Erik spilling out to land on the manure before she managed to right the thing. The children scrambled from under the tarp, their squeals a red flag to anyone listening.

Damn it. How was she supposed to get everyone out if she couldn't push the damn cart?

Parker stepped into the street, turning away from the main street, eyeing the homes for another way to escape. At least no one heard the chained creep shout. She hoped.

How was she supposed to get everyone out of here?

Her gaze landed on a wagon parked several houses down the street. A wagon complete with a horse. Taking it would be stealing. More like borrowing. And the closest she ever got to a horse was watching a Western. Once. It didn't look hard in the movie.

A quick glance showed no one watching her. Now or never. Parker drew in a breath and jogged to the wagon. An empty wagon. All the better. She gave the horse a pat and climbed into the seat, picking up the reins. She shook them. The horse stomped its foot. She shook the reins again. The horse stood still. Definitely harder than it looked on film.

Damn it.

Parker climbed down, grabbed the horse by the halter and yanked. This time the horse moved. Turning it with a wagon attached proved difficult, but at least no one came out of the house to watch her descent into criminal activity.

Conduct unbecoming of an officer.

On this she'd have to agree.

The children stood at the gate when she arrived, their eyes wide as they stared at the horse. Leaving them to gape, she pushed Jamie, still on the cart, out the gate and parked the cart by the wagon. The children helped her move him into the wagon and then she repeated the process for Erik.

Once again she covered the men with the tarp, then dumped several shovelfuls of manure around them. Jathan and Flanna climbed in and slid under the tarp. Ready to go.

Parker shoved the cart back inside and shut the gate behind her. No sense in having an overly observant neighbor notice an open gate.

Should she use the main street? Or a side street? She didn't know the side streets, provided there were side streets. The main street might be crowded, but it was a direct shot to the gates. And her load stank. Who wanted to get in the way of a wagon of manure?

Since she still had no idea how to get the damn horse to walk without her leading it, she grabbed the animal by the halter and started walking. The horse huffed and snorted, and Parker jumped. She gave one last look to the house she took the wagon from, but no one seemed aware she stole the thing.

She gave the horse a pat. "I promise you'll be returned. Eventually."

As if it understood her, it snorted, head nodding as they walked to the main street. As hoped, people took one sniff of the wagon and hustled out of her way. Now for the guards.

But the guards seemed more intent on searching people entering the city than leaving it.

Thank god.

Parker kept walking beside the horse until the town disappeared around the bend in the road. She flipped back the tarp. Four green eyes stared at her.

"We're out of the town."

"I've never been out of town." Flanna straightened. "Can we get down?"

"Yes, as long as you walk next to the wagon."

"Where are we going?"

"We're still going to Draconia."

"Where's that?"

Good question. How long did it take for the drug to wear off?

Voices chattered through the trees, buyers or

sellers heading to town. She gestured for the kids to walk close to her and grabbed the horse's halter. They couldn't stay on the side of the road all day waiting for Erik and Jamie to wake.

Damn it.

****

Jamie woke to his bed moving. Why was his bed moving? And by the Goddess, what was that stench? Did someone play a joke on him and dump manure into his house?

High-pitched children's voice giggled.

Children?

Jamie sat, batting at heavy material covering him. The movement stopped, jolting him forward as he threw off the covering. Bright sun splashed against his face and he blinked his eyes at the assault. Trees, road. Where...

Hogsbreath. Halflings. Parker. Oh, Goddess, where was Parker?

Fear lent strength to his limbs, propelling him out of the wagon, only to drop to his knees as he hit the ground.

"Hey, now," Parker knelt beside him, touching his arm, "careful there. You've been drugged."

Drugged? He remembered fighting and then...nothing. But Parker appeared to be all right. Jamie grabbed her, wrapping his arms around her waist, running a hand through her hair. His. And she was safe.

"What happened?" He released his grip around her waist, but kept a hand on her arm.

"You and Erik were drugged by these two creeps."

"Creeps?"

"Bad guys."

"I remember fighting a Watcher and then nothing."

"You gave me a fright. I thought you were dead."

"I'm glad I'm not."

"Yeah, me too. So after I realized you weren't, dead that is, I found the children—"

"The Halflings?"

"Yep. A girl and a boy." Her jaw tensed. "He kept them chained." Words gritted between clenched lips. "Chains. On children."

"I'll kill them."

"I already did. Well, one of them anyway."

Jamie's mouth popped open and he forced it to close. "You killed one?"

Her eyes focused on his hand resting against her arm. "He came at me. The tall blond. So I knocked him down the stairs. The other one is chained to the bed." Her gaze snapped to his, one side of her mouth kicking up. "With the same chains he used on the kids. After that we stuck you both in a wagon I had to steal, covered you with a tarp and manure and rolled you out of town. I wasn't sure if they would be looking for us or not."

Shock vied with relief for attention. What was more surprising? That she killed a Watcher, a ferocious warrior, or that he underestimated her ability in a crisis?

A punch of shame filled his gut. Never underestimate a female. Not even a human one. And never underestimate his mate.

Provided she still wanted to be his mate.

"You did good." Without Parker, he and Erik would still be in the house.

Or dead.

Jamie squeezed his eyes shut, tingles speeding

along his limbs like racing dragons. Parker kissed his cheek.

"I thought you'd never wake. I'm so glad you're all right. You had me worried."

Small whispers sounded behind him, pitched low, but not low enough to escape his hearing. "Do you think he's mean like the other men?"

A snarl crossed his lip as his fingers cranked into a fist. Little ones should not ask that about males. Ever. They should remain protected, sheltered, not treated like trash to be used or thrown out on a whim.

Parker's grip tightened on his as she sucked in air. "Jathan and Flanna," she pointed to each as she named them, "come meet Jamie. I promise, he won't hurt you."

Jamie twisted the snarl into a smile. "Hello, there." He turned, facing the young ones, and kept his voice even so as not to frighten them more. They stood by the back of the wagon, clothes ragged, faces smudged, hair so dirty it appeared more brown than red. The boy was taller by a finger's width, but they both appeared to be no older than eight.

Had he ever before found Halflings in this poor condition?

"Where is Draconia?" the boy asked, his body poised to run if needed.

Jamie's nails bit into his palm. "To the north. Would you like to visit?"

"I want to go home," the girl said.

"I told you, we can't go home since Mother's dead. It's them or nothing."

She sniffed.

"Draconia is a great place. There are even dragons.

Have you ever seen a dragon?"

They shook their heads, eyes wide. "Dragons eat you."

"Not these dragons. These dragons can change into males."

"You can change into a dragon?"

A familiar ache slapped his chest. He wished. "No, I can't. But he can." Jamie pointed to a snoring Erik. Was that manure cuddling next to him like a lover?

Jamie pressed his lips together to smother the chuckle. No wonder he smelled like manure. At least Parker hadn't dumped him in the pile.

"He doesn't look like a dragon."

"Wait until he wakes. Then you can ask him to change."

"Don't be silly."

"I'm not. Have you ever been able to do something no one else can?"

Jathan shook his head, but Flanna nodded. Her brother poked her in the side with his elbow. "Hush."

"What can you do?"

"Nothing." Jathan stepped in front of her, arms crossed.

Right. But he wouldn't press the issue.

"Can you take them back?" Parker patted his arm.

"Not without you, and I don't want to leave Erik here alone."

"Should we make camp?"

"He should wake up." He hoped. "We were knocked out at the same time."

"Maybe he got a higher dose."

"Maybe he's trying to figure out why he smells like horse shat." Erik propped himself on an elbow, nose wrinkling.

"Ah. The sleepy dragon wakes."

"Where am I? Scratch that. Why am I covered in manure?"

Parker giggled, biting off the sound with a cough. The little ones poked their heads around the corner of the wagon.

"He doesn't look like a dragon." Jathan tilted his head.

Flanna shook her head.

"Halflings. What did I miss?"

"A lot. This is Jathan and Flanna. The smelly male is Erik."

The little ones stepped closer to Parker as Erik jumped out of the wagon, his hands brushing off specks of manure.

"Did you have to cover me in the stuff?"

Parker stood and grabbed Jamie's hand, pulling him up. "I had to make it look convincing. No one wanted to mess with a wagon full of manure."

"Catch me up on what I missed."

Jamie told what he knew, Parker filling in the gaps.

"I want to know what a Watcher was doing here." Erik's eyes narrowed.

"You and me both."

"What's a Watcher?" Parker asked.

"The blond male. They're a class of warriors that used to guard the Draconi."

Parker raised a brow. "Why do Draconi need guardians? They're dragons with magic."

Jamie shrugged. "Good question. The answer has been lost, but what matters is that about twenty years ago they rebelled against us, attacking our towns—"

"They thought we didn't have magic and they should overthrow our rule—" Erik interjected.

"Which was ridiculous because we didn't rule them. We allowed them to live on our lands in exchange for their expertise in guarding us."

"What we don't know is why we needed guardians. The old scrolls were water damaged."

"As I said, they attacked us, and we threw the majority of them out of Draconia. The fact that one took up residence in a town this close to our borders is disturbing."

"He wasn't the only one." Jathan stepped forward.

"What do you mean?"

"The man who built the wall had blond hair. He's the one who took the children."

"What do you mean, took the children?" Parker's glare could ignite wet wood.

"The orphans. Like us. They'd round them up and sell us off. But they took an interest in us and kept us."

"They sold children?"

Jathan nodded.

"Were there any others that had red hair like you?" Jamie asked.

Jathan shook his head. "Only us. They said we were special."

"You are. You're part Draconi, like me. And Erik."

"I'm not part. I'm full-blooded." Erik slapped his chest. "We're here to take you home."

"Why?"

"That's what we do. Find special children like you and take you to Draconia."

"What if we don't want to go?"

"Would you rather go back to your village?"

Flanna and Jathan turned the direction of the village, their heads cocking to the side, mirror images of each other. "No," Jathan pointed. "Who's coming?"

Jamie spun, focusing on the road where it disappeared behind a bend of trees. Bridles jingled in the distance, the clomp-clomp of horse hooves growing closer. How could he have missed that noise?

"We need—" *to leave*, but the words died on his lips as an arrow slammed into Parker's shoulder, knocking her to the ground. Short gasps of air whimpered through her clenched lips as one hand pressed against the wound.

A roar shook the air, dripping from the overhanging leaves like drops of rain. It took Jamie a second to realize the sound came from his lips, a cry of fear laced with rage. Steam built in his throat, escaped from his ears, a prelude to an impending fireball.

Talons replaced his fingers, his face lengthened into a snout, scales ran from his hands up his arms, pricking the skin of his neck. His body elongated, thickened, wings sprouting from his shoulder blades.

A dragon. He finally managed to turn into a dragon.

Not that he had time to wallow in the joy of the moment.

His mate lay injured. All thoughts except protecting Parker fled. A full-chested roar ripped up his throat, out his lips, turning the air into reverberations of thunder. The lead horses shied, rearing away from the deafening roar, their riders tumbling to the ground. He needed to kill them all. Kill them for harming his mate.

He sucked in a deep breath, using it to fuel the steam in his throat into fire. Charring their arses sounded like a good plan.

Before he could release the blast, Erik smacked him on the flank. "Take her and go! I'll get the children."

Jamie snarled, snapping his teeth at his friend. Who repeated the hit, returning the snarl with one of his own. "Come on, scout! Snap out of it! I can't hold this shield forever!"

Right. A shield. Beads of sweat danced across Erik's brow, down his cheeks. Drugs and magic were not a good combination.

Neither was allowing an injury to his mate to go un-avenged.

Arrows bounced off Erik's shield, small pings of flying death. Death. Jamie glanced to Parker. Back to the incoming threat.

"Go! She needs help, not vengeance."

Jamie closed his eyes and focused on tamping down the rage, the steam, the fireball. Parker needed healing more than she needed him to defend her. His instincts thought otherwise. Bloody male instincts.

Another round of arrows struck Erik's shield, closer this time. A tremor ran through his friend, white lines appeared around his mouth.

As much as he hated to admit it, Erik was right. Parker needed help. The children needed returned to Draconia. And two still-recovering-from-being-drugged males could come back and fight another day.

A quick shake of his body and the scales disappeared, his face returning to normal, talons shrinking into fingers, wings retracting into shoulder blades. He bent and lifted a jaw-clenched Parker into his arms trying not to jostle her injury. The pulse of rage beat under his skin, through his veins, as he watched the color drain from her face. Erik grabbed the cowering children, nodded to Jamie, and disappeared.

So much for the rule of not showing others the Draconi skill of transportation. With a burst of power, Jamie followed Erik into a transport, crossing the ward lines as if they didn't exist, streaming across Draconia faster than a dragon could fly. He landed in the Temple Courtyard, the place all Draconi went for healing. The place where the priestesses lived, the recipients of the Goddess's power. The place Thoren specifically warned him against taking Parker. He swallowed.

Pop! Erik and the children appeared beside him.

"Where. Are. We?" White lines bracketed Parker's lips.

Was he going to listen to Thoren's cautionary words? Or take his mate inside for healing?

Was he really thinking he had a choice?

Jamie strode toward the tall doors of the Temple. "This is the Temple of the Goddess. It's where Keara performs healings."

"You're. Taking me. To her?"

"Yes."

"The children?"

"There're right here," Erik fell into step beside him, dragging the two wide-eyed children by the arm.

"What happens?"

"Keara or a priestess will treat you."

"Not me. Them."

The doors opened, a white-robed priestess gesturing them inside before he could answer.

"Why is the human—"

Jamie interrupted her. "This is my mate and Keara

269

needs to heal her."

The female's brows shot up. "Of course. This way please. And the children?"

"They need to be treated also." He lowered his voice to Parker. "They'll be taken care of."

She nodded and pressed her eyes closed. Bad sign. She usually took in her surroundings as if she needed to memorize every detail in the room. The priestess couldn't take them to the healing wing fast enough.

His mind told him the walk to one of the healing rooms took less than a minute, but it felt like forever. Forever until the priestess flung open a door. Forever until he laid Parker on the bed. Forever until Keara appeared, her worried gaze morphing into healing calm.

"Oh my. Let's see if we can get that arrow out."

"Don't let anyone else come in."

"Why? Her humanity—"

"Didn't Thoren tell you?"

"Tell me what?"

She carries titanium inside her arm. He didn't want me to bring her here in case it harmed the priestesses.

Keara's eyes flared as his mind-spoken words sank in. She glanced at Parker, held out her hand palm up and formed an energy ball. Closing her fist, she extinguished the flame. "All right, then. You," she gestured to the priestess, "need to leave. Take the children to another room and treat them as needed. Do not disturb us."

"Yes, Healer." The click of the door signaled her departure.

"How far is its reach?"

"Not far. I can touch her and work magic—"

"You can?"

"As I said. I can touch her and work magic but the effect doesn't extend far from her."

"Can magic be worked upon her?"

"Look," Parker opened pain-glazed eyes. "I don't care if you yank the thing out on two counts instead of three. Just get it out of my shoulder."

Keara's lips twitched.

"She's jesting. Do not yank it out."

Keara pressed her lips together before turning to the table next to the bed. "Do you remember your herbal lessons?"

Herbal lessons she tried to teach him ever since she found him wandering lost in the woods. The calmness of her voice wrapped around him, a gentle spell of peace. He squeezed Parker's hand.

"Some."

She placed a jar on the table before walking to his side of the bed. Parker grunted as Keara rolled her onto her side.

"The arrow doesn't go all the way through." She rolled Parker onto her back. "We're going to have to remove it before I can try healing."

"Can't you make it disappear?"

"It would still need to come out the same way it went in. Stand here," she gestured, "and hold her shoulders."

Jamie pressed his hands against Parker's shoulders as Keara indicated, his stomach twisting. She met his gaze and gave a brief nod.

"Ready? On the count of three. One…" Keara yanked out the arrow, releasing a scream from Parker. Blood trailed down her tunic, across the sheets as Keara threw the arrow to the ground.

Bile pressed against the back of his throat as nausea and rage roiled through his gut. Parker's head lolled to the side, her eyes closed. Keara held a white cloth over the wound, applying pressure to stop the bleeding.

"You can feel the pull of titanium when you touch her."

Jamie swallowed. "That's why Thoren was afraid she'd damage the energy power at the Temple and forbid me to take her here."

Keara cocked a brow. "I sincerely doubt that this little amount in her would damage the magic in the Temple. But don't tell your father that. Some things aren't worth arguing about."

"Can you heal her?"

"I will try. If it doesn't work, we'll patch her up without magic. Apply pressure so I can take a step back and try a spell."

Jamie held the cloth in place as Keara took a step back. Magic swirled around her hands, healing magic that she released at Parker's wound. The colored swirl of magic pulsed against his fingers before sinking into Parker's injury. She hissed, her eyes rolling open.

"How do you feel?" *Great word choice, Jamie. Of course she feels bad.*

Her lips twitched as if she heard his thoughts. She glanced to her shoulder, up to Keara, back to him. "It feels better with the arrow out."

"You're a bit tricky to heal." Keara waved her hand, sending another round of energy into Parker's shoulder. "But at least it seems like the magic is working. I wasn't sure if it would."

"I'm not harming you, am I? Thoren was afraid…"

Keara rolled her eyes. "It's a very small amount of titanium in you. Enough to interfere with my magic if I touch you, but not enough for you to cause chaos like a large piece of titanium does. Maybe because it's inside you and your flesh dulls the affects? I don't know. As long as I can stand here and work magic, I'm fine." She smiled and sent another wave of healing energy.

Jamie ran a finger down Parker's cheek. "I'm glad you're better."

"Remind me not to get in the way of an arrow." She blinked, glanced around the room. "Where are the children?"

"We sent them to another room, remember?"

"Oh. Right. Sorry. I was a little out of it when you brought me here."

"Understandable." He stroked her hair out of her face, the knot of worry in his gut easing as her coloring returned. Thank the Goddess Keara was able to heal her.

Balthor's voice touched his mind, loud enough to draw attention, but not the painful drop-to-your-knees call the Council used to use when Alviss was leader. *Your presence is requested in the Council Chambers in fifteen minutes.*

"I need to report for the mission debriefing."

"I'll go with you." Parker tried to push up, but he pressed her against the bed.

"No. You will stay here and rest. And heal."

Her eyes flashed. "I was part of the mission, and I will report. Besides, what are you going to tell them? You were unconscious through most of it."

Keara cleared her throat. "Pull the cloth away from her shoulder, Jamie. Let's see if the wound is healed."

Parker held his gaze. How could he allow her to leave the healing ward? She needed rest. What kind of a mate would he be if he didn't protect her?

You can't protect me from all harm, Jamie. Sometimes you have to let me find my own way.

He blinked as her voice slipped into his mind. How was that possible?

I don't know, but I've been hearing your voice off and on for awhile now. You tell me how it's possible. I'm new to this.

"Jamie?" Keara tapped his shoulder. "Please remove the cloth from her wound."

"I don't want her to report to the Council."

"Just remove the cloth. I need to see." Keara pushed against his hand until he lifted the cloth.

Applying pressure to a wound was a little hard to do when shock turned his limbs into loose strings.

Parker heard his thoughts? He could mind-speak to her without directly sending her his thoughts? The only way he knew of a human being able to mind-speak was if a Draconi projected their thoughts directly into the human's mind. No projection, no mind-speaking.

"It's sealed. The wound will need longer to completely heal, and her arm will be stiff for some time. But if she wants to go with you—"

Keara's words hung in the air, heavy with suggestion.

Parker might want to leave him, but he still needed to protect her. Especially from the Council. What would they do if they discovered the titanium she carried?

You cannot always protect me. If I'm to stay here…

If? His heart thudded, an erratic beat of hope.

If I stay here, I will need a job. I can't stay home

all day and tend house. That's not me.

Jamie swallowed. Of course it wasn't, and he was a dragon's arse to think she'd be happy doing nothing. What female was? A ripple of hope spread through his chest. *Do you mean to stay?*

I—she closed her eyes, pressing her lips together.

"Maybe I should leave you two alone." Keara dropped the bloody cloth into a bowl. "She may attend the Council meeting, but do not move that arm." She opened the drawer on the bedside table and pulled out a sling. "Make sure she wears this. I'll be outside if you need me." Giving Parker's good arm a squeeze, Keara picked up the bowl and walked out the door, closing it behind her.

Jamie's heart pounded like an overtaxed dragon. Was it possible she wanted to stay with him? His breath hitched, his voice escaping on a reedy plea. "Do you? Want to stay? Here I mean. With me?" *Good one, Jamie. Way to sound confident.*

Parker pushed up on her elbow, and Jamie helped her sit upright, her face inches from his, the heat of her skin brushing warmth across his flesh. She grabbed his hand. Swallowed.

"I love you."

Joy burst in his heart. She loved him. His mate loved him.

"But," his breath stopped when she spoke, the unfurled joy shriveling as her face grew grave, "but, as I said, I cannot live where I am not respected. Where I am not allowed to leave the house. That's not me. I need to feel useful. I need to work helping people."

"Females work."

"But they don't leave. They don't hunt down

275

criminals. They don't do what I'm trained to do. Are you willing to let me go on missions with you?"

Interesting. One really could feel blood drain from their face. She wanted to go on more missions with him? To be exposed to danger?

He had to admit she saved his arse on this mission. He and Erik would still be back in Hogsbreath, or dead—he shuddered—if not for Parker. She could help on missions, she proved her abilities. Even if he didn't like the idea.

"What if you get hurt again?"

"I get hurt again. It's a risk any time I go to work. It's not something I try to do. I'm careful. But things happen. You know that."

"I don't know if I can see you harmed. Males are supposed to protect females, not drag them into danger."

"Even if protecting me means losing me?"

He swallowed. Females did not go on missions. Neither did mated males for that matter.

A sword of ice stabbed into his chest at the thought of no more missions. Parker's brows rose, a knowing look in her eye.

Right. If he couldn't stand the thought of giving up work he loved, how could he ask her to?

But what would the Council say about her partnering with him on missions?

"I don't want to lose you. I love you, Parker."

A smile tinged her lips, her eyes sad. "Sometimes love isn't enough."

"If you don't think you can live here," Jamie drew in a breath, the enormity of his offer a heavy weight on his shoulders, "I will move to your world. I'll live there."

"It doesn't solve the problem. I would still be in danger. You would still need to cope with that. And I'd feel bad for asking you to leave."

"You'd be giving up your life to live here too."

"Not in the same way. You have more connections. A family. Friends. My family is dead. My friends don't come around anymore. It's a little hard to be friends when you work all the time."

"Sounds lonely."

"It is what it is."

"I don't want you to leave."

"I don't want to leave you either."

"I'll ask the Council if you can start going on missions with me." He could ask. And maybe that thrill of fear for her safety would subside if they went on more missions.

"We should go. They're expecting you."

We. Yes. We. The knowledge no longer seemed so scary.

Jamie grabbed the sling. "Keara will kill me if you don't put this on." He helped her adjust her arm in the sling.

She grabbed his hand. "Ready?"

"Always."

Giving her hand a squeeze, he transported them to outside the Council Chambers. The tall wooden doors had never looked more forbidding. He released a held breath. Would the Council listen to his request?

Chapter Twenty-One

Parker stood in the middle of a round stone room, the high ceilings and marble floors filling the air with a chill that had nothing to do with the temperature and everything to do with the half circle of men sitting on carved wooden chairs. Given the air of judgment hanging around she should be paying more attention to the proceedings.

But once she gave her speech on the children's rescue, the questions no longer pertained to her. She should be listening, gaining some understanding of the society, learning like she usually did in wrap-up meetings. Not now. Despite the gravity of thirteen male faces, despite the scary-ass power wafting around them like a foul odor, her thoughts fixated on her conversation with Jamie.

Did she really offer to stay here? To stay in a strange place with people who would fear her because she carried a titanium screw, of all things? To live with a man she loved, a man she wanted more than she ever wanted to apprehend a perp.

Was he worth giving up her job?

Sounds lonely.

He pegged that right. Her life was lonely. Until Jamie appeared, her job was her life. Picking up extra shifts, forgoing time off, if they needed her, she was there. All. The. Time.

What would her life be like without her job?

More time for herself. For spending time with others. For forming friendships.

For love.

If she stayed here, if Jamie lived up to his placating words, if she went on missions with him, maybe she could discover the ring of men who used children as slaves. And destroy that trade.

Jamie squeezed her hand and her thoughts jumped from speculation to reality. She needed to concentrate on the proceedings. Damn it.

"I respectfully ask that Parker be paired with me for missions." Jamie's words dropped like an explosion, repercussions rippling across faces, a shockwave of disbelief.

Even Erik's mouth popped open.

The leader, the male sitting in the middle of the semi-circle, leaned forward. "Your magic is not strong enough to go without another Draconi. Besides, females do not leave Draconia."

"She's human," Thoren waved a hand in her direction, "and she proved herself an asset. We could make an exception. Jamie's magic has improved since he found his mate. If both of them wish to continue going on missions, we should make an exception for mated males and females."

"It hasn't been done before."

"Many things we've done over the last twenty years haven't been done before."

The leader cracked a smile. "True. But we don't want to put Jamie in unnecessary danger."

Hot rage stabbed into her chest. They were discussing her man like he lacked abilities. Whether or not he had magic or used it was irrelevant to her. She loved him for himself. Loved being with him, loved talking to him, loved, ahem, other things. Her nails bit into her palms. "There is nothing wrong with Jamie. Stop acting like there is."

Thirteen sets of eyes focused on her, a gun to her target. Parker clenched her teeth. They would not intimidate her. She had faced worse. Like the hot rage of injustice when her boss took her badge and gun.

Granted, her boss lacked that creepy magical vibe circling the Council, but still, parting with her badge and gun felt worse.

One side of the leader's lips twitched. "Ah, she is a good match for the lad. Don't you think, son?"

Thoren glanced at her then focused on his father. His father was the Council leader? Interesting. "In more ways that you know."

"What say the rest of you?" Jamie's grandfather looked at the other men. "By acting on his suggestion we would be keeping two reconnaissance specialists and forming two different teams. We could pair a trainee with Erik."

A heated discussion followed. Parker smiled at Jamie. "Thank you. I know you don't want to put me in danger, and I appreciate you considering my view."

"If they don't agree to it, I'll return with you."

Parker shook her head. "As I said before, I couldn't take you away from your family."

"They aren't as important to me as you."

"Maybe not, but eventually you'd regret it and resent me."

His mouth opened, shut, as if he decided against speaking. Emotions played across his face, too fast for her to catch. She tried linking to his mind, but he either had no thoughts or shut her out.

Was she really going to leave Jamie if the Council forbid her from partnering with him on missions? Was she really going to leave her life and live with him if the Council allowed it? That option stopped the pounding pierce of panic shredding her heart. How strange that giving up her life, her world, her job caused less reaction than leaving Jamie. The power of love. Just like the song.

The Council's discussion buzzed past her ears, a rush of storm-laden air. Not that she heard their words. They might be deciding her career, but she already made the life changing decision.

She'd never return to Denver. Jamie was more important than her job. The thought of being without her badge, her gun, no longer sent chills racing across her skin. She no longer needed to drown reality with multiple drinks.

"Jamie and Parker, we have reached a decision." The leader's words caused a wave of quiet to pass through the room. A chill sank into her bones, forcing her lips together. A spell?

Clear evidence she believed in magic if that was her first thought. In less time than it took an armed robber to fire a gun she went from not believing in magic to knowing its reality.

"Allowing females to partner on reconnaissance missions has never been done before. However, Parker is human, not Draconi. She's also proven herself and in her land is part of the security force. By forbidding her to perform her training, we will be causing her harm. Harming a female is forbidden. Therefore we have decided to allow Parker to partner with Jamie. A new partner will be found for Erik. Do you have any questions?"

Jamie smiled, the expression mirrored in a glow of happiness on her face. Erik clapped Jamie on the shoulder as Thoren stood and moved toward them. And then Parker was caught in a hug, Jamie's arms clasping her waist, lifting her, swinging her in a circle. He set her down, and his mouth melded with hers, searing her, branding her his lover, his mate. Hot fire slammed into her veins, an answering scorch of heat shooting straight to her core. She wrapped her arms around his neck, her lips opening to his. The room faded into background noise, taking with it the knowledge she was kissing another on display.

Parker stiffened, and Jamie pulled away. What would they think of her public display of affection?

Apparently nothing, judging by the grins and back slaps Jamie received, along with the handshakes for her. Their names drifted by on a haze of happiness, names she needed to remember for her new job.

"Welcome to the family," Thoren pulled her into a hug. "I hope you'll forgive me for the other night."

What did she say to that? "I'll work on it."

He nodded. "Would you come to dinner? Keara would love to have you again."

Jamie pulled her to his side, wrapping an arm around her shoulders. "We'd love to, but first, we need to discuss some things. In private. If you'll excuse us?"

Thoren nodded and Jamie practically dragged her out the tall wooden doors. Once they stood outside her grabbed both her hands, turning to face her.

"Will you stay? Perform the mating ceremony with

me?"

"Is that like getting married?"

"Most mates undergo a ceremony in the Temple with the High Priestesses officiating. We're mates, and nothing will change that, but I want us to be official."

"I would be honored to be your mate. Wait a minute. What about the aging thing? If you live for centuries, what will you do when I'm gone?"

"We can bond our life-forces to extend your life. Or so I've heard. I will have to ask a priestess."

"And that would make me live as long as you?"

"That's the hope."

"I'll take it." She squeezed his hand. "Now tell me about the ceremony. What do I need to know? We don't get married in the nude, do we?"

A grin split his lips. "I like the sound of that."

"I'm sure you do. Seriously though."

"No. You only have to be nude for what comes afterward." He waggled his brows.

"Now that sounds like fun."

"I love you. I'm glad you're staying, but if you ever want to return…"

"No. I don't think I will. I love you, Jamie, and you wouldn't be happy in my world."

"I want you to be happy here without resenting me for making you stay."

"You didn't make me. I chose. Besides, according to the children, their capture was not an isolated event. I aim to shut down the child slave operation and you can help me."

"I'd like nothing better. Well, almost nothing better." He waggled his brows again. "Want to join me in my room? It's our room now."

"Would love to. I like all the rubies. It's my namesake you know."

"So you said. Ruby. I like the way your name feels on my tongue. Mind if I call you Ruby?"

"Nope. I'd like that."

"Ruby Parker, I love you."

"And I love you too, Jamie. Always."

He bent and kissed her, his lips a warm balm for her soul, his love entwining her in ribbons of joy. Her dragon, her love. Always and forever.

A word about the author…

Karilyn Bentley's love of reading stories and preference of sitting in front of a computer at home instead of in a cube, drove her to pen her own works, blending fantasy and romance mixed with a touch of funny.

Her paranormal romance novella, *Werewolves in London*, placed in the Got Wolf contest and started her writing career as an author of sexy heroes and lush fantasy worlds.

Karilyn lives in North Texas with her own hunky hero, a psycho dog nicknamed Hell Hound, a crazy puppy, and a handful of colorful saltwater fish.

You can learn more about Karilyn and her writing at www.karilynbentley.com

Sign up for Karilyn's newsletter at:
http://eepurl.com/ba_0Rf